GODS OF SOUND
THE PERILOUS PATH OF CAMERON FOSTER

By QM SCHAFFER

Published by Kylie Publishing

CHAPTER 1 ALMOST HAUNTED

A haunted house, more often than not, appears drab gray with scabs of paint peeling off its sides. Nearby trees, leafless and lifeless, often cast eerie shadows. The front walkway usually had an uneven surface as if some force beneath tried to break through. Set away from other houses, a haunted house sat alone amidst a medley of uncomfortable sounds -- the eerie hoot of an owl, a creaking stairway, unoiled door or the yowl of a mangy black cat.

What really made a house haunted was when something horrific had happened within its walls like a gruesome murder or the sight of evil spirits.

It's uncertain if that was the case with the house on Frog Tail Road. But the very sight of that place sent shivers down one's spine.

That morning Cameron Foster walked to school thinking scary thoughts. Skeletons fascinated him. Looking at the bones, he often tried to envision what the person might have looked like. One time at a museum, he cradled a human skull in both hands, wondering if someday someone might do the same with his skull. Known as Cam to his friends, he attended South Middle School, a long walk from his house but one he did every day. It struck him funny that it was called South as it was the only Middle School in town. And because of overcrowding in the elementary schools, this Middle School began in fifth grade not sixth.

Soft-spoken and at times painfully shy, Cameron was an only child with only a couple of friends and only one true interest--playing guitar. He mostly kept to himself. The only after school activity he pursued was a music class which he rarely missed. There, a music teacher helped him learn new chords and songs which he played on his hand-me-down guitar. He didn't know who it was handed down from but they didn't treat it particularly well as it was scuffed and dented. Though only 10, Cameron could play it so well that at his lesson many of the other students often stopped to watch. He was the lone guitar player as the others were taking lessons in piano, cello and violin.

Cameron sported a ratty nest of long blondish brown hair, always uncombed and in disarray. His mother had never taken him for a single haircut unlike other guys at school who had crewcuts, undercuts, fades or the occasional buzz cut.

Today was somewhat special for Cameron as he had arranged his first ever playdate. Never before had a classmate come over to his house after school. His friend Tommy had badgered him for weeks to have him over. Since he had been to Tommy's house twice, it only felt right to reciprocate. Of Cameron's very few friends, Tommy topped the list. Tommy didn't fit in with any group either though he had more friends than Cameron. Tommy was overweight and freckled and wore shirts from his father's alma mater the University of Mississippi. He also had his hair pushed back with gel like someone from the fifties.

At school that day, Tommy reconfirmed three times that he was coming over to Cameron's house after school. As the hour neared, Cameron weakly smiled, now dreading the idea of a playdate. He was nervous that his mother might embarrass him in front of his only real friend.

In the school cafeteria, Cameron sat at a blonde Formica table next to Tommy and three other boys -- Arne Skilgood, who had a tilt of Brillo-like reddish brown hair; the deathly silent Gilbert Swenson and the equally quiet Martin Fenster and his chronic case of sniffles.

"Isn't that the same shirt and pants you wore yesterday?" asked Tommy, staring at Cameron's Detroit Tigers shirt and tattered blue jeans.

"That's so gay," replied Arne. "You actually notice what another guy wears every day?!"

"You know, saying something like that is bullying," said Tommy.

"Are you nuts? That didn't physically hurt anyone. It's just an expression."

"If it's offensive to one person, then you should stop saying it," said Tommy.

"And what person is offended by it? "

"My cousin would be, " said Tommy.

"Well, he's not at this table," said Arne. "I don't know why you're so upset unless of course you're gay. Are you?"

"No, Arne. I'm just fat. And I don't appreciate any fat comments just the way you don't appreciate people doing carrot top jokes."

"I don't have a carrot top," said Arne defensively.

Tommy gave a broad smile, knowing he'd hit a nerve.

Cam nervously chewed on his fingernails or at least what was left of them. They had been whittled down from sheer nerves. He'd always been a nervous kid which is why during his few years on this planet, his nails never stood a chance to grow. He pulled out a bag of crackers and chewed on them slowly.

"So, Cam, answer me," said Tommy, leaning forward, his cheeks always puffy looking. "Isn't that the same shirt you wore yesterday?"

Clearing his throat, Cam softly replied "I have a lot of the same shirts and pants,"

Arne pointed at Cam's shirt and said, "I suppose that all of your shirts have ketchup stains on the sleeve? That's the same shirt you wore yesterday."

Tommy did a double take, shaking his head at Arne in disbelief. He didn't mean for Cameron to get attacked. He wished he'd never asked the question. "Arne, don't be so annoying," he said. "It's only fifth grade. I hate to think how you'll be in sixth grade. Can we pleeeeaaasse talk about something else?"

"Okay, if I get to pick it," said Arne.

"Fine," said Tommy, happy to move on to something else.

"What about, um, dinosaurs?"

"Dinosaurs?! That's like second grade stuff," said Tommy. "Whatever. What about dinosaurs?"

"My family went to California for vacation and visited a place called the La Brea Tar Pits."

"So?" asked Tommy

Cam sat quietly, as he often did, half-listening and half-day dreaming.

Arne straightened up in his seat and leaned forward as if to reveal a great big secret. "Well, they found a lot of dinosaur bones in the tar pits. Perfectly preserved. Dinosaurs weren't all that smart. It's why they fell in."

Arne ripped open a bag of Frito's and started crunching away while talking. "Can't blame them though. Scientists say that after it rained, the rain would sit on the surface of the tar, making it look like a pond or a lake. A bird would fly down and get stuck. Then, a passing fox would spot the bird, creep up to it and also get stuck. Then a bigger animal, like a saber-tooth tiger, would approach the fox and it would get stuck. But because of its weight, it would start to slowly sink into the tar. But before it did, a big wooly mammoth, salivating over a saber-tooth tiger steak dinner, would rumble over and get stuck as well. And its weight would cause it to get sucked way down into the pit."

"How far?" asked Tommy.

"Enough to suffocate but not so far down that archaeologists couldn't find him years later," said Arne.

"That's cool, Arne," said Tommy. "What do you think, Cam?"

Cam hesitated and said "It's difficult to imagine that the earth was once overrun with oversized lizards and then they just up and disappeared."

"Anyone here been to California?" asked Arne.

They shook their heads.

"What's the furthest you've ever been?" he asked them.

Tommy shouted "Florida! Love them palm trees."

"Cam?" asked Arne,

Cam shyly shook his head.

"What's that mean? You've traveled outside of Connecticut before, right?" asked Arne. "What's the farthest place you've been?"

Annoyed, Tommy replied "Don't pick on him. Go after Gilbert or Martin for a change."

The truth is that Cameron had never been outside the state and he was embarrassed to admit it.

"But why can't he answer a simple question like that?" asked Arne.

"Well, I'm telling you he's been outside the state. So there, "said Tommy.

The lunch bell rang, marking the end of the meal. As they retreated to their classrooms, Tommy patted Cameron on the back and said "Remember, I'm coming over to your house today."

The school day came to an end much sooner than Cam would have liked as he dreaded having Tommy come to his house. It wasn't a place he was proud of. And after seeing it, Tommy might not want to be his friend anymore.

As the final school bell sounded, Tommy grabbed Cam's arm to get his attention. "So, Cam, we ready to rock n roll?" Cam gave a faint nod.

Slinging their backpacks over their shoulders, Cam and Tommy walked down the hallway and out of the school building. Cam shuffled down the sidewalk in no hurry to get home.

They walked past five streets before Cam led them into the woods, his usual shortcut down a badly maintained dirt path. Roots and rocks ready to trip them up. They came to a stream too wide to leap over. A large rock lay in the middle. Cameron knew it was tiny so he ginger-footed it over and safely to the other side. Tommy wasn't so skillful and ended up with his right sneaker totally soaked in the cold water. And now when he walked, his one sneaker squeaked.

Along the way, a series of trees rose high above the path, a tangled network of thick gnarly vines criss-crossed from tree to tree like a giant spider web. The trees appeared lifeless, the vines having choked the life out of them, leaving scars along their sides where they had wrapped around like pythons.

Soon, a house appeared, eerie and gray. Its creepy appearance prompted Tommy to exclaim "Awesome!"

Cam remained silent.

"That place looks haunted," said Tommy. "I wonder if anyone lives in it."

As they got closer, Tommy stopped, heart pounding, unwilling to go any closer as Cameron walked up its creaky front steps, bold and confident.

"What are you doing?" asked Tommy, incredulous, his eyebrows arched in concern. "Do you have some kind of death wish?"

Cameron reached for the doorknob, turned and said matter-of-factly "I'm going inside."

"Are you crazy?! Why risk your life? You're much too young to do that."

As Cameron turned the doorknob, Tommy shouted "Don't do it, Cam! It's not worth it. I can't protect you from whatever is behind that door."

"Don't worry, Tommy. It's okay," said Cam, calmly.

"It's not okay because I say it's not okay," said Tommy. "We have a play date, remember? Don't go in there. Let's just go to your house. Please. I mean, why go in there?"

Cam took a deep breath and said "Cause I live here."

Tommy walked up the front stoop. "Oh man," he said. "You sure had me fooled. This place is awesome. You sure made it look creepy and spooky. I wish I could do this to my house. I'd transform it into something scary or maybe futuristic. Here all you need is a black cat and some spider webs and you could charge admission. Actually, I see some spider webs. You just need the black cat."

Tommy stepped back to take one more look. "On second thought, it's scary enough as is. It doesn't need a thing."

With renewed confidence, Tommy followed Cameron into the house past a big spiral staircase and into a dingy kitchen. The week amber lighting amplified the dinginess making it look uncleanly.

"Ya got anything to eat?" asked Tommy, licking his lips, his stomach growling. "I'm starving. I didn't eat that much at lunch cause Arne kept me busy talking."

Uneasy, Cameron gnawed on his lower lip. Taking the initiative, Tommy opened the refrigerator but there was nothing in it except for a butter dish and a lone bottle of milk. He went over and opened some cabinets but found only dusty plates and glasses.

With enormous understatement, he said "You may need a trip to the supermarket."

Somewhat embarrassed, Cam reached into his backpack and pulled out an over-stuffed napkin. "I've got some rolls," he said.

"This from school?"

"It's food."

Tommy took a roll and quickly gobbled it up while Cameron had the other.

"What should we do?" Tommy asked. "Got any video games?"

Cameron shook his head.

"What about a ball so we can play catch?"

Cameron opened a lower cabinet and removed a lone box of rice. Grabbing a small cloth towel, he poured some rice inside, tied the end and formed a rice ball which he tossed to Tommy.

"This isn't quite what I had in mind," said Tommy. "But good use of rice. And I'm sure in Japan where rice and baseball are big this could be very popular. What else can we do?"

Cameron shrugged his shoulders.

"Show me your room," said Tommy.

Cameron grimaced.

"Come on, Cam," said Tommy. "You got to show me your room. Unless of course you have a dead body up there."

Cam stood perfectly still.

"Do you?" asked Tommy, incredulous.

"No."

"Then let me see it. I am your best friend, right?"

The two trudged up a steep flight of stairs. The lighting was dim as the overhead bulb had fizzled out. Cameron opened the door to his room, barren of wall decor or furniture except for a bed and a bureau. A sickly pea-green paint was peeling off the walls and the whole room cried out for a paint job. There also was a guitar case leaning against the bed as well as an aquarium with a grimy white towel draped over the top.

"What's in there?" asked Tommy, pointing at it.

"My good friend Robert," said Cameron, lifting off the towel and revealing a green frog with large brown eyes. It stood motionless except for its breathing. Short steady breaths. Small brown liver spots dotted its back in contrast to its belly which was the color of egg whites.

"What do you feed him?" asked Tommy.

"Bread," said Cameron. "And sometimes bugs."

"And what does he do?" asked Tommy. "I mean does he do any tricks?"

"He can hop. But mainly he's good company."

Tommy pointed to the guitar case. "You own a guitar?"

Cameron gave a nod.

"Where'd it come from and can you play it?"

Cameron opened the case and took out the beat up guitar. "Found it in this house when we moved here. It was in the attic."

"Is it haunted?" Tommy asked, taking the guitar from Cameron and strumming some notes that were as irritating as the screech of an alley cat. He handed back the guitar.

"Play something," said Tommy.

Cam sat on the edge of his bed, wiggling his finger. He then started to play, his fingers moving so fast and producing chord after chord and note after note of beautiful music. He played blues that went into hard rock that went into classical. When he finished, he gently placed the guitar down on his bed as though it had earned a well-deserved rest.

"Sweet!" said Tommy. "Man, you sure can play. How'd you learn to do it so well?"

Cam shrugged his shoulders.

"How long you been playing?

"Um, about five years I think."

"Damn you're good. You ought to be in a band or something."

A thumping noise emanated from the wall near Cameron's bedroom window. "What the hell is that?" asked Tommy.

"You really want to know? Cameron said, half-smiling. "Behind the shutters live a family of bats."

"Holy moly," exclaimed Tommy. "A whole family?"

"A colony."

"A colony?!" repeated Tommy, as he often liked to do. "Does that mean there are 13 of them? And do they hate the British?"

"Not sure how many but I haven't detected any accents," said Cameron.

"Don't they creep you out?"

"No. I heard they eat hundreds of insects every night. And cause I don't have a screen on my window, they're kind of protecting me from being bitten by mosquitoes."

"They also fit well with your haunted house theme," observed Tommy.

Cameron stood up and walked over to the window. He grabbed a flashlight by the window ledge and handed it to Tommy.

"Reach out the window and aim the beam under the shutters, Cam instructed him, while taking his guitar and clipping on a black metal capon near the bottom of the guitar neck. Capons reduce the length of the strings producing a higher sound. He started plucking the strings, producing a high sound, almost imperceptible to the human ear. But the bats heard it loud and clear. Awakened from their slumber, the bats dropped down from the shutter and frantically flew off, zigging and zagging.

"Whoa!" said Tommy. "Ultra cool."

Cameron stopped playing. "It's not dark enough for them to stay out very long. They'll soon return to get some more sleep. They have this cool radar where they send out a signal that's loud for them but barely heard by us. They can close their ear muscles enough so they don't go deaf and then they open their ears again as the echoes come in. It's echo radar."

"They sure came out of there fast."

"That's cause they hang upside down. All they need to do is drop and fly."

"This is a, um, well, unusual playdate," said Tommy. "But I kind of like it. Anything else we could do? You have a basement or an attic?"

"Yeah but they're not really..."

"Let's go to the attic," said Tommy, insistent as always. He headed out to the hallway and spotted a set of stairs that went to a third floor.

Cameron hurried to catch up as Tommy ran up the stairs, two steps at a time. At the top he saw a hatch in the ceiling that led to the attic. A rope dangled from a knob on the hatch. Tommy grabbed it and pulled it down. Cameron reluctantly helped him open a retractable ladder and they climbed into the attic.

"Do you spend much time playing up here?" asked Tommy.

"On occasion," said Cameron.

"Is that why there's a candle and matches up here?" asked Tommy, suspiciously.

"Let's first sit and appreciate the darkness," said Cameron. "It's very peaceful."

The attic was immersed in darkness except for a slant of light that came through a wooden vent at one end. To move around, he had to crouch as the ceiling, was slanted to each side. The exposed rafters lay waiting for someone's head to clonk into them. A straw broom leaned against some cardboard boxes sealed with duct tape.

Cameron often sat in the dark, gathering his thoughts and clearing his mind. Meditative, it provided him great solace. There was a time when his mother hadn't paid the bills and their electricity got shut off for a whole week. To get through that period, he brought the candle and matches to the attic and pretended he was living in another era.

Restless, Tommy began to move about as his eyes adjusted to the dark. He had all the signs of ADD, enhanced by years of playing videogames. For him, sitting calmly in an attic was akin to living in an isolation ward with no one to see and nothing to do. It was enough to drive a person insane.

Cameron started to wheeze.

"Geez, what's happening?" worried Tommy.

"I can't--"started Cameron, reaching into his pocket. "Breathe."

He fumbled for his inhaler which he carried at all times. He took three puffs before his asthma receded.

"You okay?"

"Mmmmm hmmm," said Cameron. "Asthma."

"I hope I don't catch it," said Tommy.

"You can't catch it. It gets triggered by dust, smoke, stress."

"Well, there's no smoke at least."

"My mother smokes," said Cameron, his breathing now back to normal.

"You have any brothers or sisters??

"Nope."

"Family dog?"

"Nope."

"Who are your friends?" asked Tommy.

"You."

"And that frog."

"Robert."

"So just me and froggy?"

"How many friends am I supposed to have?" asked Cameron innocently.

"There's no quota. But you should probably have more than two, especially when one is a frog."

"So, I should find another friend?"

"Probably. You know why I became your friend? Cause I saw a kid cut in front of you in line once and you didn't stand up for yourself. And another time I saw a kid push you and call you names for no reason and again you didn't do a thing. I felt bad for you. I felt you needed, um, well, a friend. You might even need a bodyguard but that can be expensive."

They heard some scuffling under the floorboards near the vent.

"What's that?" asked Tommy.

"Some grey squirrels that live up here," said Cameron.

"It's a regular barnyard, this house of yours," said Tommy.

Cameron lit a candle and headed towards the noise. An open floorboard revealed a patch of insulation, bubblegum pink, and atop it some black droppings left by some small animal.

"If someone ever asks you if you have any pets, say yes, bats and squirrels," said Tommy. "Let's make the squirrels come out."

Tommy grabbed the broom, turned it upside down and started banging the handle on the floorboards. He banged several times, like a tribal ritual, then stopped to listen. Hearing nothing, he banged again. No squirrels appeared.

"Okay, let's go back down," said Tommy. He shuffled along the rough-hewn floorboards. When he got to the hatch, he sat and dangled his legs over the side. Suddenly, he felt something sharp dig into his flesh on both calves. He let out a blood-curdling scream.

"Ahhhhhhhhhhhhhhhhhhhhhhhhhhhhhhhhhhhhhhhhhhhh!!!!!!!"

He felt his body sliding through the hatch. He grabbed onto the side, trying to keep from falling through. He wiggled his legs, struggling to pull them back up but something had a hold and wasn't letting go.

Startled by the screaming, Cameron rushed towards his friend. He slipped and bruised his head, becoming slightly disoriented.

Tommy gazed down through the hatch and saw just what had grabbed him. His mouth agape in disbelief, he saw a real-life witch. Her hair was long and spindly gray, her nose slender yet bent and her hands like two claws, nails sharp, grasping his legs. She glared at him, her mouth partly opened, showing her crooked yellow teeth. Her hazel eyes were badly bloodshot. The only thing missing was the long black hat and a flying broomstick. Maybe the broom in the attic was hers, Tommy wondered for an instant.

Tommy writhed and twisted trying to free his legs. He reached back for the broom, then handed it to her. "Here's your broomstick! Please don't hurt me. I come in peace."

He waited for the witch to cackle but she just stared, her mouth twisted, unsure who this person was and perhaps what he tasted like.

"What are you doing up there?" the witch muttered, her voice scratchy like a bourbon-soaked chain-smoking country singer.

"He's my friend," said Cameron.

"Why didn't you tell me he was here?" she asked.

"Your door was closed," said Cameron. "And I didn't want to disturb you in case you were sleeping."

She cackled. "Sleeping?! How could anyone sleep with all that banging?! What on earth were you doing up there?"

"We thought there was a squirrel problem," said Tommy.

Rubbing the back of her neck with her bony hand, she glanced at the broomstick in his hand. "Why were you handing me that? What do you think I am? A witch or something? A cleaning lady? I don't need a darn broom. Now get down from there. Now!"

There was no way for Tommy to get down as she was blocking the ladder.

"You're in the way, Ethel," said Cameron. This was his mother and she only wanted to be called by her name and not by "mom" or "mother."

Ethel, thought Tommy. Did he hear that correctly? Was this witch a friend of Cameron's? She probably kept bats as pets. And God knows what else. Suddenly this seemed like the playdate from hell.

Ethel climbed out of the way so Tommy and Cameron could come down.

"I need to get home soon," said Tommy. The two boys walked past her and down to the kitchen. She followed. She took two glasses from the kitchen cabinet, reached into the refrigerator and took out the lone glass container of milk. She removed the lid and poured a thick yellow liquid into the two glasses. She handed them to the boys. Tommy's eyes widened in despair.

"Drink up, boys," she said.

Tommy had no interest in drinking this witches brew. Being poisoned was not the way to die. But could it really be poison? Would she really kill her son this way? He would not take a sip until Cameron did. Of course, Cameron could be in on this conspiracy. He could have already drunken some elixir to protect him from the poison. Maybe, just maybe Cameron wasn't the best friend he thought he was.

Cameron seized the glass and swigged it down. A milky residue coated his lips. He wiped it off with a swoop of his sleeve. He turned to Tommy. "Your turn."

"What's in this?" Tommy asked.

"It's my own special brew," said Cameron's mother.

Taking a deep breath, Tommy scrunched his nostrils and drank it down. He waited for the poison to seep into his system, slowly shutting down his organs one by one. He felt something deep inside him. Then it happened. One long belch. That was it. No pain. No instant death. He was still alive.

Tommy took out his iPhone. "Hi mom, you can pick me up now.

A pause.

Looking over at Cameron, Tommy asked, "What street are you on?"

"Frog Tail Road."

"Frog Tail Road, mom," said Tommy into the phone.

A pause.

"What's your house number?"

"13."

"Of course. It's number 13, mom."

CHAPTER 2 MYSTERIOUS STRANGER

As Cameron arrived at school, something didn't feel right. Just outside the building was a woman straddling a motorcycle. Probably in her late twenties or early thirties, she was dressed in black leather from head to toe -- tight pants. body hugging jacket and knee-high boots. She didn't fit in at a middle school. It was highly unlikely she was anyone's mother. But who knows? Her jet black hair, pierced nose and ears added to her rock 'n roll aura as though Joan Jett had landed in suburbia. Her dark eyes focused on Cameron. As he walked by, she tapped some numbers into her iPhone, mumbling to someone on the other end.

Tommy spotted Cameron entering the building but avoided him like the plague. Cameron saw him but Tommy quickly looked away. It was obvious he didn't want to socialize. Cameron was now persona non grata.

Cameron's homeroom teacher, Mr. Milton, asked the class to take their seats while he scrawled in white script across the green chalkboard "Creative Writing--Highly Memorable Personal Experience."

"Your next writing assignment is due in three weeks," he said, touching his dated military crew cut. "I want you to write a story that takes you beyond your normal everyday life and captures something special you actually did. It must be a true experience. For example, if you visited a city like Paris, you would write about the magic of that city, the attractions, the people, the overall vibe. And try to capture its essence by touching on the many senses you experience."

A girl in the front row raised her hand. "Could the essay be on someone kind of famous that you met?"

"Who are you thinking of?" Mr. Milton asked.

"I love soccer," she replied. "And I met a woman who plays for the US soccer team."

"That would work as long as you actually met her, spent time talking to her and learned something new," he replied. "This isn't a piece of writing you can do from books or Wikipedia. Is that clear?"

Cameron observed Tommy across the room. Unlike Cameron, Tommy was usually quite talkative in class and yet today he remained quiet and sullen. Tommy felt Cameron staring at him and glared back. Point made. Cameron quickly looked away.

At lunch in the cafeteria, Cameron sat alone. He saw Tommy with Arne and a few other boys but didn't go near them. Lunch passed slowly as did the afternoon. Today being Wednesday, he had his weekly class after school with Michael Knox, a music teacher he met several years ago. Knox taught piano and guitar after school and got paid extra for those lessons. When Cameron first met him, he was unaware that he needed to pay for the lessons. Once he found out, he knew he couldn't get his mother to pay anything so he started to walk away. Knox took note and, feeling sorry for him, asked that he stay, saying he wouldn't charge him. It was a gesture done out of kindness and sympathy. And he did it before he realized how remarkably talented Cameron was on the guitar. For someone so young, he played effortlessly. A true prodigy. His finger work was so deft that he never missed a note.

Knox, who Cameron referred to as Mr. Michael, usually had 8 to 10 students after school. They convened in the cafeteria, stationing themselves ten or so feet apart. For those getting piano lessons, an upright piano was wheeled in from a side room. For any other instrument, it was the responsibility of the student to bring it with them.

The majority of the students were decent musicians but mistake-prone. Knox spoke softly, patiently, conveying a few tips each lesson so as not to overburden them. With Cameron, he acted differently. He waited until all the other students were done and then he stayed later to give Cameron special instruction. Cameron had a near photographic memory and absorbed everything he was told. When he was young, Knox himself had been a gifted musician. He pursued a career as a classical guitarist, touring the world and playing in concert halls until health problems derailed those dreams, forcing him into a life of teaching. With Cameron, he took intense interest as there was a vicarious pleasure derived from seeing him progress. Never before had he taught a student with so much ability. He found it intoxicating to be around him.

As Cameron practiced in a corner, a seventh grade pianist named Julia, her lesson done for the day, stood nearby watching him, utterly impressed. When he performed, Cameron was often oblivious of his surroundings, the music transporting him from the real world into a dream-like one. When he stopped playing, Julia applauded, completely startling him. Blushing, he smiled weakly.

"You are so darn good, dude," she said. "I've been watching you play week after week after week and I just had to say something. You always amaze me. What's your name?"

"Cameron."

"And what grade are you in?"

"Fifth."

"No-o-o! You've got to be kidding. I'm in seventh and I wished I played the piano half as well as you play the guitar. I know you didn't ask but my name is Julia. What's yours?"

"Cameron."

"You told me that already. Whoops. My mistake. Well, I gotta go. See you around, Cameron."

Julia was very pretty from her infectious smile to her blonde hair, ponytailed, that bobbed up and down when she walked. Slim and always smiling she had a natural beauty that didn't require an ounce of makeup. She always wore blue, knowing full well how it brought out the color of her radiant blue eyes. He never expected someone like that to talk to him, a lowly fifth grader, barely noticed by other fifth graders let alone one in seventh.

His daze was broken by the entrance of the woman in black leather, the same person he'd spotted on a motorcycle that morning outside the school building. It sure felt like she was following him. What could she possibly want, he thought?

To calm himself, Cameron started playing his guitar and did so amazingly well as always. He played loud and soft, fast and slow, chords and crisp notes, his fingers never tiring. The woman in leather remained the entire time, clearly there to see him, her face stoic, not betraying a single thought or emotion, except she was clearly fascinated by him.

When Cameron finish playing, he put his guitar in the case and looked up towards the woman in leather. But she was gone. He shuffled down the corridor, stopping for a sip of water at the white porcelain fountain built into the wall.

Emerging outside, carrying his guitar, he headed home. The uneven sidewalk, a victim of the winter freeze, attempted to trip him, so he kept his eyes focused on the ground. From out of nowhere he heard the rumble of a motor. Looking up, he tripped and stumbled to the ground, tightly gripping the guitar case to protect it more than himself. Staring up, he saw the woman in leather astride her motorcycle.

"You okay?" she asked.

Dusting himself off, Cameron got to his feet.

"You play really well," she said.

He gave a stunted smile.

"You been playing long?"

"A few years."

"You like music?"

He nodded.

"Ever been to a concert?"

He shook his head.

"I'd love to take you to one."

Why was this woman being so nice to him, Cameron wondered? What was it she wanted? He had no idea.

"Can I give you a ride home? she asked, touching the motorcycle seat behind her to show she had plenty of room.

"That's okay," he said.

"All right," she replied. "Maybe we'll see each other again."

She revved the engine several times, then patched out, the tires screeching as she burned rubber.

Cameron continued walking home, staring at the uneven sidewalk until he accidentally bumped into someone. A burly guy, much taller and bigger than he was. Although he didn't know him, Cameron had seen him at school. He was a seventh grader named Scott. Mean spirited guy who played football and clearly worked out a lot.

"Don't you say excuse me?" Scott said, dead serious.

"Excuse me," said Cameron, not wanting any trouble.

"Who do you think you are?" he asked.

"Me?"

"What grade are you in?" he said, rubbing his chin.

"Um, fifth."

"Fifth?! And you think it's alright to show off to other people's girlfriends?"

"I don't know what you mean?"

"Are you calling me a liar?" baited Scott.

Cameron shook his head.

"Let me clarify in case you seem too stupid to understand me," persisted Scott. "My girlfriend told me about you. She's been impressed by your guitar playing. Pisses me off, you understand?"

Cameron nodded.

"Do you like my girlfriend?"

"I don't really know her," said Cameron.

"Hand me that," said Scott gesturing towards his guitar case.

With great reluctance, Cameron handed over the guitar case, knowing he had no other choice.

Impatient, Scott grabbed the case out of Cameron's hands, unzipped it and removed the guitar. He observed the many nicks and scratches on its surface.

"You take really great care of this," he sneered, sarcastically. "Almost as good as I'm going to take care of you."

Scott plucked some notes but clearly did not know how to play. "This thing sucks. It doesn't work at all."

"Can I have it back?" Cameron asked.

"No. This thing needs to be destroyed. It needs to be taught a lesson."

"Please don't," said Cameron.

"Don't tell me what to do," snapped Scott. "If I want to smash it to bits, I will smash it to bits."

Cameron felt helpless. Even if he could grab his guitar, he could never outrun Scott. Scott continued to torment him like a game of cat and mouse.

"Let me sum this up. I don't like you and I don't like your guitar," said Scott, raising it over his head as though ready to smash it. But before he could, the deep rumble of an engine distracted him enough to stop. Barely an inch away from his leg rested the front wheel of a motorcycle, engine revving. Riding it was the woman in black leather.

Caught completely by surprise, Scott lowered the guitar.

"Give it back to him," she ordered. "Now."

Scott handed it to Cameron who put it safely into its case.

"Hop on," said the woman in leather to Cameron. Without hesitation, he slung the guitar case over his shoulder and climbed aboard. He wrapped his arms around her waist, feeling the cool black leather of her jacket against his face. With one last rev of the engine, the motorcycle sped off, leaving Scott behind, looking dazed and confused.

The wind whooshed through Cameron's hair as the cycle zoomed along the back roads, making turn after turn effortlessly. In no time, the cycle pulled up to Cameron's house. He got off and nodded.

"Thanks," he said, wondering how she knew where he lived as he never gave an address. She must have been watching him much more than he originally thought. But why? He was just a dumb old

10-year-old kid. Anyway, it didn't really matter. What mattered was he was safely back at home with his guitar intact.

"See you again," she said. And without uttering another word, she sped off.

■■■

With all the technological innovations in the world, the cork bulletin board near the front corridor of South Middle School felt old-fashioned but there it was, bolted to the cinder block wall and encased behind sliding glass. A lock prevented anyone from posting notices unless they had the key. Each notice was held in place by multi-colored push pins and included such things as an Ice Cream Social to raise money for the Glee Club, an upcoming rally for the football team and a notice for try-outs for the school musical of Annie Get Your Gun. What caught Cameron's attention as he walked past was a posting for the school's variety show, an annual assemblage of different acts from students ranging from singers to musicians to dance routines and skits, Years ago it had been called the Annual Talent Show but someone changed it to the Annual Variety Show probably after realizing there wasn't a lot of talent. And Variety was a bit of a misnomer as many of the dance routines mimed songs from syrupy pop tunes and performances were always done to today's hits.

Cameron remembered hearing Julia encouraging him to be in the Variety Show. His music teacher suggested the same. He noted the deadline to sign-up was two days away and had to be done online. He scribbled down the sign-up information on a piece of scrap paper and stuffed it in his pocket. He just needed to get his mother to do it for him as it said a parent had to take care of it.

The hallway was now alive with students. Cameron prayed he wouldn't run into Scott, the bully who had targeted him. He slinked along the side of the hall, trying to blend in, keeping his eyes staring downward at the floor. If he could have a superpower, it would be invisibility. But he'd also settle for super strength or flying. He went directly to his home room, ducking in and taking a seat discreetly out of view from passers-by. Arne noticed him and came over.

"You on a spy mission?" he asked with a sly smile, chewing on the end of a yellow pencil.

Cameron lowered his backpack to the floor.

"Who are you hiding from?" persisted Arne. "Tommy? He's already here. You two still enemies?"

"We're not enemies," said Cameron, perturbed at the suggestion. "We're just not talking to each other."

"Heard you barely escaped from Scott the other day," said Arne. Cameron gave a look of surprise. How did that information get out so fast, he wondered? "Some lady on a motorcycle helped you out. That's what they say. But I didn't buy it."

"Who'd you hear that from?" asked Cameron.

"I got my sources," said Arne, smugly sweeping his bangs from his eyes.

Cameron had wanted to put this incident behind him, hoping Scott forgot, but it didn't look like that was going to be the case.

"Someone said the lady on the cycle looked like she was in a rock band," added Arne.

"I don't know," said Cameron.

"I guess she was just a Good Samaritan....dressed in leather," said Arne.

"What's a Samaritan?"

"I think it's a tribe of people who do nothing but good deeds. But at least you escaped death."

Cameron didn't appreciate that last line. His life wasn't in jeopardy. Just his guitar was.

"Since you're good at escapes, I have one for you," said Arne. "How do you escape from quicksand."

"Quicksand? Well, I'd ask someone to throw me a life preserver," said Cameron.

"But you can't use a prop."

"Then I'd try to reach up, grab a vine and pull myself out."

"Vines are props."

"I don't know then."

"Do you want to know the answer?" asked Arne.

Cameron shrugged, half-interested.

Arne forgot the answer so he hurried across the classroom for a quick exchange with Tommy and then returned. "Quicksand is like a giant sinkhole. So, what you have to do when you fall in is first wiggle your legs slowly then spread your arms and legs apart then lean back and float like you're in a swimming pool. And then hope someone comes by with a rope or long reach."

The school bell rang and everyone took their seats. The home room teacher, Mr. Milton, exacting and humorless, reminded the class that they had two more days to complete their essays. "And remember, your essay must be based on a personal experience. No fiction. Is that understood? I hope most of you have already finished your papers. But for those who haven't, if you need help coming up with an idea, please see me after school."

Lunch time found Cameron and Tommy seated at separate tables. Arne switched back and forth, taking his lunch bag with him, chatting a bit to Tommy, then heading to Cameron. Cameron missed Tommy but he sensed that Tommy didn't want to see him so he never made an approach.

On his way to his last class of the day, Cameron got stopped in the hallway by Julia.

"Hi," she said.

Cameron tried looking away, averting any eye contact.

"Did my boyfriend say anything to you?" she asked.

"What do you mean?"

"Was my boyfriend Scott mean to you?" she asked.

He shook his head.

A familiar voice could be heard from behind her. "Yo, J, how you doing?"

Cameron saw Scott step up and hug Julia. When he turned around and saw Cameron, his smile faded fast.

"This is Cameron," said Julia. "He's the one I told you about who's really talented. Have you met before?"

Chewing on a fat wad of gum, Scott said "Don't think so. J, let's go."

He grabbed Julia by the arm and pulled her along. She gave a fleeting wave to Cameron who stood, slack-jawed. Then he took a long deep breath.

Suddenly, he felt a large hand grip his shoulder. A voice whispered in his ear. "If you ever talk to her again, you're dead. Got that?"

The hand released its grip. Cameron saw Scott heading back to Julia, yelling to her "Just had to tell your friend not to forget to come cheer for our team this weekend."

Cameron felt his heart pounding. If he could find some quicksand right now, he'd jump in and suffocate to death so he could escape middle school altogether.

CHAPTER 3 FROM WORSE TO WORST

Most of the time when Cameron came home from school, his mother lay on the couch asleep while the television muttered on. Her snores came in bursts like the rapid snorts of a pig, almost waking her each time. As he approached, he smelled her stench breath, a mix of alcohol and cigarettes.

He rarely waked her. Sometimes she slept through dinner and even into the night. Today was different though as she wanted to go to town and always preferred having him along.

He tapped her arm, gently at first, then a bit firmer until she opened one bloodshot eye. As she opened the other eye, it took a moment for Cameron to come into focus. "What do you want?" she barked in her craggy voice.

"You told me to wake you when I got home," he said.

She rubbed her eyes and squeezed her nose to suppress a sneeze. "And why would I ask you to do that?"

"Because you need to go to town," he said. "To the bank and the market. And maybe the library."

She tried standing but slipped back onto the couch. Cameron offered his arm for support. She managed to get to her feet and shuffled across the room on wobbly legs.

"Do you want me to come back when you're ready?" he asked.

"Yeah, that's a good idea," she said, rubbing her eyes.

Cameron retreated to the safety of his room and paid a visit to his frog Robert. Robert stared, blink less, his throat pulsating. Cameron splashed a small bit of water on his back, making it glisten.

"You're my best friend, Robert," he said, sprinkling in some flakes of food.

"Where are you, boy?" hollered his mother. He leaped up and ran out of the room.

He stood in the front hallway and helped her slide into her shoes. From the side table, she took a check, her purse and the car keys.

Exiting the house, they went to a detached rundown one car garage. Inside sat a badly dinged up navy blue Buick with a cracked front windshield and a large oval discolored grey spot on the hood. Clearly in need of a muffler, the car rumbled loudly when started and every time the accelerator was pressed down.

As she drove to town, going way below the 35 mile per hour speed limit, a parade of cars lined up behind her. Every bump in the road underscored the need for new shock absorbers as they bounced in their seats. And when she pushed the accelerator too much, a plume of bluish-grey smoke spewed out the exhaust pipe polluting the air.

She got the car second hand and for very little money. $2500 total. That was mainly because it had been in a very bad accident. Because the law dictated that all sellers were obligated to disclose a car's full history of repairs and accidents, she knew what she was buying. Four years ago, she learned that the previous owner's daughter, a teenage girl who'd just gotten her license, got drunk at a party and lost control of the car. It spun off the road tumbling down a steep embankment, finally slamming into a stone wall. She was dead on impact. The battered car was destined for scrap metal but a local mechanic bought it on the cheap, put in enough repairs to make it operable and then resold it. Learning of its history, Cameron nicknamed it the "car of death."

"Where are we going?" his mother asked.

"What did you say, Ethel?" asked Cameron, caught in a state of daydreaming. Oddly, she used the last name of "Weiss" whereas

Cameron went with "Foster." Cameron never knew his father as he died when he was very young and he heard very little about him.

"Where should we go first?" she repeated.

"The bank," he said. "And you need to get there before they close."

She pulled up and onto the curb, the front wheel plopping off again with a thump. "Come in with me," she said.

Cameron's preference was always to stay in the car. On rare occasions she allowed him to do so. But not today. She liked having him with her at the bank. Her hearing wasn't great and he often served as interpreter. The truth is that Cameron was embarrassed being seen in public with his mother as people gazed at her like she was a witch. Disheveled and unkempt, she did little to discourage these notions.

Every other week she received a check from the US Government. He watched her cash them, assuming it was an unemployment check.

After the bank came the market, a true torture as he eyed so many things he would love to have. Whenever he reached for a box of cereal or cookies, she made him return them to the shelf. She spent very little on food. And only when she completely ran out of bread or milk did, she go to the market. Cameron survived on very little food which explained why he was so scrawny.

Passing the cereal aisle, Ethel said, "You can get one box of cereal but it's got to last you all week."

Cameron's eyes lit up as he grabbed Frosted Flakes, tossing it into the cart. His mother added a loaf of white bread, a jar of peanut butter, a chocolate bar and a box of prunes. After the cashier rang up everything, Ethel grimaced at the total. Not having a credit card, she counted out her bills and change from a baggie in her purse. It was a deathly slow process. Cameron felt uneasy as directly behind them was a girl from his home room. She and her mother, impatient by how long it was taking, exhaled loudly. Cameron avoided all eye contact, one of his specialties, hoping this would be over soon.

Back in the car, he told his mother "We have one last stop. The library."

"What do we need there?" she grumbled.

"We need to go online so I can register for something at school," he said. "It has to be done by the parent."

"I don't have an email address," she said.

"Yes, you do," noted Cameron. "We got one for you a month ago."

"Okay. But that'll be the last stop."

Cameron saw the library as a quiet sanctuary, a place to retreat to after school. He much preferred it to his own home. He had been there enough to know where everything was. He went immediately to the computer station, logging into the South Middle School website and locating the entry information for the Variety Show.

"Just fill in the information and send it in," he instructed his mother.

She pecked away at the keys and asked Cameron to proofread it. He caught a few errors which were corrected. Just then who appeared but Arne. With a shake of his head, he signaled for Arne to go away which he did.

Looking back at the computer, Cameron asked his mother "Did you send it?"

"Think so," she said. "Let's go home."

■■

At school the next day, the unexpected happened. Tommy approached Cameron.

"I thought I'd catch you before lunch," said Tommy. "I'm not saying I'm going to be your friend because I haven't really decided if I want your friendship but I did want to offer you some advice."

"Is at about quicksand?" asked Cameron.

"No. Quicksand is not a problem you should worry about."

"I'm listening," said Cameron.

Tommy leaned in and soft whispered "You need to stand up to Scott. Bullies keep picking on people like you because they know you won't fight back or stand up to them. If you don't, he will make your life a living hell."

"I'm not sure how to do that," said Cameron.

"Don't be rude or anything," said Tommy. "But also, don't put up with his physical or verbal abuse. I know he's older, and bigger and stronger but you need to earn his respect. I'm telling you this as a friend, um, or rather a former friend. I don't plan to renew our friendship at this time but that doesn't mean I don't care what happens to you. Do you understand?"

Cameron nodded.

"Okay. Enough said. See ya around," said Tommy, walking away.

Cameron felt pleased by Tommy's caring words, imagining a day when their friendship would be revived. He remained after school for his music lesson, one of the few things he looked forward to.

Mr. Michael came over, smiling. "I've got something for you," he said, reaching into his pocket and pulling out an old iPod. "I want you to have this."

Cameron's eyes widened as he took the ivory white iPod, cradling it in his hands like it was gold.

"It's a bit dated but loaded with songs," he said.

"Thank you."

Cameron nestled in the earphones, then swiped his finger and got a song. The clarity was so magnificent it felt like The Rolling Stones had taken up space in his head to play Start Me Up.

After listening to a few songs, Mr. Michael gave him his lesson, leaving him exuberant and upbeat. The sun warmed his neck as he walked home, guitar slung on one shoulder and backpack on the other. Music played in his head all the time whether he had an iPod or not.

He sensed trouble, feeling dark shadows around him. Looking up, he saw four guys standing in his way, blocking the sidewalk. He first saw Scott and next to him was his overweight sidekick Joe and two jocks named Van and Hank.

Cameron came to a sudden halt, then stepped towards the road to go around them.

"Aren't you going to pay the toll?" said Scott. "There's no E-Z Pass here."

Cameron barely could breathe.

"Answer me when I'm talking to you," said Scott, his voice rising in anger.

Cameron saw no escape route.

Scott pointed to his guys. "Joe. Van. Escort this young man to my office."

Ever obedient, Joe and Van did as they were told, rarely thinking for themselves. Each took one of Cameron's arms, leading him to a clearing in the woods, out of sight from the road. All four surrounded Cameron, making any escape an act of futility.

"You know," said Scott. "I still don't like you much at all. I really don't. I don't like the way you look, the way you dress, the way you talk, your whole attitude. It all sucks big time."

Cameron's knees began to tremble.

"Look at me when I'm talking to you," barked Scott. "Where are your fucking manners."

Cameron looked at Scott.

"So how is Mr. Musician Man" said Scott, chuckling. His cronies laughed too.

Scott wrenched the guitar case from Cameron. Instinctively, Cameron resisted but Joe pushed him back. Scott unzipped the guitar case and pulled out the guitar. He rapped his knuckles against the wood veneer as though knocking on someone's door.

"You don't keep this in very good shape," he said, disapproving, as his finger slid along the many scrapes and scratches on it. "You mind if I play a few notes? Of course, you don't."

Tempted to speak out, Cameron kept silent instead. But a helpless anger and frustration built up inside.

Scott strummed harshly, producing the most irritating sounds, fractured chords in minor keys. "This thing sucks," he said. "I mean, I know it couldn't be me, could it?" With that he dropped the guitar to the ground, lifted his right leg and crushed it with his foot. The wood veneer splintered as his foot broke through. He then jumped on it with both feet, this time breaking the neck. The strings, once taut, now hung limp.

Chewing on his lip, his eyes unblinking, Cameron gazed down at "his friend," feeling totally helpless. His guitar remained the one thing in this world he cherished and now it had been destroyed. He felt overwhelmed with emotion and found it difficult to breathe. Gasping, he glared at Scott.

"Guess you won't be impressing my girlfriend anymore," said Scott.

Tommy's voice echoed in Cameron's head, egging him on, telling him to stand up to this bully. With a nothing-to-lose attitude, he took a step towards Scott.

"Oh my," said Scott, sarcastically. "I'm so scared. Don't come any closer."

Cameron braved another step forward.

"Brave brave brave," said Scott. "But stupid stupid stupid."

Scott signaled to Hank who knelt behind Cameron like a human ottoman. Scott gave Cameron a shove and watched him topple hard to the ground, landing on his tailbone, right next to his busted guitar.

For most of his life, Cameron never cried and today was no exception.

"Your girlfriend on the motorcycle going to rescue you today? I don't think so," said Scott.

Cameron got up and stood in front of Scott once more.

"Back for more, are we?" said Scott. His cronies grabbed Cameron by the arms, holding him in place. Scott slipped a pocketknife from his back pocket and jabbed it near his stomach. Then he cut off a clump of Cameron's hair with the knife. He did it two more times, leaving his hair a ragged mess.

Cameron then got pushed to the ground.

"Stay there," ordered Scott. "Where you belong. In the dirt."

Random thoughts cycled through Cameron's mind...his broken guitar...his chopped up hair...his drunken mother....and Tommy's words, once again, telling him to stand up to bullies. Struggling now to gain his balance, he stood up once more, spitting distance from Scott.

"What are you, deaf?!" said Scott.

Irritated by his obstinance, Scott threw a punch that grazed Cameron's mouth, knocking his lip against his front teeth and unleashing a stream of blood. Scott threw another punch, this one landing in his gut, sending him back to the ground. For one brief moment, Cameron considered staying on the ground. But Tommy's voice urged him to get up. And he did.

Scott knocked him back to the ground again. This time he hovered over, trying to stop him from standing up. Cameron somehow managed to stand up again like some inflatable clown you punched as a kid.

"You know, you're not worth any more of my time," said Scott, annoyed by Cameron's defiance. "Let's go guys."

The gang of four followed, leaving their prey behind. Cameron stood as still as a statue, expressionless, waiting patiently until they were completely out of sight. He swung his backpack onto his sore shoulder then knelt down by his guitar, a fallen comrade, and gathered what remained in his arms before hobbling out of the woods.

■■■

Until he took that first look in the mirror, Cameron had no idea how badly beaten up he was. His nose, swollen to twice its normal size, couldn't function well, causing him to breathe entirely through his mouth. His lower lip hung down; a dark gash had dried to a cancerous-looking black scab. His right eye had purplish bruising just below it. Swiveling his head, he saw the missing chunks of hair.

He took a washcloth, dampened it with warm water and dabbed it against his face. He ached everywhere. Fortunately, his mother was asleep upstairs. He heard her snores.

Opening his mouth wide, he checked his teeth from top to bottom. All were accounted for though one in the front seemed loose. A missing tooth has ruined many a face and would have been a humiliating reminder of the whole bad experience.

Cameron swigged down a glass of cold milk, his lip painfully tender, then crept quietly upstairs, peering into his mother's room. Spotting a half-full vodka bottle by her bedside, he knew he wouldn't see much of her this evening. That was a relief even though she probably wouldn't have noticed a thing wrong with him. He slipped back into the hallway just as the doorbell rang. Fortunately, his mother didn't hear it. Panicked, he hustled downstairs, taking two at a time, supporting himself on the railing.

The front door, a heavy oak, had no peephole. Cameron unlatched the door and cracked it open a few inches.

Standing there in her black leather attire was 'Leather Girl,' the only name he knew her by.

"Hi," she said. "Mind if I come in?"

"Is it important?" asked Cameron.

"I think so," she said.

Reluctantly, he undid the safety chain and opened the door.

Stepping into the house in her black leather boots, she observed his bruised face. "What happened to you?" she asked with concern.

"I tripped and fell," he said. "I'm clumsy. Really clumsy." He had no desire to tell her the truth. If she got involved now, it would only make matters worse.

Lying on the floor nearby was his busted guitar. It caught her eye but she remained silent.

"Are you busy tonight?" she asked.

"Yes," he quickly replied. "Very busy."

"Really?" she pursued, not believing him.

"I actually have a paper due tomorrow that I haven't even started," he said. "In fact, I don't even know what I'm going to write about."

"What is the assignment?" she asked.

Rubbing his neck nervously, he said, "It's supposed to be based on a personal experience I have had."

"Such as?"

"Well, it could be meeting someone important like the mayor in town," he replied.

"And what did you decide to do?" she inquired.

Shrugging his shoulders, he said "Dunno."

"Well, I have something special to offer you," she said. "Have you ever been to a rock concert before?"

He shook his head.

"Well, tonight you can change that. If it's okay with your parents, you should come with me. You won't be disappointed."

"It's just my mother and me," he said.

"So, is it a date?"

The temptation to go was strong but something didn't feel quite right. He barely knew this woman. Had only seen her twice before. Why would she want to do something nice for him? What was in it for her? He wanted to ask a million questions, starting with her name, but he couldn't overcome his shyness. And he just felt it would appear rude if he questioned her motives.

Checking her watch, she said "I'll need to know soon."

He exhaled through his sore lips, contemplating his options. As he did so, she glanced around the room, noticing a receipt from a US Government-issued check. The US Treasury, to be exact.

"I can't go because I don't have any money," he said.

"You are my guest," she replied, nixing that excuse.

"Oh. Alright. But I'm kind of sore from my fall," he said.

"This evening will make you forget all of your pain," she said. "That I promise."

Hesitating, trying to think of another excuse, Cameron gave in. "Okay then."

"Well, put on a jacket and let's go," she said.

Cameron tugged a navy blue windbreaker from the hall closet and headed outside towards her motorcycle. Two helmets hung from the handlebars. She took the one with the red and black swirl design and slipped it on her head then she put the other with the blue and black stripes on Cameron's head as gently as she could. He winced as it pressed against his sore chin but gave her a thumbs up that he was fine. She straddled the Harley, slipped down her visor and waited for Cameron to do the same. Pushing the cycle off its kickstand, she turned on the motor, revving it several times before patching out of the driveway into the dimming light.

The windblown ride took them sailing down the Merritt Parkway, a scenic two-lane road that swerved over the beautiful tree-laden terrain. They leaned into each turn, passing the slower moving cars with ease. Fortunately, the road only had cars as trucks weren't allowed.

Passing the majestic George Washington Bridge, he looked at it in awe as they soared down the West Side Highway before finally getting off an exit. Cameron had never seen New York City and was amazed at the vast number of yellow cabs and ultra tall buildings.

The traffic lights, synchronized down Ninth Avenue, allowed for a fast uninterrupted trip to Madison Square Garden. As the traffic grew heavy, she weaved in and out of the cars. Arriving at a service entrance, she flashed a laminated pass and the security guard waved her through. Inside the garage, she angled her cycle in between a Mercedes Benz 600 series and a long white stretch limousine.

Climbing off the cycle, she said "We made great time. Leave your helmet hanging on the handlebar."

Taking him by the hand, she slipped a laminated pass around his neck and hustled past two more security guards who seemed to know her. Cameron had no idea what concert they were going to see. Had he peeked at the laminated passes, he would have known but he was too preoccupied with his surroundings. They walked down a long corridor, turned, and walked down another long corridor, coming to an enormous freight elevator.

An elderly elevator operator, probably past retirement age, closed the door and the elevator lumbered up two floors. They exited and were immediately greeted by two beefy bodyguards who looked like they couldn't find shirts that fit. They each had huge muscular bodies not too different from the Incredible Hulk. Their necks were as thick as their heads and each sported an earpiece just like the secret service. Cameron could also see that they were strapped, revolvers visible, tucked in leather shoulder straps.

"They're expecting us," she said to the guards.

"Yes, they are," one of the guards said, opening the door with a Do Not Disturb: Band One Only sign on it.

Entering the room, she explained to Cameron, "This is the Green Room."

Cameron could not see the logic in her comment as there was not the faintest trace of green in the windowless room. Not even a plant. The walls were painted yellow and the furniture was a bland brown and black.

"Have a seat," she said, plopping down on a couch.

Cameron lowered himself onto the couch. He stared at a television monitor that showed a warm-up band playing in the arena. He wasn't familiar with them. On a long table was an array of food – crackers and cheese, crudité, cookies and candy.

"If you're hungry, help yourself," she said.

Cameron stood up and headed straight for the candy, taking a pack of twizzlers, skittles and peanut M&Ms. Just as he did, two men entered the room, startling him. The first one, who was holding two drumsticks, said jokingly "Leave something for us, please."

Cameron placed the candy back. "I'm just kidding you, son," he said with an Irish accent.

Leather Girl came over to greet them, giving warm hugs to both. "This is Cameron," she said.

"Cameron," said the first. "That's a nice Scottish name. You do hear it in Ireland, too. Are you Scottish?"

Cameron shrugged his shoulders. "I don't know what I am," he said softly.

"Cameron, this is Larry," said Leather Girl, making the introduction. "He started the band. Got to give him credit for that. "

Larry shook hands with Cameron whose shyness kept his eyes lowered.

"How old are you?" he asked.

"Ten."

"Have you seen us play before?"

He shook his head not certain what the band was.

"This is his first concert ever," said Leather Girl, gnawing on a carrot.

"Well, we're honored," said Larry, his short brown hair in an immaculate crewcut.

"And this is Adam," said Leather Girl.

The silver-haired musician named Adam shook hands. "You like music?" he asked.

"He's a very talented guitarist," she said. "Very."

"Coming from you that says a lot," said Adam.

"If you'll excuse me, I want to get some last bit of therapy for my hands," said Larry. "That's what the drums'll do to you." He left the room twirling his drumsticks as he went out.

Adam went over and swigged some water. As he did, the door opened again and this time the person who entered was someone Cameron was very familiar with. It was The Edge from U2 and right behind him was the band's lead singer Bono. Cameron's jaw dropped. He had never seen a celebrity in person before. It all felt surreal.

"Hi," said Cameron, feeling like he knew them. "I'm Cameron."

"So we've heard," said Bono wearing his distinctive tinted sunglasses, this pair sported pink lenses. He kissed Leather Girl on both cheeks as did the Edge, a clear indication they knew her well.

"I'm The Edge," he said, introducing himself to Cameron and wearing his trademark black knitted cap tightly fitting his head. Known as a toque, he wore it in every photo he was in.

"I love your nicknames," said Cameron.

"Do you have one?" asked Bono.

Cameron shook his head. "I don't know how I get one," he said.

"David?" said Leather Girl, turning towards The Edge. "Tell him."

"Mine came from Bono," he explained with a wry smile, a friendly glint in his eyes. "I think it was cause I have sharp features."

"And a sharp mind," added Bono. "He observes things on the edge."

"Or is it the ledge," smiled The Edge.

"And tell him yours, Paul?" she said, looking at Bono.

"I hated mine at first," said Bono. "It came from the name of an old hearing aid company called Bonovox. Me mate Guggi gave it to me. My friends felt I was going to deafen them all with my singing so this was their way to take a poke at me. The funny thing is that Bonovox means 'Good Voice'. So, it's actually rather a complimentary nickname."

"And Adam?" she asked.

"No nickname to speak of," he said. "Just a few my wife uses when she's upset."

Studying Cameron's face, Bono finally asked "And what, if I may ask, happened to you? Your eyes. Your lip. Your hair. You been stage diving?"

Cameron felt ashamed of his appearance.

"You getting picked on?" asked Bono.

Cameron kept quiet.

"You can talk to us," said The Edge in a soft thoughtful tone.

Cameron sighed. "Sometimes."

"I knew your barber couldn't be that bad," said The Edge, reaching into a tote bag and pulling out an extra black cap which he slipped on Cameron's head. "This will help."

Taking his lead, Bono took out an extra pair of tinted sunglasses and put them on Cameron, making him look like an amalgam of the two rock superstars. The glasses were a tad on the big side, after all he was just a kid, but they looked ultra cool all the same.

There was a quick rap on the door as it opened. This person had black hair, stiff as straw, parted in the middle, contrasted by a pasty white face. It was Jack White, an immensely talented rock star whose music Cameron knew and liked.

"Hey guys," he said. "Just wishing you a good show."

Recognizing Leather Girl, Jack said "This is a pleasant surprise."

They embraced after which she introduced Cameron. "Jack, this is Cameron."

"Hey man," he said, offering a high five.

"He's a great guitarist," she said.

"How old are you?" Jack asked.

"Ten," said Cameron.

"You must be good if she says so," he replied. "Did you say ten? That's freaking cool. Hope to hear you play sometime. I'm going to go take my seat. Good luck chaps. And nice to meet you, Cameron who is ten."

Cameron couldn't believe that Jack White just uttered his name. He wished he had a recording of that moment. It would live in his head forever.

Jack White left and Adam asked Cameron "You like rock music?"

Cameron gave an enthusiastic nod.

Leather Girl took an acoustic guitar from a corner of the room and handed it to Cameron. "Play something for them," she said.

Slipping the guitar strap over his neck, Cameron readied himself. "What should I play?" he asked.

"Anything," she said. "Do a quick medley."

The full-size guitar dwarfed Cameron but his small fingers weren't to be denied. He began with the catchy familiar riff from U2's own 'Vertigo' then segued into Led Zeppelin's 'Black Dog' and ended with part of a classical piece, variations on a theme by Mozart Op 9 by Fernando Sor.

The band members all looked on, impressed. "You busy tonight?" asked Bono. "You ought to be playing with us."

"Or we should be playing with you," said The Edge.

"He's really got it," said Leather Girl. "Z hasn't seen him yet but I know he'll be impressed."

"Say hi to the old man," said Bono, turning to Cameron. "Any special requests tonight?"

"I like all of your songs," said Cameron.

"Good answer," said Adam. "Smart kid."

A stagehand entered the room. "Ten minutes," he said.

"We should take our seats," said the leather girl. "Thanks guys."

Cameron could have sat in that room forever. He was on such a high and he hadn't yet heard a note of their music. He high-fived the band members as he left the room. The leather girl navigated backstage and they soon emerged into the darkened arena. Cameron could feel the intense air of anticipation as the capacity crowd waited to see U2, knowing they would be on soon.

An usher, flashlight in hand, guided them to their seats on the side front mezzanine. The advantage to these seats was they were raised so no one obscured their view. At a U2 concert, and many others, that was particularly important as most people stood the entire time. Cameron still wasn't tall enough to see a concert from the floor.

The crowd started chanting 'U2,' the noise building to a crescendo as the whole building seemed to shake. People stomped their feet in unison. Then suddenly the lights lowered even more, triggering an enormous roar from the crowd. The many faces disappeared. With a burst of light, two sudden pyrotechnical explosions erupted on the stage and the band appeared out of nowhere, delving into a high-rocking version of the already propulsive 'Vertigo.' Bono, so cool and stylish and sporting a microphone headset, roamed the stage and its catwalks, his image projected on enormous high-definition screens on either side. His expressive falsetto voice, as unique as a fingerprint, progressed from familiar song to familiar song, rockers to ballads to anthems. Larry's drumming powered the foursome, matched with Adam's strong bass lines, marching steadily together while The Edge's distinctive guitar sound, jangly and rhythmic, echoed with his signature delay. As the ambient and chiming lead guitar ventured its own way, Bono's voice cried over it, pleading his social causes to great effect.

Having never seen a rock concert before, Cameron stood, utterly mesmerized in rapturous disbelief. The whole experience surpassed any expectations he could have mustered.

The band finished its two and a half hour set, then returned for three encores. After the first, Bono paused and said "Thank you. Thank you. Thank you. We now want to close with a song for a very special person who is with us here tonight. This marks his first concert ever. He's ten and his name is Cameron. This one's for you."

Leather Girl beamed as she watched Cameron's mouth fall agape. U2 then played "I Still Haven't Found What I'm Looking For." Cameron loved that song beyond words and to have it dedicated to him was simply amazing. The crowd joined in on the chorus as they had with many of the songs that night. The arena vibrated with love and feeling and compassion as most held up their smartphones, the light from each appearing like candles from afar, dotting the arena like a prayer vigil. Where once cigarette lighters did the trick, the cellphone now prevailed as a safer and more modern alternative. As the song ended, the band took bows, gesturing their thanks to the enthusiastic crowd which responded with a roar of approval. As the band left the stage, the lights popped on, signaling the end of the encores. The concert was officially over.

Cameron wanted to preserve this night forever. He had no interest in leaving. Leather Girl seized his hand and led him backstage, an easier egress from the sea of concert-goers moving so slow and deliberate, small step after small step, towards the exits.

"Can we visit the band in the Green Room now?" Cameron asked. "I want to thank them for the most amazing night of my entire life."

Leather Girl smiled. "They are probably not in the building anymore," she replied. "Once they leave the stage, they tug off their sweaty clothes, often donning bathrobes and hop into waiting limousines or a tour bus that whisks them back to their hotel suites."

"Oh."

Leather Girl navigated them to the freight elevator and down to her waiting motorcycle. With helmets on and ready to go, she said, "Hold on good and tight. You're probably very tired and I don't want to lose you on the ride home."

"I'm not tired at all," said Cameron, energized from the whole night. As the motorcycle sped down the Merritt Parkway, Cameron's mind recaptured the concert, song by song, image by image. Before he knew it, they'd arrived back at his house.

CHAPTER 4 DEATH KNELL

The morning sunlight pierced through his bedroom window, tickling his eyes and nose and prompting a sneeze. He awoke, startled that he'd overslept and was missing school. Rubbing his tired and itchy eyes, he sat up, wondering if the previous night was all a dream. But gazing down at the floor proved it was all true. First, he saw the tinted sunglasses and black skull cap. Then, askew on the floor lay his school notebook in which he'd scribbled his personal essay, recounting the night and his conversation with the band. He had written it when he got home because he was so energized, he couldn't sleep.

Dressing quickly for school, Cameron spotted his mother by the landing.

"Morning," he said, curious to see if she'd even noticed he was missing last night. Clearly not. She didn't say a thing. She just gestured, giving a faint wave before returning to her bedroom.

Cameron felt so eager to hand in his school essay. He wished he could bring in props – the cap and sunglasses –but this assignment didn't ask for them. He half-wanted to wear the cap to school but rules forbid any headgear.

At school he ran into Arne in the hallway. "You get your paper done on time?" Arne asked, not initially noticing Cameron's battered face.

Cameron gave an enthusiastic smile.

"It was a bitch figuring out what to write," said Arne. "What did you choose?"

"U2," said Cameron.

"The rock group?" asked Arne.

"Yep."

"What about them?"

"I saw them in concert last night," said Cameron. "And I met them all."

"Sweet!" said Arne, before hesitating and adding "But did you really? This paper can't be fictional. It's got to be stuff that really happened to you."

"It all happened. I swear."

"And what happened to your face?" asked Arne. "And your hair?"

Other classmates walking past couldn't help but notice the bruise beneath his eye, his still swollen lower lip and chopped up hair.

"Bono mentioned me by name from the stage," added Cameron.

Arne looked at him skeptically now. "Well, I'm not sure I believe you but at least you had some good news there cause I saw the list posted for the variety show and your name wasn't on it."

Cameron felt immediate disappointment. "Where'd you see it?"

"It's posted online and is also on the board by the front of the school entrance," said Arne.

Cameron found time to detour past the bulletin board. Sure enough, his name was missing. Almost sixty students listed, several of whom he knew, but not him. He stepped into the main office and inquired about it. A woman there referred him to Ms. Horner, the head of the music department. He managed to catch up to her at the end of school. Ms. Horner wore wire-rim glasses and always kept her hair in a bun. She also had perfect rod-like posture and not an ounce of humor. Cameron politely approached her. "Hello Miss Horner. I think my name was left off the Variety Show list," he said.

"I have nothing to do with that," she replied. "It is handled entirely by the mothers on the committee. You need to contact them. Ms. Periwinkle is running it this year. I can give you her contact information."

She checked her smart phone. "Should I email it to you?" she asked.

"Could you write it down?"

She obliged.

Cameron went to the school library where he emailed Ms. Periwinkle, claiming a mistake had been made. Shortly after he sent it, a response came back. It simply read, "Your application was never received. Sorry. There is always next year."

How could that be, thought Cameron. He went to the library and saw his mother send in the email. Or at least he saw her type it. Could she have botched it by not hitting the send button? In all likelihood that was probably what happened. But that was less than a week ago. Surely, they could make an exception and add him.

At his next music lesson with Mr. Michael, he brought up the Variety Show.

"Do you have any influence over the Variety Show?" he asked.

"In the past they have asked me to help out," he said. "Aren't you forgetting something?"

"I got the application done in time," Cameron said defensively.

Scratching his head, Mr. Michael said "I don't know what you're talking about. I meant your guitar. You didn't bring it. Or so it seems."

Cameron didn't know what to say.

"You can borrow mine today," he said. "It's a bit bigger but it'll be good for you to practice on."

Cameron had no desire to explain what happened to his guitar. He felt oddly embarrassed by the whole thing. Eventually, he might say something. Probably that it was stolen. No point stirring up more trouble.

"What application are you talking about?" Mr. Michael asked, tuning his guitar.

"The one for the Variety Show," he replied. "They say they never got it. But I had my mother do it. I'm her witness."

"I'll fix that," he said, assuredly. Slipping out his cellphone, he tapped in a phone number. "Hello, Ms. Periwinkle," he said. "Hi. Nice to hear your voice as well. And I want you to know I'm available to help with the show if you need me this year. Absolutely. I'm calling about Cameron Foster. He told me his mother sent in the form."

There was a long pause.

"But why can't you make an exception?" he asked.

As he listened to her, he shook his head in disgust.

"I understand," he said, patiently. "But has there been anyone else who called in asking to be added?"

He held the phone away from his ear not wanting to hear her drivel.

"I think it's a real shame," he said. "This kid is a major talent and to deprive him of this special night is just not right. It's devastating for him. It is totally in your power to say yes. I hope you'll reconsider."

He ended the call and looked at Cameron. "She won't change her mind," he said. "A real bureaucrat. I'm sorry."

Cameron masked his disappointment, showing no reaction.

"I wish I could say life is fair," he added. "But sometimes it isn't. Let's practice."

Cameron's musical gift allowed him to play effortlessly even when his mind was wandering. Playing guitar was second nature like breathing. He could hear a note and instantly tell you which one it was. And he could see the notes in his head as clear as reading sheet music.

Today his mind shifted into the world of bullies and their victims. He envisioned a witness protection program that plucked out victims and gave them safe harbor at a special school. Everyone co-existed so well because they had all been bullied and didn't dare become bullies. Beautiful music wafted through the air 24/7 and large jungle-like plants dominated the landscape. But the calmness soon was broken by a voice saying over and over "Answer me when I'm talking to you."

Cameron's eyes opened. He was no longer in his guitar lesson. Somehow, he'd walked out of the school building on his way home and sat on a green park bench immersed in thought. He'd never sat on this bench before. In fact, he'd never even noticed it was there. Its likely purpose, to accommodate students waiting for rides. Because he always walked home, he never waited for a ride.

He felt mentally and physically fatigued. The many stresses in his life had preyed on his mind, rotating over and over and leaving him in a state of worry and distress. Yet he always kept them to himself. He looked over at the flagpole, the red, white and blue flopping limply at the top in a tired breeze. Below, waiting for a ride, was Tommy who made it a point not to glance over in Cameron's direction. Cameron decided not to bother him. Instead, he went over to the green slatted bench.

Cameron lowered his head in his hands and breathed deeply, trying to calm himself. He felt someone's presence. Somebody brushed up against him uncomfortably close. He scooted an inch away but this person did the same, cramping him once more. Cameron looked up, expecting to see a classmate or friend. Instead, he saw someone he knew but didn't care to see. It was Joe, one of Scott's cronies, the one who took orders, unable to think for himself.

"What are you waiting for?" asked Joe. "A ride home?"

"No. I walk home."

"Well you're not making much progress," he said, sniveling from allergies to pollen.

Cameron slid all the way to one end of the bench.

"Your hair'll grow back...in time," Joe observed.

"Why does he hate me?" Cameron asked.

"Why does who hate you?"

"Scott."

"Why do you think he hates you?"

"I don't know," said Cameron. "I try to blend in."

"He doesn't like people who blend in," said Joe. "And he also doesn't like people who don't blend in."

"Do you hate me, too?" asked Cameron.

"Well, when I'm with Scott, I have to," said Joe.

"And when you're not?"

"You're alright, I guess," he said. "I mean, I wouldn't choose to have you as a friend or be related to you or anything."

"But you don't hate me, right?"

Joe shook his head.

"What can I do?" asked Cameron.

"Well, the thing is," said Joe. "I came over here to tell you that Scott wants to see you after school tomorrow. Down by Jones Field."

Cameron blanched, all the color draining from his face, his breathing practically stopped. "Why?"

"He doesn't believe you have a friend in the world," said Joe. "He wants you to prove him wrong. Show up tomorrow with your best friend after school. Do that and he said he'd leave you alone."

Puzzled, Cameron thought about it. "Can I really trust him?" he asked.

"You don't have a whole lot of options," said Joe.

Joe rose from the bench, stretched his arms and sauntered off, his mission accomplished. Cameron noticed that Tommy was still waiting for his ride. He decided this time to approach him.

"Hi," he said.

Tommy acted deaf.

"Can I ask you something?" said Cameron.

"Why were you talking to that guy? Don't you know he's bad news?" replied Tommy, gazing at Cameron.

"He came up to me," said Cameron. "That's what I want to talk to you about. Remember that Scott guy? Well, apparently he wants to see me after school tomorrow."

"On a Friday? What a jerk."

"If I show up with my best friend, Scott promised to leave me alone," said Cameron.

"And you believe him?"

"Well, I don't have much choice," said Cameron, fidgeting with his fingers. "So, I was wondering if you might show up with me."

"And why would I do that?"

Cameron hesitated. "Because."

"We're not best friends," said Tommy. "Remember?"

"Well, I thought things were better between us and—"

A car pulled up to the curb. "I gotta go," said Tommy. "My ride's here."

And with that, Cameron's one hope vanished in a Ford Escape.

When he got home, Cameron had a rare sighting of his mother. He waved to her as she rummaged for something in the kitchen. He headed upstairs. Wanting to build some muscle, he started doing sit-ups, struggling to do a dozen. Then, he tackled push-ups which were even more difficult to do in any quantity. His face reddened from the exercise. Standing up, he flexed his arm but there was no new muscle. He was as scrawny as ever, his physique best described as anemic. He would never be able to confront a bully. As he bent down to do more push-ups, he noticed Robert in the aquarium. It occurred to him in one brilliant moment that Robert was his ticket out of Bullyville. He would bring Robert with him after school and proclaim that this was his best friend. Scott couldn't argue with that. He never said best human friend. Just best friend. Scott might even appreciate this move.

Admiring his idea, Cameron climbed into bed, staring at the ceiling, feeling much more relaxed. But then the doorbell rang and gripped him like a seizure. No one ever rang their doorbell at night. He leapt up and hurdled downstairs, only to run into his mother who was also going towards the door. She got there first, opening it with little caution. There, much to Cameron's horror, stood Leather girl, dressed in her usual black attire.

"Who are you?" his mother asked, her craggy voice sounding rude and unfriendly.

"I know her," said Cameron, nudging in front of his mother.

"Who is she?" his mother persisted. "She must have a name. Most people do."

Mumbling to himself, Cameron replied, "She's my teacher." It was all he could think to say as he really didn't know how to refer to her. A friend? No. Acquaintance? Sort of.

His mother gave her the once over. With a disapproving sneer, she said "And the school lets you dress like that? Times sure have changed."

Leather Girl straightened her posture and said "I am sorry to stop by so unexpectedly but I didn't have another way to get in touch with your son."

"Well, so be it," his mother replied, turning to walk away.

"I was hoping Cameron could join me on Saturday for a brief outing," she said. "I want to show him the power of music."

"Well, that's between you and him, my dear," she said. "I frankly don't care what you do." Sniffling and coughing at the same time, she shuffled toward the kitchen.

Leather Girl looked at Cameron. "Sorry if I caught you off guard," she said. "Are you okay?"

He gave half a nod.

"That's not very convincing," she said.

"I'm okay," he said.

"What's bothering you?"

He shrugged his shoulders.

"Come on, tell me," she persisted.

"No, really. It's nothing."

"If it's nothing, then you can tell me."

"Well, it's not 100% nothing."

"Go on."

"Well, I didn't get into the Variety Show at school," he said.

"What?!"

"They claim they didn't get my application in time," he said. "But I went to the library with my mother and saw her fill it out."

"And you saw her hit Send?"

Cameron hesitated. "Well, not really. I got distracted and didn't actually see her hit Send."

"I'll fix this," she said with confidence.

"I don't think you can," he said. "My music teacher already approached the lady in charge and she didn't budge at all."

"We'll see."

"I really wouldn't bother," he replied. "You see, I don't have a guitar to play. So even if I got into the Variety Show, it wouldn't matter."

"Leave it to me," she said. "Now, the reason I came here was to see if you can come with me on Saturday?"

"Where?"

"I can't really say," she replied, sounding mysterious. "I can tell you this. It's not another concert. I'm sorry if I'm being vague but I have to be. So, I'll pick you up. Saturday morning. 8am. I want to make sure we have plenty of time."

With a quick wave, she turned and left the house. Cameron heard her descend down the front steps. Then, after a moment of silence, he heard the vroom of her motorcycle which gradually faded as she rode off.

■■

The power of a single letter amazingly could generate fear or disappointment or love or many other things. An X often marked the treasure on a pirate's map, or an illiterate's signature or, at the end of a note, X stood for a kiss often accompanied by the letter O for a hug. Several hundred years back the letter 'A' sewn on a woman's sweater or jacket indicated adultery. V valiantly stood for victory whereas a Z joined by a few more suggested sleep.

Mix up H and C and you could either scald yourself or surprise yourself with a burst of freezing cold water. Y and N on ballots presented your opposition to or favoritism for a proposition. All of these letters, at least from Cameron's point of view, paled in comparison to the one that greeted him that morning at school. As his personal experience paper landed on his desk, his expectations of receiving a great grade were soon dashed like a rowboat slammed against the shore in a storm. Instead of an A he saw its antithesis...an F. Scrawled in red were the words "This assignment was not to do a fantasy but a personal experience. You need to either listen better to the instructions or know the difference between fiction and non-fiction. Your grade is non-fiction. An F. That is reality."

Cameron's immediate instinct was to inform Mr. Milton that his experience did happen. It felt like fantasy but it was reality. But it would be his word against Mr. Milton's, not a winning situation. Feeling it was futile, he accepted the harsh grade, a huge disappointment given his expectations.

While Cameron sat in class, listless, Leather Girl, as promised, visited the school, her goal to persuade Ms. Periwinkle to allow him to be in the variety show. Upon first meeting Leather Girl, Ms.

Periwinkle's eyes widened as though she'd seen a ghost. They were a total contrast in opposites -- one in black, the other in pinks and greens, one in leather the other in cotton swills, one looking goth, the other as preppy as a top sider.

"I was told you're the one to talk to regarding the Talent Show," Leather Girl said, hovering over the desk of a meek and intimidated, Ms. Periwinkle.

"It's a Variety Show," she replied. "We don't want to use the word Talent."

"Is that because you keep out Talent?" she retorted.

"I don't need to be insulted," she said.

Leather Girl reigned in her emotions, doing her best to remain calm. "There is a young boy, very talented I might add, who is most deserving of a spot in this Variety Show. He tried to sign up online but somehow it didn't go through."

"Well, no one else seemed to have any trouble," she responded, totally unsympathetic.

"We both know that exceptions can always be made," said Leather Girl. "Especially at this level. This boy is not only deserving but would add immensely to the night."

"I wish I could do that. I really do. But rules are rules," she replied, blinking nervously, the ultimate bureaucrat. Visibly uneasy, she could not make eye contact with Leather Girl. "If I were to make an exception for him it would open up the floodgates."

"Floodgates? How many kids signed up late that want to be in the show?"

Her lack of a response gave a strong indication that the answer was none or very few.

"You need to do the right thing or I will," said Leather Girl. "That's all I have to say."

Leather Girl headed down the hallway, her boots clicking on the linoleum. Her very appearance provoked looks from students heading to their next classes. Cameron was one of them. Stopping with his mouth agape, he was surprised to see her.

"I just met with the woman in charge of the Variety Show," she said.

"Oh," he replied, then with a tinge of hope, asked "What happened?"

"Um, you're in," she said, watching a grin break across his face. "See you tomorrow. Good and early."

As she strode out of the building, Tommy, who had been watching the whole encounter, came over to Cameron "Who's that?" he asked. "Your rock n roll girlfriend?"

Cameron gave a shrug and headed to his next class before the bell sounded.

That day followed a predictable cadence. Very monotone and boring. The last hour of school was often torturously slow but not today. It went by fast. Cameron would have preferred that time stood still. His concentration was non-existent as his mind played out his pending encounter with Scott after school. He envisioned the worst, his nose broken and eyes blackened from a steady rain of fists. Then, he thought of a more positive scenario where he met up with Scott who admired his courage for appearing. Fat chance of that happening.

As the school bell sounded, Cameron shuffled off to his locker. Twirling the chamber of his Master lock, he was so distracted he momentarily forgot his combination. It took two more attempts before he got it unlocked. He flung open the metal door which clanged against the adjacent locker and removed a large jar, its lid perforated with a dozen holes. Inside, staring aimlessly into space sat

Robert in that three-point frog pose. Blinkless as always, his green skin glistened.

"Hey, Robert," said Cameron, peering into the jar. "How'd you like your first day of school? Kind of sucks, doesn't it?"

Cameron opened his backpack and tucked the jar inside. He zipped it partially shut as the jar was quite large. He headed out of the school building, peering ahead for any sighting of Scott and his cronies. His natural instinct taught him to avoid danger not to walk right into it. But if he didn't show up, his problems would grow exponentially. Not wise to dis Scott.

Arriving at the appointed place, Cameron waited with a sense of dread. With his head lowered, he scuffed his shoes against the dirt before feeling a sudden grip around the back of his neck. Scott had arrived. And to no one's surprise, so did his three cronies Joe, Van and Hank.

"Hey there!" said Scott loudly. "You miss me?!"

Cameron kept silent.

"Did you hear what I said to you?" he asked.

Cameron nodded.

"I told you, in fact I instructed you quite clearly to do what?" Scott asked.

"Come here after school," said Cameron.

"And with whom?"

"My best friend."

"Exactly!" snapped Scott. "Now, unless your best friend is three inches tall, I don't see anybody here with you."

"He is," said Cameron.

"He is what?"

"Three inches tall. Or maybe two inches."

His cronies looked at one another totally confused.

"Well, unless I'm blind, I don't see a soul," said Scott, unamused.

Cameron lowered his backpack to the ground and crouched to one knee. He started to unzip it.

"What are you doing?" asked Scott. "Pulling out a gun?"

"No, "said Cameron, tugging the jar from the backpack.

"And what the hell is that?" snapped Scott, peering at the jar, trying to focus on what was inside. "Oh my. It's a goddamn frog."

"That's Robert," said Cameron with pride. "He's my best friend."

Scott snickered. "We got a comedian here. You can't have an animal as your best friend."

One of Scott's cronies Van piped in, "Actually, a dog is considered man's best friend."

"Van?" said Scott. "Shut up."

"Can I go now?" asked Cameron. "I did what you asked."

Turning to his friends, Scott asked "He wants to know if he can go now?"

Hesitant at first, the friends all laughed.

"Don't you like our company?" asked Scott.

Cameron gnawed on his lower lip, uncertain what to do.

"You think you're so clever," said Scott. "Can't wait to tell your few friends you out-thought me, right? Ain't gonna happen. If you'd have played by my rules and brought a real best friend, well, things would be different. But this here? A freakin' frog? Did you really think you were gonna get away with this? It's insulting."

Scott seized the jar from Cameron. He eyed the frog, studying his breathing and stillness. Von crouched behind Cameron and Scott gave him a shove, sending him tumbling to the ground. "You never learn, do you?" Scott said, chuckling. Cameron's head smacked down hard against the ground. He sat up, dizzy and nauseous.

"Leave him alone!" called out a familiar voice. Cameron sat up, rubbing his head and saw Tommy approaching.

"Who the hell are you?" asked Scott, squinting at Tommy.

"I'm his best friend," said Tommy, defiantly.

Cameron looked relieved to see Tommy, even though they were outnumbered. A breeze rustled the leaves.

Caught off guard, Scott didn't know what to do. "How do I know you're his best friend?" he asked.

"Because I said I am," said Tommy. "So, you need to leave him alone now."

"Wait," said Scott. "I don't like being lied to. Your friend here lied to me. He said this green little frog was his best friend. Not cool."

With that, Scott raised the jar over his head and sent it crashing down against a large rock jutting out of the ground. The jar completely shattered. Cameron winced, concerned about Robert. His frog lay against the rock, badly cut from the shards. He breathed slightly, then his breathing ceased. Cameron picked up his limp body, cradling it in one hand before placing him in his backpack. Without a moment's thought, he slung the backpack over his shoulder and ran home, more distraught than he had ever been.

"Should we go after him?" asked Von.

Taking a moment to ponder things, Scott said "No. We're done with him for the day. We have a new person here to deal with. What's your name, fatso?"

"Tommy," he replied, gazing down the road where Cameron was almost out of sight.

"Tommy," said Scott. "Well, Tommy, you've been very bold today. Foolishly so. And I think you need to be taught some manners so you don't repeat foolish actions like this."

"I was just helping my friend," he replied, less defiant than before.

"So you were," said Scott, shoving him in the chest. Tommy almost fell over but caught his balance. Scott shoved him two more times, knocking him to the ground.

"Time for a little soccer practice," said Scott, kicking Tommy in the stomach, causing him to double over in pain. As he lay curled in the fetal position, Scott's right foot caught him square on the cheekbone leaving the start of a bruise.

Scott pulled him up by his hair and started slapping his face.

"Hold him," he yelled to his cronies. Two of them grabbed his arms while Scott proceeded to punch him in the stomach. Tommy fell to the ground, sobbing spastically.

"Let's go guys," said Scott. "His appointment is over."

They walked away, leaving Tommy writhing on the ground.

CHAPTER 5 THE POWER OF MUSIC

As the sun rose, the birds started chirping their morning songs. Cameron opened his eyes slowly. By the side of his bed lay a brown shoebox. Inside was the limp green body of Robert.

On a small table in his room was a grey stone the size of a softball. Cameron took out a red sharpie and scribbled "Robert R.I.P". He then carried the rock and shoebox down to the kitchen, resting it on the peeling Formica countertop. He searched through the kitchen drawers and pulled out a large serving spoon.

Cameron stepped outside into the backyard, carrying the rock, shoebox and spoon. The lawn extended a few dozen feet from the house before abruptly giving way to the woods. Cameron went right to that point, kneeled down and brushed aside a layer of dead leaves exposing a soil so dark it resembled coffee grounds. Using the large spoon, he dug into the earth, removing small amounts of dirt. Some stubborn gnarly roots and a few fist-sized rocks slowed the process but he persevered until he'd carved out a hole a foot deep and wide, just the right size to hold the shoebox. He lowered the box gently into the hole and pushed the loose soil back to where it came until the box was totally covered and a slight mound appeared. As a final touch, he placed the rock with Robert's name on it atop the mound, completing the burial.

Sitting in the kitchen, he reflected on the joy this simple little frog had given him. There were countless nights when he discussed his problems with Robert, sharing his deepest thoughts, not that any of them were really that deep. And Robert, the great listener, sat riveted in his glass home, a great source of comfort. Now that he was gone, Cameron felt an emptiness, a hole in his life. He never should have exposed Robert to those cowards. Never. A knock on the door interrupted his fond memories of Robert. Worried the knocking might awaken his mother and put her in a nasty state, he rushed to the front door, stumbling over his backpack as he reached for the doorknob. It was Leather Girl. Upon seeing her, it dawned on him that they were supposed to get together today. The weekend arrived so fast, he'd forgotten all about it. He couldn't remember where she wanted to take him. Maybe she never told him. There was a certain mystique about her and everything she did. Why, he still didn't even know her name.

"Hi," said Cameron, catching his breath. "I'm a little behind this morning but I can get ready quickly."

Leather Girl stepped into the foyer, sidestepping the backpack. "Take your time," she paused, her black helmet dangling in her right hand. "Up to a point."

Cameron disappeared upstairs, leaving her alone. She went to move his backpack when she noticed a school paper sticking out of the top. On it in red ink was written "Grade F." She slipped it out and read the teacher's comments doubting Cameron had met U2. She carefully placed the paper back into the backpack and leaned against the wall, waiting for Cameron to return.

He came back down, sporting a navy blue windbreaker, decent apparel for a ride on a motorcycle.

"Ready?" she asked.

Nodding, he followed her out of the house.

"I've been meaning to ask you," she said. "Did you get back that paper you had to do on your personal experience?"

Caught off guard, he stumbled around for a response, settling on "It's hard to remember. We have so much homework and so many assignments."

"Well, you had a great personal experience," she said. "I can't imagine any other kid could have written a better paper than you did."

He produced a sickly smile.

The extra motorcycle helmet rested on the seat. Cameron grabbed it, slipping it on snugly, then straddled the bike behind her.

"Hold on tight," she said. "We've got an hour's drive."

Cameron wrapped his arms around her waist and let his mind wander. He found the motorcycle rides totally relaxing and meditative, calmed by the rumble of the motor and his wandering thoughts. As the cycle shot up and down hills, Cameron's stomach experienced that rollercoaster feeling, tense and full of butterflies, anticipating every turn. With each curve in the road, he clung on even tighter, leaning in, then settling upright before leaning the other way. It all had a rhythmic feel, your body forever moving with the motion of the cycle, something you wouldn't experience from riding a car or bus.

Leather Girl drifted off the main route, taking back roads that twisted and turned, challenging the bike. But she was so adept, she sailed along effortlessly in total control. She soon came upon the entrance to someone's property. Skirted on each side was a stone wall as tall as a grown man and behind it a wrought-iron fence twice that height. Atop the entrance, instead of a lantern or a gargoyle was a sculpted guitar cut from marble. Was this a music school or something, Cameron wondered?

Pulling up to the entrance, she took out a remote from her pocket and pushed a button, opening the large wrought-iron gate. The gate had one letter etched into it – a big Z. She sped through and it closed behind her with a clank. Along the driveway were perfectly sculpted crabapple trees whose branches extended across the driveway, nearly touching the trees on the other side and forming a kind of umbrella of shade. Each tree was planted the exact same distance apart giving it a beautiful symmetry. This driveway wound back for a good half mile before circling in front of an enormous mansion.

The mansion was big and intimidating, resembling an English country house owned by a duke or duchess. It had two large stories and a third smaller story. Made of bricks and mortar, the mansion had ivy curling up its sides and planter boxes nestled under each window. Curtains were drawn indicating the people inside relished their privacy. To one side, connected to the main house was a conservatory while the other side seemed like an entrance for the help. The large front door, made of thick oak, had an equally large brass knocker. It needed to be large for anyone to hear it in such a big place.

In front of the mansion was a circular driveway made of white and grey cobblestone, not a kind surface for a motorcycle to travel on. And in the center of the front courtyard was a stately fountain, three-tiered with water cascading out of each large bowl.

Cameron got off the motorcycle and started walking towards the front door.

"What are you doing?" asked Leather Girl.

"Aren't we supposed to go inside?" he asked.

"No," she said. "Follow me."

Leaving their helmets by the motorcycle, they walked around the side of the mansion past the conservatory. Cameron peeked in and saw a veritable greenhouse of plants, including some magnificent purple, pink and white orchids. Leather Girl hustled him around to the back of the mansion to a beautiful courtyard lined with Greek and Roman sculptures of figures like Apollo and Diana. Further out was a maze of hedge rows, meticulously manicured, then a beautiful pond followed by a large field.

It was an enormous piece of property without a single neighboring house in view.

Leather Girl approached a large padlocked shed. She dialed a few numbers. Popping open the door, she unveiled a room full of electric guitars, hanging on the walls, all in different vibrant colors. She took one down. It was shaped like the capital letter A with a pattern of green and blue stripes. Hanging beneath each guitar was a black silk bag the size of a shoebox. She took one down, then locked up the shed. On a white wrought-iron table near the shed stood two coffee pots – one with coffee and the other with hot chocolate.

"Coffee or hot chocolate?" she asked.

"The latter," he replied, prompting her to pour him a generous cup of hot chocolate that went right to the brim like an infinity pool. She opted for coffee.

They pulled two heavy wrought iron chairs up to the table, the metal screeching against the stone terrace. They savored their hot beverages, scanning the beautiful landscape before them. It was a tranquil contrast from the noisy motorcycle ride. She finished ahead of him and waited patiently for his last sip.

"Okay," she said, standing. "Let's get to work."

Handing him the blue and green guitar, she carried the small black bag. As they walked towards the maze of hedge rows, several faces peered out from the windows of the mansion, watching them with great curiosity.

"May I ask you a question?" Cameron said, staring in awe at the beautiful surroundings.

"You may," she said.

"Who owns this place?" he asked.

She stopped, staring back at the mansion and seeing the faces duck out of sight. "A man," she said. "A quite powerful man. Maybe someday you'll meet him. It all depends."

"Depends on what?"

"Depends on whether you're qualified to meet him," she said.

"Qualified?"

"It's nothing you can prepare for," she replied. "Either you're in or you're not. It's no big deal."

"Can I ask his name?"

"Too much information too soon is not a good thing," she replied, mysteriously.

"Well, I think his name starts with a Z," said Cameron.

Her eyebrows rose, surprised to hear him say that. "How did you know that?"

"There was a big Z on the front gate," he replied.

She laughed. "So, there was. He's referred to as Z3. That's all I'll say for now."

"Sounds like a name from Star Wars," said Cameron.

"Let's go out to the field over there," she said, pointing the way.

They walked through the hedge rows, all rising higher than Cameron and nearly as tall as her. Clearly, they provided a fun place to play hide and seek. Emerging from the large shrubs, they walked under a trellis of vines, soon spotting a beautiful pond the size of three mansions. A small wooden dock angled out from the shore about six feet. Tied to a cleat on the dock was a small rowboat, its oars sticking out like wooden wings. In the center of the pond floating about were a hundred or so ducks, a feathered armada of mallards with a mix of emerald and brown speckled heads.

"Let's walk around the pond," she said. "I'm not into rowing right now. Nor am I into spending a social moment with a bunch of ducks."

They walked along a dirt path that wound closely to the edge of the pond. The mansion appeared much further away as they emerged on the other side. They now stood on the edge of a giant wheat field that was part lawn. Several large metal sculptures, some red, some green and some blue, were placed around it. One of the sculptures, a modern yellow one, was seared in half, with both broken chunks lying next to one another.

Cameron thought he saw several people standing across the field amongst the wheat.

"Who are they?" he asked.

"They?" she replied. "Look a little closer. Those are dummies."

Cameron squinted and could see that none of them were real.

"Try strumming the guitar," she said.

He put the strap around his neck and played a few chords. The guitar sounded soft and muted as an unplugged electric guitar would.

"Now, turn on that switch," she said, pointing to a knob on the front of it. He twisted it on. "It has a built in generator," she noted. "It is immensely powerful. Doesn't need an electrical outlet. Now, try it."

Cameron's fingers nimbly climbed up and down the guitar neck as he played a medley of rock songs. The sound was loud and vibrant, amazingly so.

"Whoa, this is really cool," he said.

She reached into the black bag and took out a headset attached to a wire that ended with a brass plug. It also possessed two suction-cups attached to separate wires. She took the headset to show Cameron how it worked. She gently placed the headset over his ears and put the padded suction cups on each of his temples. Then, she turned off the power on the guitar.

"Now," she said. "You must listen to me very carefully. No fooling around, okay? Because if mishandled, this can cause major problems."

Cameron promised to be cautious.

"What will happen is this," she said. "When I turn on the guitar, you will be able to control it with your fingers and your mind working together. By that, I mean your mind will be able to take the power chords or notes and direct them at a target. Your fingers will generate power and also help with accuracy. I'm not about to provide you with the whole scientific description. Someone else will do that if and when the time is right. But please don't be upset if the guitar doesn't work for you. I have seen many many people fail at using it. Trust me on that. An average guitar player would pick this up with the headpiece in place and have no results whatsoever. As I said, that may be the case with you. It's something we won't know until you try. And don't feel bad if nothing special happens. I have seen some mean guitar players who couldn't affect a single note let alone a single chord."

"Do you play guitar?" Cameron asked.

"Right now, I'm only interested in hearing you play," she said as she turned on the power.

Cameron held it up and started playing some chords. The music came out loud and clear, prompting a few ducks to take flight.

"You must concentrate," she said, then pointed to the dummies. "Focus your mind on a target and play."

Cameron tried again but failed to achieve what she had hoped he would.

"Do you have any inner anger you can draw upon?" she asked.

He shrugged his shoulders.

"Maybe you're healthier than I thought," she said. "Let me see that guitar for a moment."

Cameron slid the guitar over his head and handed it to her. She let it dangle from her neck as she put on the headset and then the suction cups on her temples. With the power off, she toyed with a few notes, her fingers fumbling clumsily around. It didn't appear as though she could play much of anything. Then, she turned on the power switch, and two fingers played two notes over and over and over, quite rapidly. She stared straight ahead, focused on one of the dummies. In a split second the dummy suddenly toppled backwards as though hit by an intensely heavy wind or an invisible laser beam. Responding to this hit came a frantic fluttering of wings as every last duck took to flight in a frightened hurry. The noise from the guitar had clearly scared them away.

"Whoa!" exclaimed Cameron. "How did you ever do that?"

Smiling, she replied "I guess I had a bunch of anger to fuel my focus. Do you want to try again?"

Cameron nodded. She handed him the guitar and once again put the headset and suction cups in place. He took a deep breath and gazed over at the dummies. He started playing, fast and furious, the music flawless. She smiled at his dexterity and fluency. He was even better than she'd remembered. But as hard and fast as he played, he could not generate that special power that she did. He stopped playing and, disappointed, handed back the guitar.

"I'm sorry," he said, disappointed.

"There's nothing to be sorry about," she replied. "Really. As I told you before, there are a lot of great guitarists who can't do it."

"But you could do it," he said.

"Beginner's luck," she replied. "Let's head back to the house."

As they headed back, Cameron marveled at the beauty of the terrain. The whole place felt magical; green and serene which was a funny contrast to the girl in black leather. She looked city-like in this rural setting. He suddenly felt sad. He had let her down. He couldn't play the guitar the way she had hoped.

"This is an amazing sounding guitar," said Cameron. "The best I've ever played."

"It is very unique," she agreed. "What happened to your guitar?"

Cameron hesitated and said "It broke."

"Do you have a backup?" she asked.

He shook his head.

"So how do you plan to play guitar?"

Shrugging his shoulders, he said "I don't know."

"We'll have to work on that one," she said.

They reached the impeccably manicured hedge rows. Stepping off the walkway, Cameron felt the hedge row with his fingers. It looked so perfectly square and box-like but was rough and spiny to the touch. As they approached the mansion. Cameron didn't notice the many faces peering out from different windows. Leather Girl saw them and shook her head, prompting those peeping toms to disappear from sight.

She approached the shed and started dialing the combination for the lock before Cameron interrupted her. "Could I borrow this guitar until I get a replacement?"

"Absolutely not," she said, watching his face turn solemn. She continued dialing the combination, soon popping open the lock. "This is not a normal guitar that could easily be replaced. It's very special and can be very powerful."

"Not in my hands," he said.

She did feel sorry for him. Sorry that he didn't have a guitar and also sorry that he didn't possess the ability to harness its special power. What would happen if he borrowed it for just a week, she thought? Probably nothing. Of course, there was always that slight chance that he could lose it or have it stolen. And the rules were implicit that no guitars were to leave the premises. But rules were a man-made concoction that she didn't always tend to abide by. Turning her gaze towards Cameron, she couldn't help but be moved by his sad face.

"I'll tell you what," she said. "I am going against all my better instincts but I'm going to let you borrow it. For one week only. But you must not lose it or lend it to anyone, do you understand?"

He nodded, wide-eyed.

"Okay," she said, locking the shed. "Let's head back."

Cameron had tucked the black bag inside his shirt and slung the guitar across his shoulder. They climbed aboard the motorcycle and zoomed off. Cameron felt the guitar against his back. It gave him a feeling of immense satisfaction.

■■■

When Cameron awoke the next morning, he felt his visit to the mansion was all a dream. But then to confirm it all happened, he reached under his bed and took out the special blue and green guitar. He played a few chords before putting it back. Leaving it under his bed was the safest place since he didn't have a guitar lesson today.

Cameron arrived on time at school and noticed a white stretch limousine parked outside. That was unusual. Its dark tinted windows prevented anyone from seeing inside. Who would come to school in a limo?

Cameron spotted Tommy getting out of a Camry and went over to say hi. Tommy, his face bruised, ignored him. He said "hi" again but Tommy didn't respond.

"Tommy, what's wrong?"

"What's wrong?! I came to help you out with those punk ass kids and you ditched me. That's what's wrong. What kind of friend are you?"

"I'm sorry."

"Well, sorry doesn't cut it," said Tommy.

"I was upset cause they killed my friend Robert," explained Cameron.

Tommy just shook his head, expressing his continued disappointment. "The worse thing is because I came to help you, I am now on their hit list. They told me I had to show up after school at the end of the week. They obviously picked the end of the week to make me sweat and worry which is what I've been doing."

"I'll come with you," offered Cameron.

"You? Come with me?! Are you kidding? That would make things a hundred times worse. They hate you. They merely despise me. Best you stay away. You've been nothing but bad news."

Although Cameron was heading to the same class as Tommy, he deliberately kept his distance. Tommy made it loud and clear he didn't want him around.

On the way to class, Cameron did a double take, spotting Leather Girl outside Mr. Milton's classroom.

"Hi. What are you doing here?" he asked with concern.

"I had to talk to your teacher," she said.

"Mr. Milton?"

"Yes."

"What for?"

"Your grade in the class," she said.

"I'd really rather you didn't do that," he said. "Mr. Milton is a very tough man and he doesn't seem to like me or anyone else for that matter."

"Well, you should have told me that earlier," she replied. "What's done is done."

"I have to go before I'm late," said Cameron, dashing to his classroom and bumping into Mr. Milton on the way.

Mr. Milton gathered some papers off his desk and ran through a few announcements before a voice came over the loudspeaker. "Good morning. Today is Monday the 25th and the schedule is Day E. Just a few announcements. Chorus practice today will be held in the cafeteria after school. Band practice has been cancelled because Mr. Skillings is out. And now, please stand for the Pledge of Allegiance. I pledge allegiance to the flag of the United States of America and to the Republic for which it stands one nation under God indivisible with liberty and justice for all. Thank you and have a great day."

Mr. Milton paced in front of the class. "Before we begin today's lesson, we have a visitor." Mr. Milton walked over to the classroom door and opened it. "You can come in," he said.

Leather Girl stepped into the room. Cameron's mouth fell slack-jawed. What on earth was she doing now, he thought. He wanted to turn invisible or crawl under a rock.

"I don't want to take up too much of your time," she said. "But one of your students did a personal experience paper and didn't receive the proper grade. Everything in his story was accurate. Everything. I was there and witnessed it all. My word may not mean much because who am I? I barely factored in the story. But there is someone who was there who can serve as a witness. "

Turning towards the door, she called out "Jack!"

No one appeared.

"Jack!" she called again.

Then, appearing through the door came Jack White, the rock star.

"This is Jack White," said Leather Girl. "He is a rock star who was at the concert the other night. Jack is here as a witness."

"I bear witness," said Jack.

"I had another witness who doesn't seem to have made it," said Leather Girl. "So, I'm very pleased that Jack could be here."

"Thank you," said Jack. "I am a musician and have been a long time. I've been in a lot of bands. And I am here as a favor to my good friend over there."

"Jack was backstage with Cameron at the U2 concert and can verify that all of Cameron's story is true, right Jack?"

"Yep."

At that moment, the classroom door opened again and in came a very familiar face – Bono from U2. Many of the children recognized him as did Mr. Milton whose look of utter surprise was priceless.

"I thought you couldn't make it," said Leather Girl, walking up and giving him a hug.

"I re-arranged my schedule," he replied, so recognizable with his oversized tinted sunglasses. "This is a might early for me. But I didn't want to let you down. Or Cameron."

Cameron smiled at the sound of his name. The kids in the classroom seemed utterly amazed, especially Tommy.

Bono gave Jack White a hug. "Jack was filling in for you," said Leather Girl.

"My opening act," joked Bono, unzipping his brown leather jacket. "So, what have I missed?"

"I wanted to prove to Mr. Milton that Cameron's special visit to your concert actually happened," said Leather Girl.

Bono walked over to Cameron's desk and gave him a high five. "Cameron here was our special guest the other night at one of our concerts," he said. "And he even played some guitar for us in the green room. He's a cool dude."

Leather Girl turned to Mr. Milton. "Is there anything else you'd like to ask us?"

Mr. Milton stammered "Um, um, no. I think the point has been clearly made. It's just that when I read his essay, it didn't ring true. It seemed like a dream."

"Well, you could say it was a dream come true," said Leather Girl.

"Class," said Mr. Milton. "Do you have any questions for our guests?"

The students sat motionless, a mix of shyness and amazement. Finally, Tommy raised his hand.

"Yes, Tommy," said Mr. Milton.

"I wanted to ask Jack White if he is related to Jack Black?"

Jack White smiled. "We both love music. Other than that, no."

A young blonde-haired girl raised her hand.

"Yes, Alison," said Mr. Milton.

"I wanted to ask Mr. Bono if that is his real name."

Bono smiled and replied, "I get asked that a lot. My given name is Paul."

"That's my name, too," said a boy in the back of the class, eliciting giggles from several of the children.

Mr. Milton cleared his throat and said "I'd just like to thank our guests for coming here today. This was a total surprise. But a pleasant one."

Leather Girl walked over to Cameron and whispered in his ear, "Take real good care of that guitar." He gave a firm nod.

Jack White gave Cameron a pat on the shoulder as did Bono. The three exited the classroom, waving to the students as they departed.

Mr. Milton walked over to Cameron's desk. "Cameron," he said. "If you don't mind, could you bring your essay to school tomorrow? I'd like to re-read it and re-consider your grade."

Cameron smiled.

"OK. Now, let's get today's lesson underway," said Mr. Milton.

The rest of the day, Cameron fell in and out of daydreams, amazed that Bono and Jack White had actually visited his school on his behalf. It was the coolest thing that ever happened to him.

At home that afternoon, he went straight to his room and checked under his bed. The blue and green guitar was still there. He began practicing with it. The sound quality was superior to any he had heard. And he could play it without an amp because it seemed to have one built in. He found the black bag with the headset and decided to go outside to try them. It was a windless day. He put on the headset and then the suction cups. Plugging the headset into the guitar, he turned it on.

Looking across the lawn, Cameron eyed a wooden birdhouse, dangling from a tree limb. He set down the guitar, removing the headset, walked over and peered inside. No birds were living there. In fact, the floor of the birdhouse had entirely rotted through. He walked back towards the house, slung the guitar over his shoulder and plugged in the headset. Concentrating on the birdhouse, he started playing several chords and notes, fast then slow. He stared intently at the birdhouse, its red-chipped paint the last remnant of color. As hard as he concentrated and played, the result was the same. Nothing. Nothing at all. He couldn't make the birdhouse move. It hung perfectly still.

Cameron scratched his head, wondering what he could do differently. He remembered hearing Leather Girl tell him how he had to channel his anger through the head set and into the guitar. But just how much anger did he really need? Taking one deep breath, he focused on it again. Playing fast and furious, he tried unsuccessfully. Frustrated, he headed back to the house when he noticed a brown toad near a pile of dead leaves. The toad reminded him of Robert and he felt an anger over Robert's death. He went back and focused on the birdhouse, channeling that anger through the headset and started to play.

"Cameron!" shouted his mother, standing on the porch. Startled, he walked towards her, not wanting her to call him twice. She was not a patient woman. What Cameron didn't know was that as he turned around, his guitar had obliterated the birdhouse. It shattered into nothingness, leaving just a string dangling behind. He had the power of music but he didn't know it. At least not yet.

■■■

The next day Cameron handed in his somewhat crumpled personal essay to Mr. Milton and got it back the following day. The previous grade and comments, all done in red ink, had been crossed off and in their place were new comments written in green ink that read: "I apologize for questioning the truth of your original essay. Upon first reading it, your story appeared to be a fantasy. It simply didn't ring true. But upon re-reading it and now being fully aware that all you wrote was true, I can say that this is the best personal essay I have ever read in my 20 years of teaching. And I reward you an A++."

An A++? Did such a grade even exist? Cameron re-read the comments twice before displaying a smug and contented expression. He would long guard and cherish this paper. And as annoyed as he was that Leather Girl showed up in his class without forewarning him, he now appreciated what she had done. How she managed to get two rock stars to show up was beyond him. How did she have such strong relationships? He couldn't imagine what it took to create such a bond of friendship and loyalty.

Shuffling down the school corridor, Cameron checked the announcements on the bulletin board and spotted a list of Variety Show rehearsal times. He ran his finger down the list but couldn't find his name. He checked again but still couldn't find it. Leather Girl told him he was going to be in the show. It must be a mistake. He wanted to see if she could fix it but he didn't know how to get in touch with her. In fact, he still didn't know her name. He would have to patiently wait for her to contact him. She had to contact him again as he had one of the special guitars which she'd need to get back.

Cameron had a guitar lesson after school. He deliberately left the special guitar at home so it wouldn't get stolen at school. He planned to rush home to get it for his lesson. He ran most of the way, stopping for a few quick breaths. The front door creaked open, its rusty hinges desperate for oil.

"Is that you, Cameron?" his mother said, coming out of the kitchen dressed in a tattered pink bathrobe.

He didn't respond but instead snuck up to his room. He slid his backpack under his bed then pulled out the guitar. He debated whether or not to take the headset with him. He wouldn't use it in his lesson. But maybe on the way home, he might give it a try. He pulled the headset out of the black bag and hung it around his neck. Then picking up the guitar, he started towards the door. Hearing his mother coming upstairs, he retreated and hid under his bed. As she entered his bedroom, he saw her feet in fluffy pink slippers. She paused, looking around the room and listening closely. Then, she left. He crawled out from under the bed and tiptoed downstairs, emerging from the house with a huge sigh of relief.

Nearing school, Cameron noticed five kids somewhat obscured in a small wooded area. He recognized one of them instantly -- Tommy. He was being shoved around by Scott and company. Tommy was their new target. Cameron wanted to intervene but knew it would be futile and could make things even worse.

He removed the blue and green guitar from its case and put the strap around his neck. Then he put on the headset, applied the suction cups to his temples and plugged it into the guitar. It was a prayer whether he could get it to work. He flicked on the power switch. He was about 50 yards away from them. He glared intently, his anger building, thinking about the cruel things these guys had done.

Tommy lay helpless on the ground as they proceeded to kick him. They had their backs to Cameron who started strumming slowly, then faster and faster. He felt a kick from the guitar just as one might from firing a gun and a surge of power invisible to the naked eye burst forth. The first boy Van was knocked down to the ground hard. Cameron wielded the guitar in a sweeping motion, moving from left to right. He couldn't see the damage he exacted but it was clear that his guitar had great effect. As the invisible beam sliced across the three, it pierced deeply into the rear ends of three of them, sending them falling to the ground in agonizing pain.

Surprised at the damage he had done, Cameron turned off the guitar and returned it to its case, tucking the headset inside his pants. He crouched down, peering as best he could to see what had happened. Three of them writhed about on the ground. They had reversed places with Tommy who now stood over them. The fourth guy lay on the ground, apparently unconscious or maybe dead. Cameron rubbed the back of his neck, uncertain what to do next. He moved towards them, keeping himself hidden behind some bushes. The fourth guy Joe, who had initially appeared motionless, rose to his feet, completely stunned.

"What the hell just happened?" he said.

Scott peered up, in great agony, and exclaimed "Aw Jesus Christ, my ass is on fire! Oh my God it hurts like hell!"

The other guys, also hit, screamed obscenities.

"Maybe it was a lightning strike," Joe said, unable to find a rational explanation.

"A what?!" exclaimed Scott. "What are you, a goddamn weatherman?"

"There's nothing but blue sky," moaned one of the guys on the ground. "There's no damn lightning. And if there were, we would have heard thunder. Oh God, it hurts."

The fourth guy clung to his explanation "It could be one of those freak things like when the moon is hidden by the sun and totally disappears."

"This ain't a damn eclipse," said Scott. "Put me out of my misery someone! Please! Oh my God! My ass!"

Tommy glanced over confounded at what had just occurred. He walked backwards, ever so slowly, trying to distance himself. As he got about twenty feet away, he walked off, nonchalant.

"Do something, wouldja?!" Scott shouted at Joe who was the only one standing.

"Like what?" he asked.

"Call 9-1-1 for Christ sake!" shouted Scott.

"Okay. What's the number?" Joe asked.

"What do you think it is, you moron idiot asshole?!" screamed Scott.

Joe hesitated, thinking.

"It's 9-1-1!" yelled Scott. "Oh my God."

Cameron decided it best to leave for his guitar class. It would provide him with an alibi. He circled back towards the road and with his guitar case in hand, looked as innocent and nonchalant as could be.

■■

For Cameron and many of his classmates, Friday was the day they liked best as it marked the end of the school week with a full weekend ahead to enjoy. But Cameron dreaded this particular Friday, worried that Scott might suspect him. After all, who else might have come to Tommy's rescue?

Standing by his desk in his homeroom, Cameron was surprised when Tommy approached him. "Did you hear what happened yesterday?" Tommy asked.

Cameron acted ignorant. "No. What?"

"You know those guys who were picking on you and then me?" asked Tommy. "Well, they won't be doing much of that anymore."

"Why?"

Tommy looked around the room. "Well, nobody really knows," he said. "Three of them got their asses burned. It was like someone took a light saber and cut them an inch deep. These guys won't be sitting down anytime soon."

"Are they at school today?"

"No way. I think they're in a hospital. I'm sure they'll be out of school for a while."

Mr. Milton closed the classroom door and stepped over to his desk.

"The funny thing is they were really beating on me badly and then out of nowhere comes some force that disabled them," said Tommy. "It was an act of God. Like some angel of mercy. And the one who didn't get his ass burned, well, he's kind of loopy."

"How do you know that?"

Tommy smiled. "Cause I had to go down to the police department last night as a witness. That one guy pointed me out. But the police didn't think for a minute I had anything to do with it. The one guy kept saying he thought it was from lightning. Lightning? It was a beautiful day yesterday. It would have been more believable if he'd have said an alien force."

"So, what's going to be done?" asked Cameron.

Tommy shrugged his shoulders. "One thing I know that has to be done is those three guys are going to need to buy some new pants."

Cameron and Tommy shared a laugh before Mr. Milton asked for everyone's attention.

The morning announcements came over the scratchy intercom, boring and repetitive, spoken in a disinterested monotone by the vice principal. But the day's final announcement caught Cameron's attention.

"Yesterday afternoon," the voice said. "An incident occurred after school fairly nearby though not officially on school grounds. Four boys, excuse me, three boys suffered severe first degree burns on parts of their bodies. While the local police are investigating, we ask that anyone who can shed any light on what might have happened to please alert the proper authorities. Thank you."

Cameron felt his heart race, jumpstarted by the announcement. His hand nervously tapped a pencil on his desk while his right foot tapped on the floor. He was a bundle of nerves.

"Is everything all right?" asked Mr. Milton, waking Cameron from his daydream.

Cameron's face flushed with embarrassment.

"I think so."

On the way to his next class, Cameron corralled Tommy in the hallway.

"Are you all right?" he asked.

"Well, I'm here, aren't I? And no thanks to you. Those guys who went after me are going to think I somehow had something to do with their burnt butts."

Cameron wanted very much to tell Tommy exactly what happened but didn't feel comfortable yet. For one, Tommy never would have believed him. But more importantly, Cameron could not afford to disclose anything about the special guitar and its incredible power. Leather Girl would not be pleased to know he used it in such a way. She was nice enough to lend it to him for his guitar lesson because she assumed no harm would be done.

Turning to Tommy, Cameron said assuredly "Sounds like they won't be bothering you for quite some time."

"When they heal, and they will heal, they're going to go after me. No question about it."

"Tommy," Cameron said. "As your friend, I promise you, you will be safe."

"You promise? Scrawny little you? That's a good laugh. What are you going to do? Frighten them with your physique?"

Arne walked over. "Anyone have any good jokes?" he asked.

They both shook their heads and walked away.

When Cameron got home, he noticed a bat slicing through the air, much earlier than usual. It zigged and zagged, cutting fast angles, before settling under a shutter. He stepped onto the front porch and opened the door. Out of nowhere, a grey squirrel raced by him and into the house.

"Oh crap!" he said, chasing after it.

The squirrel went into the kitchen. Cameron spotted it on top of a counter, its wispy gray tail twitching nervously. He went back into the hallway and placed two chairs on their sides in an attempt to block it from heading upstairs. Hoping to get the squirrel to leave the house, he opened the front door, aware that a dozen more squirrels could sneak in.

Back to the kitchen, he grabbed a broom and maneuvered himself to the side of the squirrel. It stared at him with almond eyes, making short staccato movements, clearly confused. In a panic, it leapt off the counter and ran in a circle around the perimeter of the kitchen. Cameron chased after it, holding the broom close to the floor right behind it. They went around the kitchen two times before the squirrel made a break for the hallway. It hesitated, almost climbing through the chairs, but at the last moment made a dash out the open front door.

Cameron slammed the door shut, leaning with his back against it like some beleaguered victim in a horror movie. He straightened up the chairs and put the broom away. It was then that he sensed something was wrong. With all the commotion downstairs, he was certain by now he would have heard his mother shout her patented "What the hell is going on down there?" She often shouted through her door which slightly muffled her voice. But not a word was uttered.

He went upstairs, cautious and vigilant, walking softly so he could hear every little sound. Near the top of the stairs, he noticed her door was ajar. That was unusual as she valued her privacy and usually kept it closed. As he entered, he first saw her foot sticking out as she lay motionless and lifeless on the floor.

He knelt down and softly jostled her shoulder.

"Are you all right?" he asked with concern.

She didn't respond.

He shook her again. Nothing. Placing his hands under her shoulders, he dragged her towards the wall, propping her against it so she was sitting up. He went to the bathroom, returning with a cold damp washcloth which he placed on her forehead. She didn't respond. Feeling uneasy, he turned and accidentally stepped on her foot.

"Ahhhh!" she screamed out, her eyes opening. She mumbled something rather incoherent. Cameron almost jumped out of his skin.

"Should I call a doctor?" he asked, uncertain whether or not her condition was life-threatening.

She gave a discouraging shake of the head which was anything but convincing. She didn't seem well as evidenced by her uneven and labored breathing. For the first time Cameron wondered what would happen if she died. Where would he go? Who would take care of him? How would he eat? Would he drop out of school? She wasn't the best parent in the world but she was all he knew. And she had somehow managed to keep him alive for the majority of his life. He didn't feel particularly close to her or like he knew her at all. But maybe that was normal.

After what felt like an eternity, her breathing normalized into a regular rhythm. He assisted her as she rose to her feet and shuffled towards her bed. She laid down, one foot dangling off the side, and quickly drifted off to sleep.

He watched her closely, feeling relief. He took a deep breath to calm himself, when suddenly he heard a knock on the door. He ran downstairs, nearly taking a tumble. He reached for the knob but had second thoughts and went to a side window to peer out through the white veneer curtains. He knew full well who was there by the sight of her motorcycle.

Cameron crawled on his hands and knees towards the kitchen. He scooted to the wall, his back pressed against it, waiting for the knocking to subside, hoping she would get frustrated and leave. A minute passed with no more knocking. Then two minutes went by. He started to stand when he caught a glimpse of her passing outside the kitchen window. She squinted and peered in. Cameron dove to the floor and out of her line of sight. He rolled under a table like some cowboy staying out of harm's way and waited.

After a period of time, he snuck upstairs, stopping after each step to listen for any suspicious noises. When he reached the top, he nervously yawned, stretching his hands towards the ceiling before turning towards his room. He gasped at the sight of Leather Girl lying on his bed. She had climbed through the window as it was left slightly ajar.

Cameron couldn't help but think that she looked like a latter-day Catwoman, clad in her black leather and skilled at scaling heights. He couldn't quite figure out the purpose of her black leather gloves as they were fingerless from the knuckles out. No real protection for her fingers.

"You have some explaining to do," she said with a searing glare.

Cameron fumbled for a chair, desperately needing to sit and steady his nerves.

"Well?" she persisted.

His eyes scanned the floor as he tried to gather his thoughts.

"Well?" he replied, stalling. "What are you referring to exactly?"

She sighed, not interested in playing games. "The guitar you borrowed," she said.

"Oh," he replied. "You see, um, my mother hasn't been well lately so I thought you might have been referring to that."

Shaking her head, she said, "No. I'm just curious about the guitar."

"What have you heard?"

She stood up from the bed, "I think you know," she said. "I just need to hear it from you. I want your explanation whatever it may be."

Cameron rocked back and forth on his chair, pushing off with his feet like it was a rocking chair. "I took the guitar to school for a music lesson," he said. "And on the way there, I saw these guys picking on a friend of mine. So, I used the guitar on them."

"Used the guitar?" she said. "You put on the headgear and aimed your sound at them?"

He nodded.

"And this was after you promised you would only use it for practice?!" she said.

Cameron stammered. "I wanted to help my friend. And I didn't think it would work. I failed when I was at that house you took me to. I surprised myself when it worked so well."

"What you did could have ended very badly," she noted. "You're lucky. Very lucky."

He breathed deeply, relieved to have gotten this out in the open. "Can I ask you something?"

"Yes. But I'm done not with you yet."

"Okay. For the variety show that you said I'm a part of, I'm not down on the list for any rehearsals."

"There wasn't space for everyone to rehearse," she said. "It doesn't matter where you rehearse. Just practice at home. Because you signed up late, they want to be discreet about latecomers as there were many who didn't make the cut."

"Oh."

"Now, I have one more thing to ask you," she said. "I need you to come back to the mansion tomorrow. I'll pick you up and bring you there."

"What for?"

"I need to see you practice out by the field again," she added. "And I need you to meet someone."

"Who?"

"The person who owns the house," she said.

"The Z guy?"

She nodded.

"I'm supposed to go to the market with my mother tomorrow," he noted. "And she hasn't been feeling well so she needs my help."

"You must come with me," she said. "Work out your schedule as best you can. But be ready in the morning."

Leather Girl walked towards the door, then, having second thoughts, she stepped over to the window and climbed out. In an instant, she was gone.

■■

His mother's snoring reassured him that she was at least breathing. He quietly pulled her bedroom door closed.

Cameron kept his promise to go with Leather Girl back to the mansion. She showed up at sunrise, the air chilly from the night. A carpet of dew covered the ground. Cameron stepped outside carrying the special guitar in its case. As he straddled the back of the motorcycle, Leather Girl didn't exchange a single word. She just hit the throttle and off they went. His mind wandered as they zoomed along, arriving there before he knew it.

The grounds around the mansion were as spectacular as he remembered them, perfectly groomed with no loose debris, sticks or leaves anywhere in sight. She led the way to the pond. Trailing behind them was a boy, probably in his late teens, wearing a pair of dark sunglasses. His long blonde hair was tied back in a ponytail. Cameron didn't notice him at first and was startled when he caught his first glimpse.

"He lives here," comforted Leather Girl.

"What's his name?" Cameron whispered.

"Everyone calls him Pluto," she replied.

Cameron remembered learning about Pluto at school, particularly the controversy over whether or not it was a planet. For centuries it was thought to be one of nine planets circling the sun. And being furthest away, it was known to be little more than an icy mass. But scientists more recently downgraded it to a dwarf planet, one of 50 that scientists knew about. Quite a demotion from planet to dwarf. Cameron seemed puzzled as to why this particular guy trailing them was called Pluto. He was far from a dwarf.

"Hi," said Cameron. Pluto remained quiet and mysterious behind his shades.

Pointing to a dozen or so mannequins lined up 100 yards away, Leather Girl said "Those are your targets, okay? So, strap on the guitar and headgear and listen to my instructions."

Cameron took the guitar from its case, slinging it over his shoulder, then donned the headset, pressing in the ear buds and placing the suction cups to his temples.

"I want you to knock down the third mannequin on the left," she instructed. "And I want you to slightly rock the fourth mannequin next to it."

Cameron glanced at both mannequins which were clad in red plaid shirts and jeans. From a distance they appeared like real people. He focused with great concentration, then started plucking rapidly on the strings. In a fraction of a second, the third mannequin tumbled over. His fingers slowed as he eyed the fourth mannequin and with a masterful touch got it to rock slowly in place without falling over.

"Now, knock over the dummy on the far right and far left, then make the middle one with the purplish shirt spin around," she said.

Pluto lowered his sunglasses, peering over them to make out the color of the purple one. Cameron inhaled deeply, reloading his mind with the images of these three mannequins. He lifted his guitar and executed her request with perfection. Turning towards her for approval, he was surprised when she barely acknowledged what he had accomplished.

"Try knocking off one of the buttons on its shirt," she said.

Cameron stared hard at the dummy to the far left. He could barely make out the buttons, which were the size of a dime. He grasped his guitar, then placed his fingers on the strings and began to play slowly, then a sudden quick plucking, then slow again. The buttons popped off one by one.

Pluto and Leather Girl looked at one another.

"You're quite the sharpshooter," said Pluto. "What's your name again?"

"Cameron," he replied.

"Cameron the sharpshooter," Pluto noted. "I'm calling you C Sharp. That's the name you'll go by."

A broad smile crossed Cameron's face.

"Is that all we need to do?" Cameron asked.

Shaking her head, Leather Girl said, "No. No, it isn't. You have to meet someone before you leave."

"Who's that?"

"The owner of this property," she replied.

"What was his name?" Cameron inquired.

Leather Girl glanced at Pluto who nodded his approval. "Z3," she said. "I'm going to bring you to his waiting room."

Inside the enormous house, Pluto disappeared upstairs as Leather Girl took Cameron to a small room, about six by six feet, with a built-in desk against the wall and a swivel chair tucked underneath.

"Let me put you here for now," she said as Cameron sat in the chair.

"Is this the waiting room?" he asked, noticing a closed door at one end.

"It's a waiting room for the waiting room," she said. "Just wait here and you'll be allowed in the waiting room soon."

Leather Girl left, closing the door behind. Swiveling in his chair, Cameron stared at the blank white walls. There was little else for him to do. He started to twiddle his thumbs, going slow then gradually faster and faster. Next, he stretched his arms towards the ceiling and made elastic faces.

The door to the waiting room slipped open and an Asian man appeared holding a large red duster in his hand. "You can come in," he said, stepping aside. "I'm just cleaning."

Cameron went into the official waiting room. It was a good size with dramatic artwork on the walls. One wall had a large Japanese flag – a white canvas with a large red circle in the center. On the other three walls were versions of the Japanese flag done Andy Warhol-style. One, a green background with a bright yellow circle in the middle; another, a black background with an orange circle in the center and the final wall, a yellow background with a blue circle. A dizzying sight, for sure, making one's eyes vibrate slightly.

 The room had a red couch with big yellow pillows, a comforting sight and one that Cameron indulged in, plopping himself down. Across the room were three large Oriental vases in yellow, orange and green, each resting on a small table. On a side table near the couch stood a small green vase. The room had two jungle-like palms and a brass container with magnificent peacock feathers towering five to six feet tall.

Cameron noticed that two French doors in solid brass lay on the other side of the room. He assumed these led into the office of Z3. He stared at the doors, expecting them to open at any minute. Newly polished, the doors gave off a magnificent shiny glow. Etched on each were designs of nature – waterfalls, crooked pathways, crashing waves and snow-capped peaks.

An hour went by. With nothing to busy himself with, Cameron felt the time stand still. The Asian man re-entered, still carrying his red duster. He grinned at Cameron, then started dusting the palms. He got on his knees and reached the duster under the couch. Then he stood up again and continued dusting. When he got to the two brass doors, he took a dust cloth from his back pocket, breathed a foggy mist on a part of the door and polished it until it glistened even more.

The man stepped back proudly, turning to Cameron who gave an encouraging nod. The man went over to the three large vases and started dusting them. He used his breath again, this time on the yellow vase, rubbing the dust cloth counterclockwise, then the same on the orange vase. When he got to the green one, his red duster bumped it too hard. It staggered about on the tabletop. Before he could grab it, it fell to the floor, shattering into a hundred pieces. The man held his hands to his head in a panic, his face terror-stricken. He glanced at the brass doors, hesitant, wondering if they might open from the noise. Holding his breath, he turned and hustled from the room closing the door behind him.

Cameron leapt up from the couch, staring at the green shards of pottery, wondering how expensive this vase must be. Anyone who entered the room now would assume that Cameron broke it. He couldn't help but look guilty even though he was innocent. He heard the brass doors rattle for a moment and expected them to open. But they didn't. He paced around the room, first back and forth and then in a circle, reversing direction every now and then, trying to think what to do. Time passed slowly and still no one entered. Cameron sat back on the couch. He waited and waited.

The white door opened and in came the Asian man. Instead of his duster he carried a broom and dustpan. Under his arm was a black plastic bag. He swept the shards into the dustpan and dumped them into the trash bag. When he had cleaned the entire mess, he lay his broom and pan on the floor, went over to the small green vase and placed it where the large one used to be.

"What are you doing?" asked Cameron.

"Covering my tracks," he said, proudly.

"You're not going to fool anyone," said Cameron. "They're going to notice the big vase is missing." That was an understatement as the small vase measured a mere 8 inches tall versus the large vases which were about three feet in height.

"Not to worry," the Asian man replied.

Cameron sat up. " I don't want to be blamed," he said.

"Why?"

"I'm kind of in trouble as is," he said.

"And who are you waiting to see?" he asked.

"Somebody named Z3," he said. "You must know who that is, of course."

"Oh, yes," said the man, giving a solemn nod. "Oh, yes."

"I don't have a good feeling about this meeting," he said.

"What's your name?" the old man asked.

"Well, it was Cameron," he said. "But they told me today I was to go by C Sharp."

The man nodded.

"Do you play the guitar?" the man asked.

He nodded.

"How many guitars do you own?" he asked.

"None right now," said Cameron.

"So how do you play the guitar then?" he asked.

"I had borrowed a guitar," he said.

"You didn't have your own?"

Cameron scratched his head. "I did but it got broken."

"You didn't take good care of it?"

"No, I did. But these guys I ran into, well, they didn't."

"So, you borrowed a guitar?"

He nodded.

"From where?

"Here."

""Were you able to use it?"

Almost beaming, Cameron said "I sure did."

"And?"

"I used it against some guys who were picking on my friend. I didn't think it was actually going to work."

"Did you kill any of them?"

He shook his head.

The Asian man sidled up to Cameron and whispered, "Do you know why you're here?"

Cameron turned to face him and said "For discipline?"

"Possibly, yes, but more importantly, you are under consideration," he said, taking a step back.

"Consideration?"

"Yes, for a spot," he said. "Have you ever heard of the Dalai Lama?"

Cameron shook his head.

"How old are you?

"Ten."

"Well, the Dalai Lama was chosen when he was 15," he said.

"Was he good at guitar?"

The older man laughed, shaking his head. "No, no. no. There were signs. Signs that he was the one. And when he was approached, he passed the first test very well."

"What test was that?"

"Well, it took four years to find him and when they did, he was shown a number of different objects, some of which were owned by the previous Dalai Lama," he said. "And he had to show them which ones the previous Dalai Lama owned and which ones he didn't."

"What did that prove?"

"Well, they believed that when the Dalai Lama died, he was reborn in someone else," he said.

"Seriously? That doesn't make any sense. How?"

"Reincarnation," he said. "That's what it is called. So, they search for him in another person. The current Dalai Lama was the 14th incarnation of the original soul."

"This sounds like something out of a comic book. You know, an origination story."

"We found you because of a search."

"Did I used to be someone else?" Cameron asked.

He shook his head. "The search for you had nothing to do with reincarnation. There were other factors."

There was a sudden knock on the door. The old man looked concerned. He shuffled over to the corner of the room, hiding behind a Japanese room divider – a six foot tall piece of artwork that folded in half. Cameron wondered why he hid. The door opened and in walked Leather Girl.

"Did you meet him yet?"

Cameron shook his head.

Leather Girl scratched her head. "Well, I think we should go."

"Okay, said Cameron. "Very rude of him."

Leather Girl smiled. "He's different, that's all."

They walked to the door. "Wait here," she said, disappearing around the corner. Cameron could hear voices upstairs that sounded like kids his age or older. After a short period of time, Leather Girl returned.

"We can go," she said.

"Okay," he replied. "One thing, though."

"What's that?

He took a deep swallow. "Can I still borrow the guitar? I need it for the Variety Show next week."

"The answer is no."

"Okay" came his solemn reply.

CHAPTER 6 THE SHOW

Signs were everywhere around school proclaiming the upcoming Student Variety Show.

After school each day, Variety Show contestants flooded the gym for final practice sessions. Sign-up sheets were posted with call times. They practiced in order of appearance, with people quickly moving props around for the next act. Timing was everything as they wanted to avoid long gaps between acts.

Cameron noticed an announcement for the final dress rehearsal on Thursday. Below it was a list of every act in order of appearance. He scanned through all 58 but didn't see his name. Leather Girl was obviously misinformed. He had been left out. Period.

The truth was that even if he was going to be in the show, he wouldn't be able to perform since he no longer owned a guitar. Sullen, he slinked down the hall, accidentally bumping into a girl he knew in class, Cindy Thompson, who played piano.

"Sorry," he said.

"Hi Cameron," she said. "I was surprised you didn't sign up for the Variety Show."

"I thought I had but somehow my name wasn't on the list."

"Too bad," she said sweetly, sweeping her blonde bangs from her eyes. "I've seen how good you are."

"Thanks."

Cameron's curiosity led him to the school auditorium where rehearsals were taking place. He slipped into the back of the spacious theater where dozens of students waited to rehearse their acts. There was a girl performing ballet with all the clunky grace of a horse. And following her was the world's worst juggler, a mop-topped kid who couldn't keep three balls in the air for more than three seconds.

Cameron felt a tap on his shoulder. He turned and saw a grownup staring down at him.

"Excuse me but are you part of the show?" she asked, lifting her clapboard. "What's your name?"

"Cameron," he replied.

"Your full name."

"Cameron Foster."

"Foster, Foster," she said as her finger moved down the list. "I don't see it here. Is there any other name you would go by?"

Another name? How many names did she think he had? He wasn't a spy or anything. "No," he said.

"Well then I'm afraid I am going to have to ask you to leave," she replied with authority. "The only people permitted in this area are those in the show."

Cameron obediently headed for the exit and made the lonely walk home.

On his front porch stood two large boxes. A very unusual site as they rarely received any packages. His mother must have ordered something as he sure hadn't. But up close he saw that both boxes were addressed to him. He carried them into the kitchen one at a time.

One package was quite heavy whereas the larger box was more manageable. With a scissors, he sliced along the crease of the longer box where a clear packing tape held it together. His eyes brightened at the sight of its contents -- a new guitar. But not just any guitar.

This was a hand-crafted Gibson J-30 acoustic electric. He lifted it from the box, cradling it in his arms like a newborn. His heart fluttered as he placed it on the counter and opened the second heavier box. It contained a 50 watt Vox amp with a cord for his guitar. Taped to the amp was a small envelope. He opened it up and read the handwritten scrawl. All it said was "Turn over the guitar."

Cameron did as instructed. On the back, scrawled in black Sharpie, it read "To Cameron, Play it well as I know you will. Peace xx Bono. PS I played this in Capetown."

Beyond elated, he never ever dreamt of owning a guitar as good as this one. He held it up, staring lovingly at each string and the wood veneer. His broad smile, though, diminished before a wave of sadness descended on him. As great as this guitar was, he wouldn't be able to play it at the Variety Show because he wasn't on the list. Why did Leather Girl mislead him?

Cameron set up his new Vox amp at the kitchen counter. He took an electric cord and connected the amp to the guitar. The amp produced a burst of feedback when first turned on. Lowering the volume, he started to play. The guitar produced a rich deep acoustic sound, the quality one might hear in a concert hall.

As a token of appreciation, he began playing some U2 songs he knew, starting with New Year's Day then Desire and I Will Follow, one blending into the next. When he finished, he took a bow before an imaginary crowd.

Playing this wondrous instrument brought him out of his funk. He heard stomping upstairs. His mother was probably going to come down and complain about the noise. He held his breath so he could hear better. All was quiet, the stomping had stopped. Carefully, he carried the amp and guitar to his room. He flipped over the guitar checking out Bono's signature one more time to make sure it wasn't all a dream. This was real.

Friday afternoon arrived with many children anticipating that night's Variety Show. Several classrooms reverted into last minute rehearsal halls where students could get in a final practice before the big night.

"Hi Cameron," yelled Arne. "You going to the show tonight?"

Cameron was definitely curious to see some of the acts, especially ones involving people he knew. But to sit there and watch, knowing he couldn't perform, was too painful a thought.

"I can't," he replied.

"How come?"

"Cause my mother planned something else for me," he said.

Cameron hung around the hallways watching all the last minute preparations. At four o'clock, he headed home, encountering his mother in the kitchen where she was making a piece of toast.

She looked up, blankly, staring at him. "We have to go to the market tomorrow," she said, before breaking into a hacking cough.

"Are you okay?" he asked with concern.

She continued to cough, her eyes bloodshot and face beet red. She nodded unconvincingly.

"I'm going to my room," he said.

When he got upstairs and took out his new guitar, it instantly brightened his mood. For the next two hours, he played, song after song. Many of them, he had never played before. He knew how they sounded and played them by ear, remarkably close to how he remembered them. Taking a break, he lay on his bed, looking at his bedside clock. It was 6:45pm. What else would he do this evening to distract himself so he didn't dwell on the Variety Show he was missing.

He heard a crunch of gravel outside the house. He went downstairs and peered through a side window, spotting an old green Cadillac with big fins. Probably someone lost, he figured. It certainly wasn't anyone he knew or anyone his mother knew as she had no friends. He waited for someone to get out of the car. The door opened squeakily and out appeared a black boot and black leather pants. It was Leather Girl. He opened the front door.

"Sorry I'm late," she said. "I had to borrow a car. Couldn't use the bike tonight. And there was really bad traffic. Being in a car I couldn't do any lane splitting. You ready?"

Cameron looked at her quizzical.

"Tonight is the Variety Show, right?" she asked.

He nodded.

"Then, let's go," she said.

"I'm not in the show," he replied. "I don't know why you keep saying I am."

Leather Girl stepped further into the house, ignoring him. "Where's your new guitar?"

"How'd you know I got a new guitar?"

She simply smiled.

"It's upstairs."

"And the amp?"

"Same."

"Grab them and let's go."

They loaded the guitar and amp into the backseat of the car.

"Couldn't have done this with the bike," she replied.

They drove off, the large car occupying half the road. By school, the main parking lot was completely full. Many cars were parked on portions of the lawn and some on the street. She drove to the back of the school near the auditorium. In the glove compartment, she pulled out a blue handicapped pass and tucked it inside the front windshield so it was visible from the outside.

"You're not handicapped," said Cameron.

She smiled. "I'm borrowing this car from someone who is," she replied. "And if I carried your amp a mile away, I might just be. I follow rules. Just not all the time."

Checking the time, Cameron saw it was 7:15pm. "The show started already," he said.

"We're fine," she replied. "You're not scheduled to go on until the very end."

When they entered the school, Leather Girl led them backstage where a number of adults and some children had congregated. With most of the adults dressed up in preppy attire, Leather Girl stood out like a sore thumb.

"Can I help you?" said a woman, in her thirties, clutching a notepad.

"We're leaving his amp back here," Leather Girl replied.

"And what is the name?" she asked.

"Vox."

She looked down her list. "I don't see a Vox," she replied.

"That's the name of the amp," replied Leather Girl.

"I need the name of the act," she said.

"It's Cameron," Cameron replied.

"Your last name is Cameron?" she asked.

"No. That's my first name," Cameron replied.

Another woman came over. "Dorothy?" she asked. "I need you."

"I'll be back," the woman named Dorothy said to Leather Girl.

Muttering under her breath, Leather Girl said "And, so will we? Let's tuck the amp under here." Pushing the amp into a corner, she tugged over a large garbage container to help conceal it.

Leather Girl hustled out of the backstage area before Dorothy returned. Cameron dutifully followed, carrying his guitar. They emerged from backstage and walked around to the back of the auditorium. The place was packed, every seat filled. Standing room only. A number of people stood in the back watching the interminable proceedings. Talent was a scarce commodity as was creativity and originality.

Three girls came out, dressed in different colored leotards – one all pink, another all yellow and the third all lime green. They somersaulted onto the stage like runaway Easter eggs. As the music began, it blared Kelley Clarkson's Stronger, prompting them to leap to their feet. Then, they proceeded to sway back and forth to the music. Looking at one another for the next cue, they each kicked a leg in the air, then spun around and repeated the same steps. It was a monotonous performance. One that made the song feel long. And if Kelley Clarkson were around, she probably could have sued for defamation of a song. When it ended, they all smiled, curtsied and strode off to moderate applause.

The next act was a girl dressed like a cheerleader, holding a baton. In the program book she was listed as Majorette Margie. She tossed the baton into the air, helicoptered around and caught it with ease, moving it behind her back then up in the air again. She then lay on her back and caught it on the way down. She stood and tossed it up again, missing the catch. She awkwardly scooped it up and started spinning it around, faster and faster. She moved towards the back of the stage and threw it into the air. She waited a moment, then another and another, before realizing the baton wasn't coming down. It had gotten stuck on something. A parent came out from the wings to help find it. All the while, the music, a Christina Aguilera song, continued to play, making it appear that this was all part of the act. As the song wound down, the baton fell from above, landing on the majorette's head. Startled, she almost cried, reigning in the tears through sheer will power. She picked up the baton and ran off. The audience applauded out of respect though there was some snickering.

Next came a young boy who could have won the worst dress-up competition. He wore a black top hat and black suit, the sleeves and pants much too big. On his face was a bushy black mustache, adhered crookedly beneath his nose. On a table he placed his top hat, reached in and pulled out a rabbit. If it were a real rabbit, it would have been rather impressive. Instead, this was a stuffed toy rabbit that obviously had been crammed into the hat. He then took out a red handkerchief which he tucked into his hand, making it appear to disappear. As he pulled both hands back as if to say "ta da," a fake rubber thumb flew off of his hand with part of the red handkerchief dangling out, betraying his secret. For his final act, he took out a coin, held it up, closed his hand, reopened it and the coin was gone. Decent trick but not on a big stage where the audience couldn't even see the coin as it was so small. He received a smattering of applause, most likely from his parents and relatives.

Out next were six girls dressed as weightlifters. Rags were stuffed into their sleeves to give the appearance of muscles. In front of them was a weight - basically a silver broomstick handle with two silver Styrofoam bowling ball-like objects at each end. The music began, and yes, once again it was Kelley Clarkson's Stronger, the fourth time someone had used that music. As it played, the girls lifted weights. Although it made sense to use a song called Stronger., the act was little more than dead weight generating minimal applause.

A stagehand, most likely one of the fathers, carried a chair onto the stage for a young boy who had a dummy with red hair and freckles. The boy had dyed his own hair bright orangey red and had large brown freckles drawn onto his face so he mirrored his dummy although it looked more like a bad case of measles. He proceeded to do a ventriloquist act.

"Hi there," he said to the dummy. "What's your name?"

"Red. Dummy."

"Your name is Red Dummy?"

"No, dummy. I'm saying my name is Red. And I'm calling you a dummy."

"But I'm not a dummy," the boy said.

"With an act like this, you sure are," said the dummy.

The banter was a tad grating though not entirely awful. But the boy's ventriloquist skills were virtually non-existent. He couldn't throw his voice at all. The only thing he did to differentiate himself from the dummy was to use an Irish accent whenever the dummy spoke. But he messed up several times, doing the Irish accent for himself. It wasn't a great act but at least it wasn't accompanied by that Kelley Clarkson song.

Leather Girl and Cameron looked at one another in disbelief.

Another act was a young boy who did impersonations. Impersonations can be artful if you don't have to explain who they are. But for the ones he did – Justin Bieber, Donald Trump and Lindsay Lohan – you needed to hear who he was doing or you wouldn't have had a clue.

Another girl group came out, this time four of them, doing a gymnastic routine to... Kelley Clarkson's Stronger. All four girls were obviously gymnasts and they tumbled across blue rubber mats placed on stage. They were the most talented of the Kelley Clarkson acts so far but that wasn't saying a lot.

Fortunately, every act was limited to two minutes but multiplied by 58 acts it amounted to three long hours that felt eternal. There was an off key flutist, a kid who sang a song while someone next to him did sign language, another magic act, this time from a girl doing card tricks which no one could see and two more Kelley Clarkson songs with accompanying acts. People started turning their heads, talking to one another every time Stronger came on. It was as though it was the only song on the planet.

The show wound down with the 58th act, a kid who came on stage and read the Declaration of Independence while wearing a Minuteman hat. The audience remained seated. Out of respect for the other children in the show, parents were discouraged from leaving after their own child performed otherwise many would have left by then.

Leather Girl nudged Cameron and they headed backstage. Most of the parent volunteers had vacated the stage as had the performers. The ones remaining were gathering up their things. Leather Girl took hold of the amp and stood in the wings of the theater, watching Ms. Periwinkle make final remarks. Ms. Periwinkle had overdressed for the occasion, wearing high heels, a pearl necklace and a fancy navy blue dress.

"Do you know what you're going to play?" Leather Girl asked Cameron.

"No."

"Well, you better figure it out fast," she said. "You're performing once she's done. And you'll have two minutes."

"How do I know when two minutes is up?" he asked.

"I'll wave," she said.

Ms. Periwinkle droned on. Thanking all the parents who volunteered. Dozens of names. She thanked the music department, including Ms. Becker who accompanied several acts on the piano. And she thanked those who helped with set decorations, tickets, brochures, those parents who made cookies and brownies and the custodial staff.

Cameron nervously turned to Leather Girl. "I think the whole show is over," he said. "It doesn't sound like she knows I'm going to perform."

"It's a surprise for everyone," said Leather Girl. "I told you that. Now, I've got to get out there. Can you grab that stool and carry it out?"

While Ms. Periwinkle spoke, Leather Girl carried out the amp to the center of the stage, plugging it into an outlet located on the floor. It produced some feedback, causing Ms. Periwinkle to look back.

"Don't mind me," said Leather Girl, nonchalantly.

Ms. Periwinkle appeared very surprised to see her. She looked back at the sea of people and continued to speak.

"I also want to thank our wonderful principal," she said. "And let's not forget all the veterans overseas."

Where did that come from? I could see the Super Bowl recognizing the vets but it seemed out of place in a school variety show. Leather Girl situated Cameron on his stool and plugged his guitar into the amp. Cameron sat on the stage looking all alone.

"And so, that concludes this year's variety show. Thank you all."

At that moment, a young ponytailed girl emerged from the wings on cue carrying a large bouquet of red roses for Ms. Periwinkle. Leather Girl gently took the microphone from Ms. Periwinkle so she could more easily hold the flowers.

"Anything else to say?" Leather Girl asked, holding the microphone towards Ms. Periwinkle's mouth.

"Thank you all for the lovely flowers," she said as a few parents started to stand, getting ready to leave.

Leather Girl cleared her throat then held up the microphone. Excuse me," she said. "I just want to say, Ms. Periwinkle did a wonderful job with tonight's variety show. There was only one thing missing. A young boy who I have gotten to know had tried to sign up for the show. He submitted his registration on time but somehow it was received a day late. I know there is bureaucracy everywhere but it seemed so wrong to deprive him of the chance to play his two minutes. You are welcome to leave as the official variety show is over. But I now have a two-minute talent show that I hope those who stay can appreciate. This is Cameron Foster. He plays guitar. Take it away Cameron."

The parents who had begun to stand re-took their seats.

Cameron was baffled. It all happened so fast he couldn't digest it. All he could do was play. He waited as Leather Girl stepped to the side. Then with lightning fast fingers he played the beginning of an intricate classical song for Spanish guitar, gracefully slipping into the last two minutes of the Eagles Hotel California, then into part of the heavier Black Dog by Led Zeppelin, his fingers dancing up and down the guitar and finally ending with the opening of a song he just learned the other day, one called "I'm Going Home" made famous by Alvin Lee at Woodstock. The song demanded the most agile guitar playing as it ricocheted from highs to lows at a manically fast speed. He looked over at Leather Girl to see if his time was up. She had actually let him go six minutes because he had kept the audience enthralled. When he stopped, she gestured for him to take a bow which he did. The crowd stood on their feet and gave him the most enthusiastic applause of the night with many piercing whistles of appreciation. Cameron stood like a deer in headlights uncertain what to do next. Leather Girl returned, grabbed the mike

She helped Cameron unplug his amp and place the guitar back in its case. The stool, owned by the school, remained on stage.

Ms. Periwinkle encountered them as they walked off. "That was highly inappropriate," she said.

Leather Girl smiled. "We're sorry you don't like Led Zeppelin or The Beatles or Tarrega or...um..."

"Alvin Lee," said Cameron.

"Yes, Alvin Lee."

"That's not what I meant," said an indignant Ms. Periwinkle. "We spent a lot of time on this event and I don't appreciate you crashing it this way. We have very specific rules."

"We respectfully disagree," said Leather Girl. "We waited and waited and waited through three painful hours until the show was done. We then waited through your remarks and offered the audience a great finale that, as I mentioned, was separate from your variety show. Have a pleasant night and please dress a little differently next time. This isn't a prom."

Leather Girl had to restrain herself from saying even more. She walked off the stage. Looking back for Cameron, she saw him surrounded by several older teenagers. She got closer and overheard them talking.

"Man, you were awesome," said a teenage boy with shoulder-length hair. "I mean, geez, how long have you been playing?"

Cameron hesitated, counting the years in his head. "Five years," he replied.

"You in a band?" he asked.

Cameron shook his head.

"Well, I'm part of a band and we could use someone like you," he said. "Of course, you'll probably first want to hear how we play together, what music we like and stuff like that. But you rock."

Cameron stood in disbelief. The very idea that he could be playing in a band with high school students overwhelmed him. It was beyond cool. He couldn't believe it.

A girl approached, probably 15, and asked "How old are you?"

"Ten," Cameron said.

"Wow. You're going to be really good. What am I saying?!" she smacked her hand against her forehead. "You already are really good. Ten? That's sick. I'm sending this video to all my friends," she said, holding up her iPhone.

Leather Girl waited patiently while Cameron soaked in the adulation. Then, spotting a quiet moment, she took him by the arm and escorted him off. Ms. Periwinkle remained backstage, looking totally flustered. Walking by, Leather Girl turned, looked her directly in the eyes and said "Peace and out."

Cameron smiled weakly at Ms. Periwinkle and added "Peace." As Cameron walked off, his beloved music teacher Mr. Michael high-fived him.

The green Cadillac ambled down the road, pulling up to Cameron's house. Leather Girl sat in the car. She glanced over at Cameron who sat perfectly still, not wanting to get out, relishing the night. Not wanting him to feel rushed, she stared out through the windshield, watching the night bugs flying into the amber headlights. Cameron rubbed the back of his neck, nervously.

"Thanks," he said, simply.

She smiled, giving him an appreciative nod.

He opened his door. She took that as her cue to do the same, walking to the trunk to take out his amp. She carried it up the front steps and through the door. Leaving it just inside, she headed out.

Cameron said "Can I ask you something?"

"Sure."

He quickly sorted through his thoughts. "Well, this is going to sound strange but I've always referred to you as 'Leather Girl' in my head because I don't know your name."

She looked amused.

"Could you tell me what it is?" he asked, expecting to hear something ultra-cool.

She paused for one very long moment and said "Hillary."

"Hillary?" he repeated.

She nodded. "But no one ever calls me that."

She went to her car and before getting in said one final word "You were great tonight. You really impressed everyone, including me."

The car drove off. Cameron watched its rear taillights fade into the night.

He went to his bedroom and put away his guitar. He put on a different t-shirt since he owned no pajamas and brushed his teeth. But something wasn't right. He stepped out into the hallway and noticed the light in his mother's room was still illuminated. She never kept it on this late.

He squeezed the doorknob, turning it slightly, just enough so he could push the door open. He peered into the room but didn't see anything. He took a few steps before he noticed two feet extended out by the bed. Walking around for a better view, he saw his mother lying on the floor, her mouth agape, her skin blue. Blood, now dried, coated both nostrils. It didn't take a medical examiner or coroner to know that she was stone cold dead. It was at this moment that Cameron's life was going to change forever.

CHAPTER 7 A NEW DAY

Outside the window stood a large weeping willow, its branches and light green leaves cascading to the ground. Cameron found it so beautiful and strange looking that he couldn't turn away from it. It swayed gently, seeming to come alive in the breeze.

"What's your name again?" said a police officer, tapping a computer keyboard as he sat across from Cameron at a wood table.

"Cameron."

"Your full name."

"Cameron Foster," he replied.

Drumming his fingers, the officer exhaled loudly. "Somehow you got lost in the system," he said. "I can't find you anywhere. As far as this computer is concerned, you don't exist."

Cameron glanced down at his body from his feet to his stomach to his arms and chest to acknowledge, at least to himself, that he did indeed exist.

The officer watched and smirked before jotting down more information.

"Okay," said the officer. "Never easy. Never easy. Well, we're going to assume you do exist and add you to the system. I have to put an address here for you but you don't really have one right now."

"Can you put down the police department since that's where I am?" asked Cameron.

"I could put the 1939 World's Fair but it's not accurate," he replied, chewing on a piece of gum. "You're a ward of the state."

"Why a reward?"

"A ward," he said. "That means the state owns your fate. They are responsible for looking after your well-being."

The phone rang. "Hello? Uh, huh," he said. "Yep, he's here with me now." He peered into a corner at two large black plastic garbage bags. "Yeah, his stuff is here. I understand. No, that's okay. I'm fine. So, you'll be able to get here tomorrow then? Okay. I'll figure something out. Thanks." He hung up and turned towards Cameron. "Your social worker can't come down tonight," he replied, chewing away. "Personal emergency."

"What's that mean?" Cameron asked.

"Frankly, I don't know," he said. "It's personal. Tell you what. I can't have you staying here all night so I'll take you to my place. It's not quite protocol but we're not a big bureaucratic police department here."

He stares at the clock. "I'm out of here in 20 minutes," he said. "So, why don't you busy yourself til then and we'll grab your stuff and get something to eat. That is, if you're hungry."

"Sure."

"Sure, to what?"

"Everything you said."

"I haven't officially introduced myself," the officer replied. "I'm Sgt Manning. You can call me Sarge or Phil. Your choice."

Sgt Manning finished up his desk work and filed away several folders. Then, he shut down his desktop computer and walked over to Cameron who stood near the garbage bags.

"Let's go," he said.

"I took out the aquarium," Cameron said, pointing to the rectangular glass tank on the floor. "It's got nothing in it but moss."

Sgt Manning noticed a guitar case in one of the two garbage bags. "You got a guitar here? " He said with a smile. "You're in luck. I can play you a few songs tonight."

They left the stationhouse and got into a squad car. "You been in a squad car before tonight?" he asked.

Cameron shook his head.

"Well, that's just as well."

Driving down the moonlit road, away from the main streets, Sgt Manning spotted three teenagers walking along the side of the road. With a mischievous grin, he told Cameron to push a button. Cameron obeyed and a loud police siren broke through the night air, unnerving them. They appeared frightened and rather guilty looking though they had done nothing wrong. He instructed Cameron to hit a second button and the swirling red police lights lit up atop the roof of the car. He then sped away, swerving around each corner. Cameron felt as though he were in a movie. He had been so used to his mother's slow driving that he had never experienced a fast ride in a car. The whole experience initially threw him off guard. But it didn't take long before he took great pleasure in it.

Sgt Manning soon pulled into the driveway of a small one-story house. "This is the last stop," he said, turning off the car. They carried in the two black garbage bags. "What do you have in these? A car? "

"No, that's my amp," said Cameron.

"You'll be in the first room on the left," he said. "Make yourself comfortable while I change and get dinner ready. There's a TV right there."

Cameron plunked himself down in front of the TV and began channel surfing, amazed at the wide variety of programming. He glanced around the room, noticing a cross on one wall next to a photo of the Pope. Then, he saw a pennant for the New York Giants and another for the New York Yankees. The kitchen sat just off the side of the small living room. Sgt Manning cooked a spaghetti dinner with meatballs and then made a salad. He set up tray tables and brought out the food.

"I don't know what you normally eat for dinner but I assume most kids like spaghetti," he replied.

Cameron nodded. "My mother never made dinner so this is really nice of you."

They dined in front of the television. Sgt Manning slurped a beer while Cameron sipped a large cold glass of milk. Neither spoke throughout the meal. When they finished, Sgt Manning cleared the plates and brought out two pieces of chocolate cake.

"I hope you like chocolate," he said.

Cameron's smile said it all.

At the end of the meal, Sgt Manning walked Cameron to his room. "I call this the trophy room," he said. All around were trophies – ribbons and statues. Gold athletic figures on wood stands. There were ones for football and baseball and even basketball.

"Wow," said Cameron. "Where did you get all of these? On eBay?"

Sgt Manning laughed. "eBay? Does it really look like I couldn't have won any of these? I was a good athlete in high school."

"Then what happened?" asked Cameron.

"Ha!" he snorted. "Well, I still play sports in the various leagues but I never excelled beyond my high school days. Do you play any sports?"

Cameron shook his head, gazing down.

"Hey, nothing wrong with that," he said. "So, what do you do instead?"

"I play guitar," he replied.

Sgt Manning nodded his approval. "Good for you. Let's take out that guitar now. In fact, let me show you a few things."

Cameron opened up the case. "This is a beautiful guitar," said the officer. "Where'd you get it?"

"Bono."

"Bono?"

He nodded.

"You mean, Bono as in the U2 guy?"

He nodded.

"You're funny," he said. "Bono gave you this guitar? Of course he did."

Sgt Manning picked up the guitar and began strumming. Noticing one of the strings was out of key, he paused to tune it, then slowly played a poor man's version of the Lynyrd Skynyrd classic 'Sweet Home Alabama.' He was so cautious about playing the wrong chord, it was a cringe-worthy performance.

Cameron politely smiled. "Sweet Home Alabama," he said.

"It probably could use a little work," the officer replied. "I've been practicing it for a while. Tough one to master, I guess. You want to play something?"

He handed the guitar to Cameron. "What should I play?"

"Whatever you like," he said. "Start with something basic. Something simple. Do you know 'Michael Rowed the Boat Ashore?'"

Cameron shook his head.

"What about 'Twinkle Twinkle Little Star?'"

Cameron gave a blank stare.

"Play whatever you want," he said.

'Is there a rock group you like?" Cameron asked.

"Many," he replied. "But the groups I like have some darn difficult songs to play. I mean, Lynyrd Skynyrd has a song called 'Free Bird' that is one I'd love to play but probably never will."

"I know it," said Cameron.

"You know how to play 'Free Bird'?" Sgt Manning said with amazement. "It's a long and difficult song."

"I can skip the beginning, the ballad part, and go right to the fast part if you like."

"If nothing else, I like your confidence kid," he said, amused. "Do your best and don't get frustrated."

Cameron nestled the guitar against his leg, took a pick from his pocket, closed his eyes and proceeded to play 'Free Bird' from the point where the song goes into the up tempo guitar solo. Cameron's fingers flickered quickly in this 5:12 triple guitar solo. As he played, Sgt Manning's jaw dropped lower and lower. When he finished, he opened his eyes and looked up at Sgt Manning. The Sgt stood and applauded.

'Damn, that was impressive!" he exclaimed. "Who in the world are you?"

"Cameron," he replied.

"I got to keep an eye on you, Cameron Foster. You are going places, my man. How old are you?"

"Ten...and counting," Cameron replied.

"I haven't seen a teenager let alone an adult play that well. Can you play anything else?"

For the next two hours, Cameron went through a roster of songs by Led Zeppelin, the Foo Fighters, the Rolling Stones, REM, U2, the Beatles, Nirvana, Guns n Roses and more, leaving Sgt. Manning greatly entertained and gob smacked.

"I could hear you play all night long and never get tired," said Manning. "But we've got to get some sleep as I have to get you to the station house tomorrow before the social worker arrives."

"Okay," said Cameron, wishing he could just stay with Sgt Manning.

"Let me tell you something," he replied. "You have immense talent. The only thing that's gonna hold you back is yourself. Don't be shy. Get yourself noticed. Take chances. You understand?"

"I guess."

"Thanks so much for playing for me."

Sgt. Manning stood up from the sofa, tossed the pillows aside and opened it up into a bed. The sheets were already in place.

"The bathroom's right over there," he said. "See you in the morning."

Cameron felt a special pride in receiving adulation from Sgt. Manning. In the past, he had always seen police in a different light, usually coming to his house because of a complaint about his mother. Although he was now technically homeless, he actually felt better than he ever had.

When morning came, Sgt Manning drove Cameron to Dunkin Donuts where he treated him to hot chocolate and two donuts while he nursed a cup of steaming black coffee. They sat inside, sipping at their respective drinks, both too tired to speak.

By the time they got to the stationhouse, the social worker was already there. Her name was Rose Greely. She was in her mid-thirties, had strawberry blonde hair in need of a wash and wore clothes so rumpled she must have slept in them. "I'm up to speed on the case," she said, her voice tinged with an Irish accent.

"Pleased to hear it," said Sgt Manning.

"A perfect couple has just come my way," she said.

"Is there really such a thing as a perfect couple?" asked Sgt Manning. "I'm curious to know what makes you say such a thing?"

"For starters, they're younger. Early thirties. His primary caretaker before this was much much much older than that. And they don't smoke as his former caretaker did. He has a day job but she is around. But best of all, they like rock music."

"You're right on that last point," said officer Manning. "Cameron loves rock music. And he is a major talent, I am telling you first-hand."

"You want to hear something odd?" she said.

Sgt Manning swiveled around in his chair to face Rose. She leaned in and whispered, "This is really messed up. He was a foster child. His foster father died early on so his foster mother raised him. Somehow, he slipped through the system as he never was adopted. And weirdest of all, his foster mother gave him the last name Foster even though her name was Weiss. And she collected checks all along. Anyway, at least we figured it out."

Sgt Manning nodded in agreement, then stood up from his chair and stretched. "So, how soon is this all going to happen?"

Rose took a deep breath and with immense pride said "Very soon."

∎∎

The day Cameron met his new foster parents, Carl and Sally Magid, was memorable. They had a slacker attitude, moving slow and easy, clad in casual attire and living in an unadorned house, small but immaculately kept.

They chewed gum perpetually from morning to night. Chewing was as natural to them as a cow chewing its cud.

In their living room Cameron noticed the walls had framed posters of Mick Jagger, Keith Richards and the Rolling Stones, a clear sign that this couple loved rock 'n roll.

Cameron's stomach gurgled with hunger as he hadn't eaten that day. Even gum would suffice. "Do you have any extra gum?" he asked politely.

"None that you could have," said Carl to Cameron's disappointment. "Come see your room."

Carl led Cameron to a small but freshly painted room, its walls pale yellow. It had a closet, single bed and a desk with a swivel chair. The one piece of artwork on the walls was of a guitar, lightning striking it and electrifying it in a neon blue. Cameron assumed they put up this guitar art for him as they must have heard about his love of that instrument.

 Carl gave him a quick tour of the rest of the house. For ambiance, Carl cranked up the sound of his DVD player with the Rolling Stones' classic 'Jumpin' Jack Flash'. When the song ended, it played once again. It was on repeat mode and the Magids didn't seem to notice it repeating over and over again. For Cameron, the repetition got on his nerves. His whole body tightened each time it played.

Although the house was dust-free, Cameron felt a pending asthma attack. Stress could sometimes bring them on. He reached for his inhaler and took three satisfying puffs, filling his lungs.

"What are you doing?" said Sally, catching sight of his actions.

"Helping myself breathe," he replied.

Scratching her head, she said "You're not dependent on that thing, are you? I mean, you're not some kind of juvenile junkie that's landed at our door."

He shook his head.

"I just wonder if you're all that's been advertised," she added.

Cameron had no idea what she was talking about. But he started to witness her highly critical nature. She was a hard person to impress and an easy one to disappoint.

As dinner neared, Cameron hovered near the kitchen, offering to set the table. Having never been properly schooled in the placement of utensils, he placed the spoon, knife and fork together in the center of each place. When Sally told him to get placemats, he nodded before realizing he didn't know where they kept them.

"Search around," she said. "Good way to familiarize yourself with where things are."

Cameron tugged open cupboards and drawers, finding everything but placemats. In one cupboard, he saw boxes and boxes marked 'Nicorette Gum.' These were big time gum chewers, he thought, understanding now why they didn't share their gum with him.

By the time dinner was served, Cameron had heard 'Jumping Jack Flash' about 30 straight times in a row. The words "And it's all right now" made him think, "No, it isn't at all."

"Do either of you like any other songs?" he said, asking a question that anyone in their right mind would have asked an hour ago.

They looked at one another and smiled. Sally unwrapped a new piece of Nicorette gum which she popped in her mouth. The chicklet clicked against her teeth. "When we like something, we stick with it until we get tired of it. And then, and only then, do we move on."

Cameron nodded though he didn't quite understand her logic.

"That's why we like Nicorette gum," added Carl, taking a fresh piece.

"Well, that's kind of true, Carl," said Sally. "Carl and I had smoked for a long time."

"Too long," said Carl.

"And when we got ready to stop, we got hooked on Nicorette gum."

"How long ago was that, honey?" asked Carl.

Sally leaned her head back to think. "Um, about two months now. We're only supposed to use Nicorette for three months. Then we'll need something to break our Nicorette gum addiction."

"Me in particular," said Carl. "I have to use the 4mg. strength where Sally gets away with 2mg. The good news is it's not fattening. A mere 3 calories per piece."

"And they have some nice flavors," added Sally. "My fave is Fruit Chill."

"And mine is Cinnamon Surge."

Sally brought a big pot of soup over to the table and scooped a ladle full of a tomato-y broth into Cameron's bowl. Carl's and her bowls remained empty. Starved, Cameron slurped the hot soup, nearly burning his throat. He cautiously blew on each spoonful, cooling it enough so he could sip it down. Carl and Sally sat at the table but didn't eat at all. They just watched while chewing their gum.

"This is our first family meal together," Sally proclaimed proudly, gazing at Cameron and Carl. Cameron relished the meal but an uneasiness settled in as he felt their stares. Sally cleared his empty bowl and brought over a plate of chicken, white rice and string beans. Cameron couldn't recall having a full meal like this in a long time. He had become so used to grabbing snacks or eating cereal for dinner. Before indulging on the main course, he waited for them to serve themselves. Their plates lay empty and they made no effort to get food.

The chicken tasted delicious, well-seasoned with spices that peaked his taste buds. He began to feel full. It did dawn on him how strange it was they didn't eat. He had a queasy feeling that maybe they had poisoned his food. He pondered that notion, aware that there was little he could do if they had. He wouldn't know the poison and without that knowledge he wouldn't know what antidote to get if an antidote even existed. So, he accepted his fate, feeling that death by poison may be preferable to hearing 'Jumping Jack Flash' play 100 straight times without a single solitary break.

"If you didn't know any better," said Sally with a broad smile. "You'd probably think we were trying to poison you."

"Ha!" laughed Carl. "You sure would."

"But we wouldn't do that," said Sally. "We barely know you."

"And we need the money for doing this foster parent thing," added Carl.

Cameron produced a weak smile. Changing the subject, he asked "How do you survive on so little food?"

Answering in perfect unison, they responded "Multi vitamins."

Cameron scratched his head, unable to think of a follow-up question. He knew very little about vitamins. He wiped his napkin across his mouth, signaling he was done. Before he could stand, Sally cleared his plate and delivered a bowl of strawberry ice cream, two pink scoops with a spoon stuck in one. "Thank you," said Cameron, realizing he would once again be eating alone.

Though he gobbled up the dessert quickly, he only registered one minor ice cream headache. He wished he'd eaten slower so he could have savored every bite. He didn't dare ask for more. He wanted to be on best behavior so they didn't get rid of him.

Gesturing to the bedrooms, Carl said "We saw that you own a guitar."

Cameron gave an efficient nod.

"I'd love to hear you play," said Sally, turning off the stereo.

"Instead of hearing Mick Jagger and Keith Richards play it," she said. "We'd love to hear you play Jumpin' Jack Flash."

Oh my God, thought Cameron. What did he do to deserve this? At one time, he loved the song.

Wiping off the table, Sally asked "You do know how to play, don't you?"

Cameron hesitated and said bluntly. "No."

"You don't?" exclaimed Carl with surprise in his voice. "I thought the social worker said you were musically gifted."

"I remember her saying that as well," said Sally. "She knew we were music lovers and thought you'd be a perfect match for us because of your music."

"Maybe she was referring to another kid," said Carl. "Maybe we have the wrong kid. I mean, you're fine and all but the music thing was attractive to us. Very attractive. Rock n roll, that is. Stones, in particular."

"You really can't play?" Sally asked, scratching her head, confused. "So then why do you own a guitar?"

"It was a gift," said Cameron.

"A recent gift?" said Carl. "He probably expects to learn how to play soon."

Cameron shrugged his shoulders.

"But you can't play a single song right now?" persisted Sally.

Cameron took a deep breath and said, "Not a note."

▪▪▪

While at Carl and Sally's, Cameron had easily memorized every word of 'Jumping Jack Flash to the point where he could sing it backwards. He hadn't set out to memorize it. But the constant repetition ingrained it in his brain. And after this experience, he told himself he would try to never play a song more than a few times in a row no matter how much he liked it. To do otherwise would be a road straight to madness.

Although today marked one week with Carl, Sally and Jack (that is, Jumping Jack), for Cameron it felt like a month. Living in this madhouse made him miss the absolute quietude he had with his late mother in her ramshackle house. Of course, there were positives here, namely, home-cooked meals and a very clean and well-kept house. But he didn't truly feel like home. He felt like a guest.

While on the surface they looked perfectly normal, Carl and Sally were always too revved up from their Nicorette gum. They never stopped moving and that made for a clean house. Sally maneuvered her vacuum cleaner like some electronic anteater, sucking up every minute speck. Carl loved going through their things and tossing stuff in the trash. It was probably why they had nothing on their bookshelves or tabletops. No knickknacks whatsoever. Carl also regularly manned an azure-blue bottle of Windex, cleaning mirrors and windows in every room.

Watching them, Cameron realized that adults weren't all-knowing and wise. Just neurotic, flawed and fallible. Just because someone was older, it didn't make them wiser.

The doorbell rang. Since Cameron moved in, they had not had a single visitor nor did they receive much mail. Carl opened the door. There stood the social worker Rose Greeley with an officer of the law. Nothing about this scene looked good to Cameron.

"Good afternoon," she said, making minimum eye contact.

"Hi," said Carl, uneasy. "What's the problem?"

"You've done nothing wrong," she said, reassuring him.

Carl breathed a sigh of relief and welcomed them into the house.

Rose peered down at a notebook and said "There's a change."

"What do you mean a change?" asked Sally, walking over, holding a duster. "Did we get the wrong child? We thought the child we got could play guitar."

"There has been a mix-up," said Rose. "Not really a mix-up but a change. Someone else had put in a request for this child and the court awarded him to them."

"So, who do we get in return?"

"That isn't clear right now," said Rose, meekly. "I'll have to get back to you. You are still potential foster parents for someone."

"Well, at least we didn't do anything wrong," said Carl. "That's always a relief when the police are involved."

Rose walked over to Cameron. "Hello," she said. "I'm sorry to be moving you from place to place. I hope this time things are permanent. Can you gather your things so we can go?"

"Won't take long," he said. "I don't have much stuff."

Cameron disappeared into his bedroom and stuffed the two black plastic trash bags full of his clothes and belongings. He brought them into the living room, then went back twice to fetch his guitar and aquarium.

"I'm ready," he declared.

Rose sensed something was off, as she'd now heard "Jumping Jack Flash" six times since she'd arrived. The officer carried Cameron's things to the squad car outside.

"You can say good-bye to your foster parents," said Rose. "Take as much time as you like."

Cameron walked over to Sally. "Thanks," he said.

She patted him on the head, feeling very little connection. A hug was clearly not in order. Then he approached Carl, offering another quick "Thanks."

Carl shook his hand. "A pleasure," he said, as if concluding a business deal.

With that, Cameron walked out the front door, hoping it would be the last time he'd ever have to hear "Jumping Jack Flash." A new chapter lay ahead and the circle of life, well, it kept circling, making him dizzy. He had absolutely no idea where his life was headed nor what family he was going to end out with. But whoever it might be, he sincerely hoped they didn't own a CD player and that Rolling Stones song. Amen.

"So much paperwork." Cameron heard those words over and over while the case worker sat before a desktop computer pecking away at the keys. Oddly, though, Cameron saw very little paperwork on the desk.

"You're Cameron Foster?" the case worker asked, swiveling in her chair, her oily black hair desperate for a shampoo.

"Yes. I am," he said, perplexed he would be asked that question after sitting in this office for an hour.

"Just checking," she said, pecking away at the keyboard.

Cameron sat stoically in an uncomfortable metal office chair dangling a yo-yo. They had given it to him as a distraction. He had never used one before so he just let it dangle on its string like a pendulum.

Cameron studied the faces of each employee that walked past, noticing the color and shape of their eyes, how deep-set they were, the destiny of their eyebrows, the width of their noses, if their teeth were crooked or yellow or cracked, how their ears sat on their heads either extended or closely pinned in, the strength of their chins as well as facial hair, freckles, short or long hair, natural or dyed and their overall mood be it happy or sad or in between. He started his own game, evaluating each face. Some people looked best straight on, others in profile, some best on the right side and others the left. He started to grade them accordingly on an A-F scale. Front A meant someone appeared the best from a frontal view whereas a Side C meant they had an average view from the side, perhaps a weak chin or bad overbite. This whole exercise kept him pre-occupied while he waited. It sure beat a three hour session with a yo-yo.

Cameron was used to spending hours upon hours alone while his mother remained locked in her bedroom. With no siblings and few friends, he busied himself by playing guitar or letting his imagination run rampant. Someone tapped his shoulder. It was a man with a shock of white hair who seemed to know him.

"Hello Cameron," he said. "I'm Martin Liptak and I'm the attorney representing the people you will soon be living with. Sorry I'm late but I expect to get this done today. Lot of documents to review and sign."

Based on his slick hair and three-piece pin-striped suit, Cameron perceived this lawyer to be someone smart and successful. His soft-spoken manner and air of dignity commanded his respect.

"Will I be going home with you?" Cameron asked.

"Yes and no. I work for the man who is interested in you. I'll be taking you there right after we finish all the paperwork."

The lawyer grabbed hold of a grey metal folding chair and slid it next to the social worker. He propped a pair of reading glasses at the end of his nose and perused a folder of documents, questioning a sentence here and there, crossing some out and initialing the changes. This went on for two more hours. Finally, the lawyer stood up, stretched and exclaimed "Finito."

He shook hands with the social worker. She smiled and said "Martin, I'll follow up on those things we discussed but there's nothing that will hold this up. I'll get you a copy of all the documents by the end of the week."

Smacking his lips proudly, he said "Works for me. Thanks for making this so easy." He turned to Cameron and said "My man, we are ready to rock n roll. Off to your new home. And this should be permanent. Foster care is a good interim step but it's a short term solution. Usually two years and you move on or get placed in a permanent home."

Cameron had felt like a pinball, bounced around from place to place with no control of his destiny. He welcomed this change.

Outside the air was cool and fresh. His stomach rumbled loudly enough to catch Liptak's attention.

"We'll have about an hour on the road so it's wise we eat before we leave," he said. "Besides, I need a cup of coffee."

They walked over to a diner and sat in a booth with red pleather seating. The faux leather seat felt cool to the touch and was much more comfortable than the office chair he'd been sitting on for much of the day. Liptak told him to order anything he wanted. Cameron obliged, asking the waitress for a cheeseburger and a milkshake.

"How do you want your cheeseburger?" she asked, her hair held back with mesh netting resembling a shower cap.

"Cooked please," he said.

"I mean do you want it rare, medium rare, medium, medium well or well done?" she asked.

Cameron glanced over at Liptak for guidance.

"I always like medium," said Liptak. "It's cooked enough so you're safe but not too much so you're not eating leather."

"Medium," said Cameron.

"And what about your milkshake?" she asked.

"Medium as well," he said.

"I mean what flavor," she asked. "Strawberry, vanilla, chocolate?"

"Strawberry."

"I'll have a burger medium, vanilla shake and bring us some fries, please," said Liptak without having to even glance at the menu.

From Cameron's perspective it was a glorious meal. Delicious and filling. He had no room for dessert though Liptak offered. Liptak paid, leaving a generous tip on the table in cash. He led Cameron back across the street where he'd left his car, a shiny black four-door Mercedes 550 with tinted windows.

"Your stuff is already in the trunk," said Liptak. "Just a couple of trash bags, guitar and an aquarium."

Cameron smiled, climbing into the passenger seat and sniffing the leather upholstery, a strong but comforting smell. Nestled in his seat, quite cozy, with his seat belt secure around his waist and shoulder, Cameron felt a rare sense of security. He last remembered hearing Liptak's car door close and the motor start up before he drifted off to sleep.

He awoke only after the car came to a complete stop and the engine was turned off. His sleepy eyes opened slightly, adjusting to the darkness. He focused in until he made out a stately mansion, one that felt eminently familiar. Climbing out of the car, he stretched his arms, trying to recall why this place looked so familiar. Before he could think any more, the front door of the house opened. Standing there, clad in black leather, was Leather Girl. He knew exactly where he was.

"Welcome home, C Sharp," she said, referring to his nickname.

Cameron gave a thankful nod.

CHAPTER 8 HOME SWEET HOME?

The melodic song of a wood thrush, fluid and flute-like, came caressing through the window only to be interrupted by the harsh sound of a blue jay and a fast-chirping chickadee. Soon there rose a whole symphony of birds introducing the morning.

Cameron's eyes fluttered open as he sat up in his fluffy bed, confused by the unfamiliar surroundings. The chiffon yellow walls, though clean and soothing to the eye, were not familiar at all. He had been so tired when he arrived last night that he took no notice of anything except the comfortable bed. In the corner of the room sat the two black trash bags holding his possessions and beside them was his guitar and the empty aquarium.

All he recalled was seeing Leather Girl greeting him when he arrived. He climbed out of bed and noticed he was wearing a pair of light blue pajamas with a pattern of yellow suns repeated over and over. Though these weren't part of his wardrobe, they fit perfectly. He'd never owned a pair of pajamas before.

He rummaged in one of the trash bags and took out a shirt and pants which he changed into. There was an eerie quiet prompting him to crack open his door to see if anyone was awake. He peeked into the hallway and saw a dozen doors all closed. Stepping softly, to keep the creaking to a minimum, he walked down the hallway to a grand stairwell. He noticed a separate stairway that went up to a third floor. This was one big house. He took one step down the stairs when every door facing the hallway suddenly opened at the same time and slammed shut. Cameron jumped out of his skin, gasping as he raced down the stairs.

On the last step, he ran smack into the old Asian man he'd encountered before. He was carrying an off-white dishrag. Cameron couldn't decide if he was a chef or a caretaker of the place.

"Slow down," the elderly man said. "What is the hurry?"

"I heard some doors slamming," said Cameron, pointing upstairs.

"Doors do that," he said.

Cameron felt foolish. "I just got here last night," he said. "I don't know what I'm supposed to do."

The Asian man held up his dishrag. "Do you like to clean?"

Cameron shrugged his shoulders. "I'd be happy to help if you want," he offered.

The Asian man nodded, appreciating the gesture. "Have you had breakfast?" he asked.

Cameron shook his head.

"Are you hungry?"

Cameron nodded.

"Well, you should get something to eat," he said. "I think you're still growing."

Cameron followed the Asian man down a hall, through a sitting room, past the living room and into a dining room. The table was set for eight people but no one had yet arrived.

On the sideboard was a serving plate of blueberry pancakes, another with scrambled eggs and a third with cold cereal. There was an urn of coffee and hot water with tea bags as well as a pitcher of orange juice, so pulpy it looked freshly squeezed. Cameron salivated at the sight of all this food. Breakfast was a meal he rarely had as his mother never rose early enough to make it nor did she ever have much food in the house.

"Is anyone else coming?" asked Cameron.

"If they're hungry, they will," he replied with a knowing smile. "Take a seat."

"Where?"

"You have a choice, don't you?"

Cameron studied each place. All had the same sized chair and place setting. There were four chairs on each side of the table but none at the end. The Asian man took one chair and put it at the head of the table. "I do not like symmetry," he said. "I like imperfection. There is a beauty in imperfection. Please, sit in this chair."

Cameron reluctantly walked over to the lone seat at the head of the table and slowly lowered himself onto it.

"Now, let me get you some food," the Asian man said, turning toward the buffet. He placed a stack of pancakes with syrup onto a plate, added some scrambled eggs and then poured a tall glass of orange juice.

"Thank you," said Cameron. "But you don't need to wait on me even if it is your job."

The Asian man smiled, then disappeared into the kitchen. Cameron sat alone at the head of the table, his small stature making him look out of place. At that same time, a young man arrived who was quite familiar looking. He had long blonde hair tied back in a ponytail and wore wrap-around sunglasses. Cameron recalled meeting him last time he was here but couldn't remember his name.

"Hi," said Cameron. "My name is—"

"I know who you are," snapped the young man. "You're C Sharp."

It then hit Cameron that this guy's nickname was Pluto. "And you are Pluto," he said.

Pluto couldn't help but notice that Cameron was seated at the head of the table. "You always sit at the head of the table?" he asked.

Cameron shook his head. He wanted to explain that it wasn't his idea. But he also didn't want to get the Asian man in trouble by saying he had encouraged him to sit there. So, he kept quiet.

Pluto went over to the buffet and piled up a plate of food, then sat as far away from Cameron as he could. Wanting to make conversation, Cameron asked "How did you get the nickname Pluto?"

"Why do you ask?" he replied with a tone of annoyance.

"Well, it's just that you always wear sunglasses and yet Pluto is the farthest planet from the sun. That is, if it's even a planet."

"I feel it's a planet," he said. "What difference does it really make? No one's going to ever live there. Too damn cold and too distant."

Cameron nodded.

"Talking about distance, you saw how those guitars worked the other day?" Pluto asked.

"Yeah. That was impressive."

"Well, none of the others here can make their guitar go as far as I can," boasted Pluto.

"How many others are there?"

"You can count, can't you?" he gestured at the place settings. "Eight total and that includes you. How old are you anyway?"

"Ten."

"Ten?! Geez. A youngster."

"And you?"

Pluto said "21. In two months." He seemed annoyed to be talking to someone so much younger.

In walked a boy with unkempt brown hair skewed in every direction. His bangs covered his eyes like a sheepdog. Cameron stared at him, trying to decipher what he looked like. Without hesitating for a moment, the kid gave him the middle finger.

What was that for, Cameron wondered? Another unfriendly person. The boy sat near Pluto who he also flipped off. Pluto ignored him completely, grabbed a plate of food and came back to the table to eat.

Taking the initiative, Cameron introduced himself. "I'm Cameron."

"No, you're not," said Pluto. "Not around here."

Cameron corrected himself. "I'm C Sharp."

The boy kept eating.

"What's your name?" Cameron asked.

The boy rudely ignored him.

"You can call him Flipper," said Pluto with a smile.

"Is it cause he's a good swimmer?" Cameron asked.

Without looking up from his food, the boy flipped off Cameron again.

"I think you can figure it out," said Pluto.

"Does he play guitar?" asked Cameron

Pluto gestured for Cameron to ask Flipper.

"Do you play guitar?" he asked.

Flipper continued eating, once more raising his middle finger.

"I tried to give him the nickname of NEC," said Pluto. "That would be for No Eye Contact. But Flipper won out."

Flipper flipped off Pluto.

"Before you ask every person who comes into this room whether or not they play guitar, the answer is yes they all play guitar," said Pluto. He stood up, stretched and yawned. Cameron felt marooned, sitting alone at one end of the table.

A teenage girl with jet black hair glided into the room, riding a skateboard. She gave Cameron a friendly smile as she leaned her skateboard against the wall. She poured herself a glass of orange juice before taking a seat next to Cameron.

"I'm Viper," she said, extending her hand. Cameron hesitated. "I don't bite," she added, encouraging him to shake it.

Three other teenagers arrived at the same time including a tall black guy named Quake, a slight Asian boy named Brick and a girl, medium build with violet hair, named Fireball.

"He wants to know your age and stuff," said Pluto.

"Is he into astrology?" asked Brick, whose obsession with people's horoscopes was widely known amongst the other kids.

"I really don't think so," said Pluto.

"Don't be so dismissive," said Brick, sweeping back his black bangs. "You can tell a lot about a person through their astrological sign and especially their moon sign."

"They'll be no mooning," joked Fireball in her Southern accent.

"I gave the new kid the name C Sharp," noted Pluto. "He's 10. Finally, someone's younger than Flipper."

Flipper expectedly flipped off Pluto.

"Go on, Vipe," encouraged Pluto.

"I'm Viper from the 51st State and I'm 15," said Viper.

"51st State?" questioned Cameron, softly, aware of only 50.

"She's from the State of Confusion," said Pluto.

"PR," she replied, giving the initials for Puerto Rico which went completely over Cameron's head. "Puerto Rico, baby."

The older Asian man emerged from the kitchen, checking the breakfast set-up to see how the food was holding up. Pluto deliberately tossed his napkin to the floor, looked over at the Asian man and said "Can you pick that up?"

Cameron winced, bothered that Pluto could be so disrespectful to the older man. The Asian man hesitated, staring back at Pluto, his face solemn and emotionless. None of the other kids at the table seemed at all concerned about what transpired. Shaking his head, Cameron decided to act. Rising from his chair, he walked towards the napkin. As he bent down to pick it up, Pluto shouted "Hey!" causing him to jump upright. "I asked him to pick it up," said Pluto. "Not you."

Cameron straightened up, contemplating what to do. He could feel the old man's pain and sorrow. He never enjoyed being singled out or picked on but he also didn't enjoy seeing it happen to others. Pluto turned and said "I'm waiting old man. Is someone hard of hearing?"

Cameron, rather defiantly, bent down and picked up the napkin. He handed it to Pluto who tossed it back on the floor. Once again, Cameron picked it up, this time depositing it on the table. He then returned to his seat at the head of the table as the older man quietly exited the room.

"You like cleaning up?" Pluto asked Cameron. "We can always use a cleaning lady here."

Rather defiant, Viper said "Pluto, must you be such a....?"

Although younger than him, Viper somehow commanded Pluto's respect as he suddenly and unexpectedly stopped saying another mean or critical word.

The three remaining people in the room, urged on by Viper, introduced themselves with thumbnail sketches. The African American teenager, well over six feet tall, maybe close to 6'3", said "I'm Earthquake but most know me as Quake or Biggie Quake when I've had a lot to eat. I just turned 17. And...."

"Where are you from?" asked Viper

"You know," he said.

"Tell our new friend," she prompted.

"Where else, Sweden," he said and with a mischievous wink and added "As you can see, we don't get a lot of sun there."

Quake cleared his throat with a few coughs and then rapped "Make no mistake I got the right attitude, Even though I hail from a very different latitude, Playing guitar with all of you, why, I got nothing but gratitude."

Viper smiled "You're the man, Quakester."

"I am not your typical Swede," he said. "Most Swedes are quite, um, shy and reserved. When they meet you, they never look up from the ground.

Cameron felt like an honorary Swede as he often rarely looked a person in the face.

"Do you know what they call an extroverted Swede?" Quake asked.

"You mean, like someone really outgoing?" Viper asked.

"Yeah," said Quake. "Any idea?" No one responded.

"An extroverted Swede is someone who will look at your shoes," he said.

They all had to think about it a moment. Quake laughed out loud.

"Any way, that's all I have to say," said Quake. "For now."

The next boy, his hair black as shoe polish, said "I'm Brick. I'm a year younger than Quake which puts me at 16. I am from China." He put on his patented green tie-back headband.

"How'd you get that name?" Cameron asked.

"Flipper gave it to me," he said. "I practice yoga every day. I used to always use a rubber mat to sit on. One day Flipper challenged me to do three hours of yoga on the back patio. It was made of brick. Tough on one's rear. But I did all three hours. And my reward was that nickname. Ha."

The last person stood up, sporting violet hair, spiked with mousse. "I'm Fireball," she said. "15. From somewhere down South where peaches are a big deal. I did School of Rock down there. Was in their All Stars band. Toured cross country in the summer. That may be how I got discovered."

"And tell him who gave you your nickname," said Viper.

"Well gee, I did bestow it," said Fireball, exaggerating a Southern drawl.

"You're not supposed to give yourself your own nickname," Viper added. "But somehow, that rule was broken."

"Everyone knows my fascination with fire," she said. "So, the nickname fit."

"But the hair doesn't," noted Viper. "Fire is red."

"Viper, stick to skateboarding," said Fireball. "You know nothing about fire. Red flames are the least hot. They're like 1500 degrees Fahrenheit. Then you have orange at 2100, yellow at 2500, blue at 3000 degrees. I'm of the school that violet glows the hottest though some point to light blue. So, my purple hair is much more meaningful than if it were red."

Cameron liked her explanation.

Pluto rose from his seat. "See you all later," he said, leaving the room. Most of the others followed shortly thereafter, leaving just Cameron, Viper and Flipper behind.

"What happens now?" asked Cameron.

"Classes," Viper noted. "You have a private tutor for your fifth grade subjects – math, science, English and all. Then there are some group classes. You should have a weekly schedule printed on your desk or you can pull it up on the computer screen in your room. If you get confused, you can always come and ask me. I'm your neighbor. First door on the right as you leave your room."

"Thank you," said Cameron, trying to remember her name. "Snake."

"Not snake," she said. "Viper."

"Viper," he said, correcting himself. "Which is a snake."

"Would it help your memory if I bit you in the neck?" she asked.

Cameron scratched his head.

"I'm kidding," she said, pretending to grade Cameron using an invisible pencil and pad. She added "Sense of humor: 2."

Viper spun around and exited the room, saying "Later gator."

Flipper remained the last of them to leave. Fearful of being flipped off again, Cameron had no interest in speaking to or looking at Flipper. Flipper sidled up near him and whispered "Do you know what a cult is?"

Cameron had heard the word but didn't know its full meaning. He assumed it had a negative connotation. There was a long silence before Flipper quietly explained "A cult is a group of people with an extreme ideology that they believe in, often with weird and bizarre rituals and beliefs. And many people in a cult are basically brainwashed to the point where they can't think clearly and follow every dictum the cult sets out."

Cameron's eyes widened as everything suddenly felt creepy.

"Beware," said Flipper.

With renewed concern, Cameron asked "What do you mean?"

Flipper smiled and whispered "I grew up in Vegas so I'm used to surveillance. Every casino had cameras. You were watched all the time. Same is true here. They want everyone to fall in line. So that's why I say beware."

He hustled quickly from the room, leaving Cameron alone with the realization that this whole seemingly wonderful place was too good to be true.

■■■

Back on the desk in his room lay the schedule of classes, leading off with Language Arts followed by Math, Social Studies and Science. He was relieved to see no foreign language requirement. Listed after those classes was "Lunch Break" then simply "Afternoon Classes" with no specifics.

Above the desk was a wall clock, indicating 8:55am, five minutes until his first class. The problem was he didn't know where to go and there was no one there to ask. He peeked outside his door hoping to catch someone in the hallway who might know but no one was around. No sooner had he closed the door when he heard a knock.

"Come in," he said, watching the door open slowly, revealing a woman in her early thirties, petite with short-cropped blonde hair and wire-rimmed glasses. Cradled in her arms were several pounds of textbooks.

"Hello," she said, politely. "My name is Ms. Pennebaker. Pauline Pennebaker. You can call me Pauline. In case you want to know about my background, I've taught school for ten years, all different curriculums, no real specialty, and I've been a tutor here for two years and four months to be exact. I've been assigned to you for your morning schedule. I understand your name is Cameron but your name here is C Sharp. I'm happy to use either one. Whatever you prefer."

"C Sharp is fine," said Cameron, completely amenable although he was not yet used to the nickname.

"Very well," she said. "I've seen your past academic records so I know where you stand in terms of various courses. I am here to teach you fifth grade subjects. Any other courses such as music theory are done separately in the afternoon. What goes on then tends to be secretive."

"When will I know what my afternoon schedule is?" Cameron asked.

"In the afternoon I'd imagine," she replied, not very helpful. "You'll be joined by the others then. They are all at various grade levels. You have the distinction of being the youngest."

Cameron nodded, aware of where he stood having met them all at breakfast that morning.

She leaned in and said "I hear all of you get together in the afternoon."

Cameron whispered back "Are the kids here brainwashed?"

"I honestly don't know," she said. "I have a good relationship with Viper and Fireball. We're going to begin this morning with Language Arts. In my day we called it English or Creative Writing. It's a mix of history and language."

She took out a yellow legal pad and jotted down some words. She angled the pad towards Cameron, partly obscuring it with her body. It read "Be careful. You are being watched. At all times!"

Cameron's eyes darted around the room, looking for any miniature cameras or peepholes. "Now," she said, getting his attention. "Do you like this clock here?" she pointed at the wall clock. Near the center Cameron could make out what appeared to be a small video camera. "And this corner of the room needs some paint," she said. The walls were spotless but she was once again indicating where another miniature camera had been placed. She pointed to two more cameras before getting up close to Cameron's ear and in a soft whisper saying "Lots of hidden cameras. Beware."

Cameron felt a sense of dread, like he was some kind of lab animal monitored by a slew of scientists sitting in another room concocting eerie experiments. He envisioned half a dozen of them in white lab coats, scribbling on their clipboards, registering times and ever-searching for clues to his mental well-being. But for what? What awful destiny lay ahead for him? Why couldn't he have spent just a portion of his life with a normal everyday family if such a thing existed?

"Take a seat," she said. "I'd like you to write down the word 'red' in the center of your paper." He obliged. "Now," she said. "Draw a line from red to your next word which should be something red."

Cameron wrote the word "fire."

"Now," she continued. "Write a word tied to 'burning.'

He thought for a moment then wrote 'sidewalk.'

He wrote down 30 different words at her instruction before she asked him to stop.

"I want you to look at the first word you wrote," she instructed.

Cameron said "Red."

"And now the last word you wrote."

He peered at the paper and said "Banana."

"Interesting how you can connect to a word that would seemingly have nothing to do with your first word," she said. "That's what life is. Lots of connections. And connections can lead you to the strangest and most interesting places."

The lesson continued with other writing exercises, keeping him busy as he put his thoughts to paper. When the 45-minute session was over, Miss Pennebaker left the room, then seconds later re-merged as though she was a new teacher. "Math," she said.

Cameron appeared confused and she clarified matters, saying, "I have to leave the room after each course so I can get myself primed for the next one. She went right into math, dealing with fractions before leaving the room and coming back two more times for social studies and finally science. He stood up and stretched briefly in between courses. When all his morning courses were completed, Miss Pennebaker gave him some homework, then bid him good-bye, saying she would see him tomorrow.

There seemed no place on earth where one could escape homework, he thought.

Cameron peered into the hallway but didn't see or hear anyone. He sauntered downstairs. Near the dining room was a sign indicating that lunch was served outside today. He went to the terrace but no one was there. He heard voices coming from the garden. Behind some towering hedge rows, Cameron found a table set up with eight chairs around it. Six people were already seated, eating lunch. At least he wasn't last. But then he remembered that these were the same six he saw at breakfast. Including himself, Cameron counted seven. There was no eighth person. And yet, he had been told he was the eighth. So, then who was the seventh.

He headed towards Flipper who predictably flipped him off. So, he sought a friendlier lunch mate in Viper who sat at the table with a skateboard draped across her lap.

"Can I ask you a question?" said Cameron.

A slight breeze brought a freshness to the air as different birds bestowed their signature melodic songs.

"I was told I was the eighth person," he said.

"You are."

"But how come I haven't seen a seventh person yet?"

Strutting confidently around the corner was Leather Girl. Cameron instinctively did a short wave and she waved back. "What's her name?" Cameron asked.

Viper replied, "She's the seventh person. Her name's Senza."

"Senza?" he responded.

She nodded. "It's a term used in music meaning 'without.' Senza sordido is 'without mute.'"

"Is she without music?"

Viper laughed. "No way. She is without color. Always in black. Kind of pale, right?"

Cameron finally had a name he could call her, knowing she didn't like her given name Hillary and calling her Leather Girl felt wrong. Now it was Senza. Quite original and easy to say.

She approached Cameron. "How are you?" she asked.

"Okay," he replied.

"Learning your way around?"

He nodded.

Pluto beckoned her over for a conversation that turned intense, with each periodically looking over at Cameron. Senza held up her hand like a traffic cop, the palm facing him, flat and blunt. Not taking a breath or giving him the slightest opening to speak back, she lectured him. His mouth opened but he couldn't get a word in. When she finished speaking, she sat at the table ready for lunch, acting as though nothing had happened. Large bowls rested in the center, each getting passed clockwise. There was a bowl of pasta, composed of corkscrew fusilli with tomatoes and basil, then a bowl of salad and a plate of cold cuts, mainly cheeses and sandwich meats.

After everyone had served themselves, Senza presided over the conversation, showing a level of maturity far greater than anyone else. At age 28, she was the oldest one there.

"I want to test everyone's intuition," she said.

Flipper seemed annoyed, shaking his head, totally unexcited.

"Another challenge? I'm tired of always winning," boasted Pluto, overly confident, adjusting his sunglasses.

"You almost lost last time," reminded Viper. "And to me."

"But I didn't," he said.

Senza got up from her seat, walked over to Cameron and whispered into his ear.

"Don't talk secrets to him," Pluto said. "You giving him the answers?"

"Fine," said Senza. "I was going to spare you all from hearing what the game is all about. So, bear with me as I explain it to him. "You all have pens and paper," she said. "Here's how it goes. I ask a question. Everyone writes down what they think the answer is. I then reveal it. But the questions aren't true or false. Nor are they Jeopardy like questions that you can learn from textbooks. These questions are all about your intuition. Do you know what intuition is?"

Cameron shrugged his shoulders, embarrassed to admit he didn't know.

"Intuition is from the Latin word 'intuir' which means knowledge from within," she said. "It's not based on rational or analytical thinking."

"Cognitive scientists say it's sometimes derived from associations or strong feelings," said Pluto. "Or in my case, a really good gut instinct about things."

"A super hunch," added Fireball.

"Lucky guesses," said Flipper.

"Here's the thing," she said. "It can't really be learned. You can exercise the mind, tapping its inner power, by intuiting things but it's not always reliable or accurate. Does that make sense?"

Cameron gave another shrug.

"Okay," she said. "Let's do it. Now, if you get one wrong, you drop out. The one with the greatest intuition is the last one to miss a question. Here's the first one."

She held up a poster with two paintings. The one on the left was abstract with angular lines running through different sized circles and the one on the right was a landscape of a French countryside, the nationality given away by a small French flag planted in a field.

"Which painting was done by a man and which by a woman?" she asked.

"Could they both be painted by a man?" asked Flipper.

"Yes. Or vice versa," she said. "Once you've written down your answers, raise your hand." After several minutes, all hands were raised. "Let's go around the table starting with Flipper."

Flipper said "A man painted both."

Fireball said "I have a woman doing both."

Pausing an extra moment to think, Quake said "I have a man doing the abstract and a woman doing the countryside."

Pluto said "I have the opposite. A man doing the countryside and a woman doing the abstract."

"C Sharp," said Viper. "Your turn."

Cameron said "I have the same. A man doing the countryside and a woman doing the abstract."

"And I wrote down the same as Pluto and Cameron," said Viper.

And finally, Brick said. "I have the same as Viper and the others."

Senza hesitated, then pointed to Flipper and Fireball. "You two are out," she said. "The answer is a man painted the countryside and a woman did the abstract."

Flipper growled but held back from flipping off Senza. Finally, someone was off limits.

"Okay," she said. "Another picture. This is a photo taken in Antarctica." The photo showed a sunny piece of snow-laden land with a deep blue ocean and icy blue sky."

"What season of the year was this photo taken?"

They all jotted down their answers.

Surprisingly, they all gave the same answer: "Autumn."

"Very impressive, all of you," she said, glancing at Pluto, C Sharp, Viper and Brick.

"Now, I have a piece of cloth in my right pocket. What color is it?"

Pluto, Viper and Brick all gazed at Senza as though they were trying to read her mind. She glanced back, like the best poker player, expressionless.

"Is black considered a color?" asked Brick.

"Maybe," she said. "Put down your best guess. What you feel is in there."

Cameron wrote down his answer right away, then sat waiting for the others to do the same. She called on him first. He held up his notepad and showed the word "Green."

Pluto and Brick also had green. Viper had purple.

"Viper," said Senza. "You intuited something. Yesterday, I did have a purple cloth in my pocket. But not today." She reached in and tugged out a green handkerchief.

"You guys are good," she said, producing five eggs from a brown paper bag. She lay them on the table, the tan shells touching one another. "How many of these are hard-boiled and how many are not?" she asked.

Pluto and Brick studied the eggs whereas Cameron barely looked at them. The eggs looked remarkably similar in shape, size and color. It would be incredibly difficult to discern one from the other.

"Write down your thoughts," she said. "Don't over-analyze. This is all about intuition. What you feel."

"Brick, you go first this time," she said.

Brick held up his notepad and showed the number 2. "Since these eggs haven't hatched, there's no birthdate to go by and therefore no horoscope. So, this is a pie-in-the sky guess. Two hard-boiled eggs," he said.

Pluto raised his notepad showing "4." To Pluto's annoyance, Cameron held his notepad up also showing "4."

"The moment of truth has arrived," she said. "The answer is 4. Okay, now, these eggs are numbered 1-5, one is closest to me and 5 is furthest. Which egg is the lone uncooked egg?"

Cameron wrote down the number 2 and Pluto wrote down the number 5.

"This is the final test," she said. "Pluto, take the egg that you chose, the number 5 egg, with moderate force, crack it over C Sharp's head."

Pluto did, causing Cameron to wince as the egg was hardboiled and didn't give much. Disappointed, Pluto peeled off bits of the cracked shell, revealing no yellowy yolk just the rubbery white stuff.

"And Cameron, take the egg you chose, number two, and crack it over Pluto's head," she said.

Cameron reached for the egg. Looking uneasy, he reluctantly raised the tan orb and brought it down on Pluto's head. It cracked open, the gooey yellow yolk oozing down Pluto's forehead, sending him into a rage. He gritted his teeth trying to hold back his anger.

The others stared in amazement -- amazed that Pluto had lost and amazed that he had been so humiliated.

Pluto leapt from his chair, taking a napkin to wipe off the yolk. In a huff, he strode toward the mansion.

"Pluto," yelled Senza. "I expect you to be back later today for meditation. He never looked back or acknowledged that he heard her.

"You are awesome," said Viper, admiring Cameron and his low-key attitude.

Cameron didn't enjoy the victory as he felt it put him in a difficult spot for any future relationship with Pluto. Pluto never liked him before and now he had a reason to truly hate him.

Senza whispered to Cameron "I knew you had intuition," she said.

"How?" he asked. "How'd you know?"

Her eyes brightened. "Because I have intuition. Better than anyone here. And my intuition was that you had intuition. A nice trait to have."

"I'm glad we have something in common," he said.

"I watched you and you trusted your inner feelings, the voice in your head, the emotions in your heart. If we did this game again tonight, you'd win again. It was no accident. That I am sure."

"I'd rather have lost than have Pluto hate me," said Cameron.

She shook her head. "Pluto needs to come down to earth," she said. "His ego's been sky high...until now."

"Did you ever feel that this place was like a cult?" he asked her.

She rolled her eyes. "Is that what your intuition says?"

"Well, there are cameras everywhere and something doesn't feel right," he said.

"Give your amygdala a breather," she replied. "It deserves it."

The elderly Asian man emerged and began removing the dishes. He caught Cameron's eye and nodded up at a video camera shaking his head in disapproval.

■■■

"Do you like astrology?" asked Brick, sitting on a beach towel outside the mansion. The sun had recently set and stars emerged, dotting the vast black skyscape.

"Don't get him started," said Viper.

"Jupiter's in my moon which means I have a great sense of humor," Brick said.

"That's funny," said Flipper.

"What sign are you?" Brick asked Cameron.

"Sign?" he asked.

"Yeah, your astrological sign?"

He shrugged his shoulders. It amazed him how loud the crickets were. And the periodic hoot of a night owl made it feel like some kind of creature concert.

"Must we do this now?" said Viper. "Can't you tell him something more useful? Like the sound of toilets flushing is in E flat?!"

"Where did you ever hear that?" asked Brick. "Musicaltoilets.com?"

"It's common knowledge," replied Viper, defensive.

"You ever meditate?" asked Brick, shifting subjects.

Cameron didn't know what he meant.

Brick continued "Are you able to calm your mind?"

Cameron shrugged. "I let my mind wander a lot," he said.

"Do you know what the words 'tabula rasa' mean?"

Cameron did not.

Brick's steady stream of questions amounted to a constant interrogation. Each question made Cameron feel more inadequate as he knew none of the answers.

Brick pointed to the night sky. "Tabula rasa means a blank slate," he said. "When your mind becomes a tabula rasa, it means you clear it of everything else. Like a blackboard upon which you've just erased all the chalk scribblings."

Cameron gazed up, trying to grasp the concept.

"You want a clear mind to meditate effectively," he added. "I like meditation outside at night because there's a tabula rasa right above you and few distractions," said Brick.

Suspicious, Cameron felt this was a disguised form of brainwashing. They wanted to clear his mind so they could load it up with their own propaganda. Take away any individuality and make you part of a big group think.

"This is all cool," said Brick, noticing Cameron's reluctance. "I've been doing it most of my life."

"Where are you from?"

Brick smiled and said "An orphanage in Beijing."

Cameron looked at him, blankly.

"You've never heard of it?" asked Brick. "What about Hong Kong?"

"I've heard of King Kong," said Cameron. "But that's not a place."

"They're both on the other side of the world," he said. "A lot more people than here. I learned to meditate there. Try it. Sit with your legs crossed and your eyes closed."

Cameron obeyed, stifling any breathing so he remained as quiet as possible.

"You're allowed to breath," said Brick. "Breathing's in fact key. Deep breaths through your nose. Exhale slowly through your mouth. Get that heart rate down. Keep your posture even straighter. That's it. If you begin meditation with a swirl of emotions and thoughts in your head, you should put those aside. Try transferring negative feelings into positive ones. A mantra can help. It's a unique phrase you repeat over and over again to distract you from your many thoughts and feelings. I can't tell you my mantra but it's a series of meaningless words that harmlessly occupy my mind. I don't want to throw too much more at you but another thing I do is visualization.

Visualize either a pure white light or invisible sound waves. How do you visualize the invisible; the same way you visualize the wind. Can you try this?"

Cameron's suspicions subsided, listening to Brick's calm and soothing voice. He breathed in deeply, holding his breath then releasing, and repeating this over and over. He felt a stillness, a calm, a serenity as his focus went inward, envisioning a pure white light. His mind drifted as he felt transported into nothingness, all his thoughts suspended. He lost track of time as a certain tranquility set in that was only disturbed by a voice calling him.

"C Sharp. C Sharp. C Sharp," said a soft voice. Not quite used to his nickname, Cameron took a moment for it to register.

"Where am I?" he asked.

"Outside," said Brick. "You did great, man."

Cameron appeared utterly confused.

"You got into heavy meditation," said Brick, checking his watch. "For 90 minutes. Usually beginners complain about it being boring but you dove in like you've done it your entire life."

"I've had a lot of alone time," he said.

"Let me check your pulse," he said, seizing Cameron's wrist while looking at the second hand on his watch. "Wow, that's sick. You got your heart rate down to 36 beats a minute. I've never seen anyone below 46. 36 fewer and you'd be technically dead. 36 is a really good number. I'm impressed. Your level of concentration is stunning."

Flipper, Viper, Fireball and Quake all arrived, holding beach towels. Senza came shortly thereafter, prodding Pluto who reluctantly came.

"I brought you a towel," she said.

"Don't need it," he replied, preferring to sit on the cool grass.

On cue, they sat on their towels, legs crisscrossed in the lotus position, and proceeded to meditate. Cameron tried as well but this time he couldn't concentrate. All of them there was a big distraction. Instead, he wondered who all these kids were and how they came to be here. Unable to meditate, he sat with his eyes closed.

When they were finished, Senza reached into a sack and handed everyone a flashlight.

"Around the rim...twice," she said, everyone nodded knowingly. "And no shortcuts."

Around the rim meant running around the perimeter of the property, about two miles. The property was encircled by a rather menacing looking ten-foot tall wrought iron fence that discouraged any potential trespassers. About three feet from the fence was a dirt path, downtrodden from people running on it over a period of time. This path clearly had a lot of runners. Pluto took off first, taking the lead as he often liked to do, while the others followed behind at different rates.

"And no skateboarding, Viper!" shouted Senza, causing Viper to turn around and deposit her tiger-striped skateboard on her towel. She soon caught up to Cameron at the back of the pack. Not very athletic, Cameron struggled along, trying not to fall too far behind. Viper slowed her gait to run side by side with him. She did so for a while but with her patience thinning, she started to run faster, leaving him behind, the human caboose.

A deep pain seized Cameron's lungs, followed by a shortness of breath. An asthma attack was looming. He started to panic, mildly at first, worrying about his shortness of breath and whether or not he should stop running. Approaching the front gate of the property, he saw a figure on the other side of the wrought-iron fence. It was a man, his face initially hidden in the shadows. The man gripped the iron bars, pressing his face against them so he could peer through like a desperate prisoner.

As Cameron grew closer, he could see that the man had dark black scraggly hair, a black mustache and unshaven stubble. The skin on his face was acne-scarred. Across his left side from between his eyebrows to down his nose and along his cheek was a four inch scar, possibly the result of a knife fight. His face, tired and drawn, carried a permanent unfriendly scowl. Only his eyes, two dark orbs with a soft gaze, showed any compassion.

"Scuse me," he said with a strong Hispanic accent, his eyes darting about frantically. "Important I talk to owner of house. Very important. Can you help?"

Cameron stopped, bent over, quite winded, his hands pressed against his knees. He felt light-headed. Panting profusely, his throat tightened. Cameron wasn't able to help this man or anyone else for that matter as he could barely help himself.

"Please, I beg you," the man said, reaching into his jacket pocket. "I no trouble. I have information, important, before is too late."

Cameron gazed at the man's face which went in and out of focus. He saw his mouth mumbling words but they were totally silent to his ears. Cameron staggered around, then clutched his chest, collapsing to the ground. Seeing him fall and wanting no trouble, the Hispanic man panicked and disappeared into the darkness.

When you're asleep or in a daze, time passed quickly. As Cameron's eyes fluttered open, he was unaware how long he had been unconscious. He lay in bed, an oxygen mask strapped to his face, breathing in a steady stream of pure oxygen. Sitting on a chair in the far corner of the room was a nurse dressed in white including her sneaker-like footwear.

"Remain calm," she said, her voice gentle. She stood and removed the mask from his face. "You had everyone scared last night."

Cameron looked bewildered, trying to remember how he got here.

"Do you recall what happened to you?" asked the nurse, chewing on the eraser of her pencil.

He nervously scratched his head. "I remember gasping for air," he said. "Probably my asthma."

"It happened while you were running around the property," she replied.

Cameron sat up in bed, dry-mouthed, and reached for a glass of water on his bedside table. He gulped it all down.

"You're quite dehydrated," she said. "But your pulse and blood pressure are all normal now."

There was a knock on the door and Senza stepped in. "You appear to be alive," she said.

Cameron forced a weak smile.

Turning to the nurse, Senza asked "How long until he can function normally?"

The nurse replied "All his vital signs have improved and are in the normal range. He needs to carry an inhaler and I wouldn't recommend any long jogs. But other than that, I think he's going to be fine."

"Any other restrictions?" she asked, looking him over.

"No. Just plenty of rest," said the nurse.

Cameron felt pleased that Senza showed concern. He jokingly wanted to say "Thanks, Mom" but realized that might not be received well. He couldn't actually envision her as anyone's mom dressed the way she was in all leather.

Senza patted Cameron on the leg and left the room.

The nurse said "It could have been a lot worse if you weren't found right away. If you need anything, just push that button next to your bed and someone will come."

She left the room.

Cameron stared at the walls, his eyes spotting the hidden cameras. He started feeling hungry and reached for the button. He raised his finger, ready to push it but didn't want to inconvenience anyone. His stomach grumbled. He stood up gradually and paced around the room. He glanced at the clock, realizing that he wouldn't be eating anytime soon. He took a deep sigh then went back and pushed the button. In a few minutes someone knocked on the door.

"Come in," he said.

The door opened, revealing the old Asian man. Wearing a red robe with Japanese symbols on it, he bowed at the sight of Cameron.

"Sorry to trouble you," said Cameron. "I'm hungry."

The Asian man smiled, curled his finger and signaled for Cameron to follow him. They headed downstairs, the mansion feeling uncomfortably quiet with no one around. He led Cameron into the kitchen where he found a banana and a box of crackers to satiate his appetite.

Cameron sat at a counter, ravenous, savoring every bite while the Asian man looked on approvingly. When Cameron finished, the Asian man said "Psssst. Follow me." He then led Cameron to a door to the side of the massive kitchen.

He pulled out a key that hung around his neck on a silver chain. He unlocked three locks on the door, then quietly opened it, shushing Cameron so he'd know to be quiet. The two descended the stairs, each step creaking. The stairs wound down almost two stories worth before another door faced them. The Asian man once again removed his key and opened the door.

Down a partial hallway, they came upon a large room resembling a TV studio. A huge pane of glass, the size of a garage door, stood between them and the studio. Inside, there were five seats at a control panel facing a wall of TV monitors, probably 30 altogether. Each monitor focused on a different room in the house as well as the premises outside. On one monitor, Cameron could see his room, bed unmade and schoolbooks piled on his desk. Two men, their backs towards Cameron, sat closely watching the monitors, unaware of his presence.

"I want you to hide behind this glass," said the Asian man. "I will get their attention and ask them to put something on the monitors you might be interested in."

"Are we supposed to be down here?" Cameron asked nervously. "It doesn't seem like we are."

"I bring them food," he said. "Let me see if they want anything."

Cameron obediently crouched beneath the pane while the Asian man entered the studio, greeting the men. They turned the monitors on one site.

The Asian man signaled for Cameron to look at the monitors. He did as he was told. There, captured in a freeze frame, was a familiar-looking face. Though slightly shadowed, the familiar face became apparent when Cameron noticed it staring from behind a wrought iron fence. This was the man he'd encountered the other night when he collapsed.

The Asian man left the room with Cameron following closely behind as they went back upstairs.

"Thanks for taking me down there," said Cameron. "I don't want you to get in trouble."

"I'm trying to find answers just like you are," said the Asian man.

"They have cameras everywhere," said Cameron. "Inside and outside."

"Did the face you saw mean anything to you?" the Asian man asked.

Cameron gave a strong nod. "That man was there the night I collapsed," said Cameron. "He was trying to get my attention through the bars. Said he had something important to tell."

"I wonder if he might have sprayed you with something to make you collapse."

Cameron scratched his head, giving it a second thought. "I don't think so."

"I heard people wondering who that man was and what he wanted," said the Asian man. "He had appeared once before, maybe a month earlier, but ran off. They captured an image of him then. I just hope he doesn't intend to harm anyone."

"Can't they enhance his image and find out who he is?" asked Cameron.

"Apparently, they did. I overheard someone saying he wasn't a citizen so there are very few records to confirm his identity."

"Not a citizen?"

"Appears to be an illegal immigrant. And you seem to be the only one who saw him," said the Asian man.

When Cameron returned to his room, he felt something wasn't right. Maybe this was a cult and that man outside the property wanted to warn him about it. Or maybe he wanted to kill the owner of this mansion. What kind of home requires extensive surveillance like this? If it were all totally legal, they wouldn't need all these cameras. Cameron's mind played that evening over and over, trying to piece it together. He couldn't get that man's face out of his head. It kept appearing, looking sad and desperate, just the way he felt right now.

He kicked off his shoes, plopped on his bed, waved at one of the cameras and fell asleep.

CHAPTER 9 AUSSIE LUNCH

Cameron slept for a full day.

When he awoke, he felt much improved, enough to participate fully in his school lessons with Ms. Pennebaker.

At lunch, everyone greeted him with kindness, all except Pluto, who maintained his distain, not going near him nor offering a single word of encouragement. Even Flipper refrained from flipping him off, at least at this meal.

"You don't look so bad," said Flipper.

"I feel fine," Cameron replied.

Viper had a small steel ratchet that she used to tighten the wheels on her beloved skateboard. She finished her task, then parked the skateboard under the table near her seat. Looking at Senza, she said "Don't you think C Sharp should do an Australian lunch today?"

Senza looked him over. "Seems good."

"I'm not Australian," Cameron said.

There was a mix of laughter.

"It's just the name of the game," said Viper. "No one here is Australian that I know of."

"The game is quite simple," said Brick. "You go under the table with one other person and have a meal together there. And you have to keep up a dialogue the whole time. And the people sitting at the table can't talk but have to tune you out. If they for any reason listen to what you're saying and either react verbally or physically, they are counted out."

Cameron nodded his understanding. "But why Australian?"

"It's merely called Australian because you're Down Under....the table," said Fireball, her hair dyed a deeper purple today. "But you're not gonna burn up down there."

Cameron saw little purpose to the game. It seemed like something a cult might do. Clearly, the others had already played this game before which meant the pressure was on him to play it. Was this game a mandate from Z3? Cameron had never even seen a photo of that elusive and mysterious man. Maybe he didn't even exist but was a fabrication of this cult?

"So, who is going to go Australian with C Sharp?" asked Senza, staring directly at an uncomfortable Pluto who vigorously shook his head.

"It's a good bonding experience," said Senza.

"N period O period," said Pluto bluntly.

"Quake?" she asked. "You game?"

Quake agreed, stooping down and shuffling his rear end under the table. Cameron followed his lead and sat cross-legged, facing him.

Quake rapped "I got my man Sharp as my partner in crime, We're out to beat your asses with our wits and some rhyme, And when we're victorious it will all be sublime."

The Asian man entered the room and slid a few bowls of food under the table as though feeding some dogs. He also gently pushed some clean empty plates but no utensils. This was a hands-only meal.

The others sat eating at the table in silence, acting oblivious to what was happening below.

Quake kicked off the conversation. "You play bass, man?"

Cameron nodded.

"Look at the thumb and fingers on my right hand," said Quake. "And compare them with my left hand. Pretty awesome, eh? Plucking them fat strings all the time has given my fingers a workout. Made them bulk up with callouses."

"I toughen my fingers by tapping," said Cameron. "For warm-up I do Eruption by Van Halen."

"You know who Flea is?" Quake asked. "With the Red Hot Chili Peppers. He uses Super Glue on his fingers. It forms a callous. These two fingers of mine are stuck together from Super Glue."

Cameron examined Quake's fingers. They looked fine. Quake signaled to him to be quiet. He was merely saying that to get attention from above.

"If I try to separate them, the skin pulls off," said Quake. "Ahhhhh."

At that moment, Flipper glanced under the table, unable to resist his curiosity.

"You're out," smiled Quake, prompting Flipper to flip him off.

"How do you remove Super Glue?" asked C Sharp.

Quake smiled. "Search through your rock n roll arsenal and take out the nail polish remover. Your fingers are pretty sore after that. So, what someone once told me to do was to soak them in pickle juice. It builds callouses. All that vinegar is palliative. Good word there. Palliative."

Flipper remarked "I suck at this game."

"I got one for you," said Quake. "I read somewhere that a hippo, a pigeon and a salmon all have something in common. Do you know what it is?"

Cameron shook his head.

"This is the kind of thing a bass player would know," said Quake. "Infrasonically is how they communicate, producing and hearing noises lower than low, for goodness sake. A frequency that humans can't hear or make, causes these animals' ears to ache keeping them awake without a break until they jump in a lake."

Cameron reached out and rolled over Viper's skateboard, setting it between Quake and himself. Taking his plate, now topped with food, he placed it on the skateboard so it served as a mini table.

"Ingenious," said Quake. "Who would have thought of having our own table under the table."

"This skateboard is the perfect size," said Cameron.

He expected Viper, who was always over-protective of her skateboards, to gaze down but she maintained her focus and ignored him.

"Oops," said Quake. "My bad. Got a bunch of food on it."

Annoyed, Viper leaned down and said "That's my property."

The skateboard was perfectly clean. It was all a bluff but a successful one.

"And she's out," said Quake.

In a huff, Viper scooped up her skateboard and cradled it on her lap, dusting it off with her napkin even though it looked clean.

Quake had eaten a banana and left the peel on his plate. He reached in his pants pocket and pulled out a pack of matches. He twisted off a match and scraped it against the pack until a small flame burst to life. He held it under the banana peel producing a noxious smell. As the match burnt out, he lit another, doing the same thing.

Obsessed with anything related to fire, Fireball fidgeted in her seat. "What in the name of God is that burning smell?" she asked aloud. "Jeez."

"Oh my!" exclaimed Quake, inciting Fireball's curiosity. Fireball crouched down and saw the burnt banana.

"And you're...."began Quake.

"Out," finished Cameron.

Only three remained in the game – Senza, Brick and Pluto. They were traditionally the best players.

Cameron and Quake went into an endless banter, discussing inane subjects from why a pair of socks can fit a lot of different foot sizes while a pair of gloves only fits one hand size to the disappointing news that Pluto is not a planet to guitar talk.

"Did you know about the guy who invited the Fender guitar?" asked Quake.

Cameron recalled reading it in a magazine. "Leo Fender," he replied. "He was a saxophonist."

"Weird, right?" said Quake.

Cameron sensed that these remaining three were going to be tough. In his head, he heard the voice of Sgt Manning urging him on: Don't be shy. Get noticed. Take chances. All his life, he'd tried to blend in. He needed to break that trend. A wild thought occurred. Completely out of character, Cameron removed his sneakers and then slid off his pants. Quake burst out laughing.

"Oh my God!" he said. "I can't believe what I'm seeing!"

Cameron's smile had a mischievous curl.

"I've never seen anyone remove their pants in this game," Quake said. "Wowser."

Brick leaned back in his chair, trying to catch a glimpse of the action under the table. Unable to see much, he bent down to look under. "You're out," said Quake.

"I just had to see for myself," he said, holding up a pair of pants then flipping them back under the table.

With Sgt Manning's voice in his head spurring him on, Cameron pushed the envelope further, this time removing his white jockey shorts.

"Holy cow!" bellowed Quake. "I've got to hold these up for all to see." Clenched in his fist, he lifted the underwear above the table.

"Naked as a jay bird," he replied. "That's all I can say."

Pluto usually displayed the greatest discipline, rarely if ever losing at Australian lunch. But even he couldn't hold back from seeing how far Cameron had actually gone. He peered under the table and his eyes widened at the sight of a naked boy curled in the fetal position. Annoyed he lost, Pluto abruptly left the room but returned for one final word.

"You know," said Pluto. "It's very hard to respect someone who will do anything to win. I would no sooner humiliate myself by removing my clothes than I would jump off a bridge. And I don't even think that was playing by the rules."

He threw up his hands and muttering to himself walked away.

When he was out of earshot, Viper said. "A nice show of poor sportsmanship there. So now we know what Pluto likes to look at. Naked people. How embarrassing is that. In fact, that's more embarrassing than taking off your pants."

Cameron slid into his underwear and then struggled to get his pants back on one leg at a time. He was disappointed at Pluto's reaction, hoping he would have appreciated his creativity.

Viper turned to Senza and said "You win, girl. But you missed one helluva show down there. C Sharp was, well, sharp, really on his game. He seems so unassuming but he somehow has what it takes."

Senza pushed her chair back, stood up and said "We'll see everyone in the field in an hour. The new guitars will be handed out then."

Viper sailed out of the room on her skateboard. The remaining kids all high-fived Cameron for his victory. Cameron felt good for once although he still didn't know what compelled him to remove his pants. Somehow, his competitive spirit rose up and took over. And he was kind of glad it did.

Quake put a coda on the whole activity with a final rap. "My man never once came unglued, Even when he had to get totally nude, He showed he was far from a prude, Just a dude, slightly lewd, in the mood for some victory food. And I'm damn proud he's living in my longitude."

■■

Viper escorted Cameron to the back of the massive mansion.

Senza had laid out a row of guitars in a multitude of colors: lime green, purple, red, yellow, orange, cornflower blue, leopard spotted and silver.

"Take your pick," said Senza. "Except the silver bass player. That's for Quake. And it's a lefty."

Viper migrated right to the red guitar and slung it comfortably around her shoulder. She then grabbed one of the wireless headsets from a large basketful of them.

"Go on C, take your pick before the others get here," Viper encouraged.

Eyeing them all, Cameron was particularly drawn to the leopard spotted one but felt he didn't have the right to take a guitar ahead of the others. "Well, maybe I should wait," he said softly.

"That's the dumbest thing I've ever heard," said Viper. "I can tell you right now who is going to pick which guitar with the exception of Senza. Tell me which guitar you want."

"They're all nice," he said, waffling.

Quake arrived, spotted the silver bass and swooped it up along with headphones. He went into a rap. "We all are running in a steeplechase, representing that club called the human race, on a dot of a planet in outer space. But all I care about is getting my bass, So I can happily play til I'm in my resting place."

Cameron loved to hear Quake's spontaneous raps even though he didn't know what he was talking about.

Flipper came next, instinctively flipping off Cameron.

"What was that for?" asked Cameron, perplexed.

"My health," said Flipper.

"Flipper will take the cornflower blue, Brick will take the lime green and Fireball will grab the purple," Viper quietly predicted and sure enough she was right.

The remaining guitars – yellow, orange and leopard – were for Senza, Pluto and C Sharp.

"Quick, pick before Pluto gets here," pleaded Viper. "He has his sights on the yellow guitar."

Viper was unaware that Pluto had walked over just as she was speaking and went right for the yellow guitar. With two guitars left, Cameron knew he had a fifty-fifty chance of getting the one he wanted. Senza looked at him and said, "Take one."

"No, you can go first," he demurred.

A wind picked up as some dark storm clouds formed overhead.

Looking up, Pluto said ""This is a slow tracking storm. We're okay for at least an hour."

Senza eyed the remaining two guitars, hesitated momentarily before stepping over and taking the leopard-spotted guitar. Cameron masked his disappointment, settling for the orange one. He looked it over, searching for the brand name – Gibson, Epiphone, Fender, Ibanez – but saw none, meaning it was probably custom-made.

"Don't forget your special headset," she reminded him. He grabbed one and put it on, watching how the others placed the suction cups against their foreheads.

The octet marched out to the field by the lake. Cameron remembered his first time there with Senza and Pluto. The guitar he'd previously used had been amazing but the new one promised to be even better. They formed a line, spaced six feet apart, armed with their guitars and wearing the special headset setups.

"These new guitars can harness energy even greater than the previous ones," Senza said. "The power of sound can be as strong as the power of light. What is the most powerful form of concentrated light?"

Pluto quickly said "The laser."

"Exactly," she said. "What Z3 has produced for you is basically the laser of sound. He has found a way to harness sound into such an intense amount of energy that it can topple walls and knock holes through almost anything. The headphones still work as they did before. They send electrical impulses from your mind to your guitar. Each of you is here because you possess the combination of strong brainwaves and special guitar skills. An average person would not be able to use these guitars. They would not be able to generate the power needed to run them. Interestingly, each of you has managed to perfect different skills with your guitar. Those same skills apply with the new guitars, too. In fact, you'll find it easier to use. I'd like to do this one at a time, leaving C Sharp until the end. I want him to see the full demonstration. Who wants to go first?"

Quake raised his hand. "As the resident bass player, I'd like to take center stage for that rare moment."

"Turn towards the lake," instructed Senza.

Turning on his wireless guitar, Quake faced the lake. His face grimaced as he began concentrating. He angled the neck of his bass guitar slightly higher then started plucking at the thick strings.

An invisible force emanated from the guitar, causing ripples across the lake that soon turned to small waves. Quake inhaled deeply then exhaled, trying to relax his mind. From the center of the lake, a deep pocket developed as a wave formed and started moving towards the other side, soon sweeping a large amount of water onto the land. Senza tapped Quake on the shoulder, signaling for him to stop. As soon as he did, the energy that had been forming in the lake ceased as well.

"Everyone needs a bass player like that," said Flipper. "That was stupid good."

"Flipper, you want to go next?" said Senza.

"Yeah. But hard to top that" he said.

Flipper readied his blue guitar. "Everyone should stand behind me," he said. "And if you have ear plugs, I'd recommend them."

"As long as we're behind you, we'll be okay," said Senza.

Flipper's guitar faced away from the lake and towards a huge forest of towering trees quite a distance away. He took a few quick breaths, almost panting, before concentrating. He started playing his guitar, fingers nimbly strumming. It produced a loud noise, with an other-worldly screech. Anyone facing it would have had their eardrums severely taxed. The noise quickly reached the trees. Birds perched on branches streamed out of the forest, flying straight up or away from the noise. Senza tapped his shoulder and he stopped playing. He saw the sky peppered with birds and sported a healthy smile of accomplishment. Then, one lone bird emerged from the forest, having withstood the aural assault. Flipper thought about flipping it off but didn't. Instead, he laughed.

"So, we've now heard and seen the power of sound," said Senza. "Pretty awesome. Now, Fireball, I'd like you to give a demo. Do it with the shrubs by the lake. Immediately following you, I want Brick to do his thing, okay?"

Brick and Fireball nodded and paired up, facing the lake.

"Did anyone know that Buddha was a Taurus?" asked Brick.

"What's that have to do with anything?" said Fireball.

"I don't know. Just thought I'd toss it out for thought," said Brick.

Fireball took her purple guitar, flicked it on and started plucking the same string over and over again. She went faster and faster until a spark appeared 100 yards away and a burst of fire emanated from it, totally destroying a bush. She did the same thing to two other bushes nearby, causing a mini wall of fire. Satisfied, Senza tapped her shoulder, signaling she could stop. Then, Brick took over. He swept his guitar back and forth while playing, moving it around an invisible box. From a distance, you could see that the bird could not advance. It was as though it had run into an invisible shield or wall. Brick had, in effect, produced a force field and a quite effective one at that.

"Push the fire back," ordered Senza. Brick moved his guitar, rocking it back and forth until the burning bushes were all pushed into the lake and extinguished.

Cameron was visibly impressed by all he had seen.

"Who's left?" asked Senza. "Viper, Pluto, C Sharp. Viper, why don't you go next?"

"With pleasure," she said.

Viper pointed to the dummies that stood between them and the forest. "For the newly initiated," she said, referring to Cameron. "I am going to send and bend a note around the dummy in the blue outfit and hit the dummy 20 yards behind it in the red outfit. You may want to step to the side so you can get a good view of this. I'm only doing it once no matter how many encores you ask for."

She waited while the group moved over so both dummies were visible.

Taking her red guitar, Viper blew on the neck like it was a smoking rifle and started to strum, efficiently and effectively. Although the notes she sent were barely audible, the sound waves were visible. They shot through the air, causing a blurry ripple much like a mirage on a hot summer day only this was a very narrow and focused ray. The notes swerved around the blue dummy then swerved back and nailed the red one, knocking it to the ground.

Flipper applauded causing Viper to smile. "Cool girl," he said.

"Pluto? You ready?"

Armed with his yellow guitar, Pluto stood tall and surveyed the property. There was a towering pine tree a half mile away.

"I have no intention of harming the tree but I'm going to try to prune the top of it," he said.

"That looks too far away," said Senza.

Pluto first aimed his guitar skyward and began plucking notes and chords. Comfortable with how it felt, he aimed his guitar towards the tree and started plucking at the highest note he could. He played frantically but the sound didn't reach it. Frustrated, he shook the guitar as though it was to blame.

"Try something closer," said Senza.

Annoyed, Pluto tried the tall pine once more. But again, he failed to reach it. He turned and aimed towards the nearby forest of trees, connecting with the top of one and sending a heavy branch tumbling down.

"Good!" said Senza.

"Oh, come on, it sucked," said Pluto. "I'm disappointed. I really am."

"No one can go farther than you," said Viper.

Pluto shook his head in disgust. No words could soothe him. Everyone else had performed well except for him.

When it came to Cameron's turn, he aimed his guitar at the forest and strummed slowly. Nothing happened. He tried some more, a bit faster, but he couldn't produce an invisible force wave. And that was deliberate on his part. He had no desire to show up Pluto who already disliked him. As tempting as it was to experiment with the guitar, he refrained.

"I have a bit of a headache today," he said, providing an excuse.

"Senza, you going to do it?" asked Fireball as some raindrops started to fall. "Celestial spit. How annoying."

As the storm clouds clustered overhead, a loud rumble of thunder emanated from the distance. Flashes of lightning appeared closer and closer. The air had that static feeling, one often experienced during thunderstorms.

Brick lifted his guitar, moving it back and forth and producing an invisible umbrella, the raindrops falling off the sides, not touching any of the others. Fireball stepped outside the invisible shield and tried sending a fireball of energy towards the clouds above. The

fireball rose 100 yards before tumbling down a few feet away.
Fireball grimaced, saying "Whoops. Close call there."

Pluto and Senza aimed their guitars at the storm cloud above,
seeming to jostle it. Finally, Quake and Flipper emerged together.
Quake got his bass rumbling like thunder while Flipper's guitar
produced a strong sound that shot up towards the heavens. The cloud
above seemed to dissipate, the vapors swirling away into
nothingness.

They waited out the rest of the storm, staying dry beneath Brick's
force field.

"How long a charge do these guitars have?" asked Brick.

Senza responded "They can go 2-3 days continuously. It's all due to
the crystal inside."

Brick lowered his guitar and stopped playing. He reached out his
hand, feeling the last few drops of rain. The storm had passed.

"Let's head back to the main house," said Senza, leading the way
back. Cameron trailed, last in line.

Viper saw him and asked if he was okay.

"I just need to tie my shoe," he said. "You can go ahead."

"Don't be disappointed. You'll get the hang of it."

She caught up with the others, leaving Cameron behind.

With everyone heading to the mansion and backs turned, Cameron
flicked on his orange guitar and aimed it at the far tree, the one that
Pluto couldn't reach. He closed his eyes partway and concentrated
fiercely, focusing on the top of it, strumming frantically, his fingers
moving across all the strings and frets. Within a split second, the top
three feet of the tree got sliced in half and tumbled to the ground.
Viper heard the noise, turning just in time to see the top of the tree
fall.

Cameron felt a great sense of accomplishment. He quickly lowered his guitar, turned it off and hurried to join the others. When he caught up to Viper, she said, "I saw what you did."

Cameron feigned confusion.

"You just reached the top of that darn tree, the same one Pluto couldn't reach," she said.

"I think it got severed from the storm," said Cameron.

Viper stared at him, not finding him at all credible.

"You're good," she said. "Really good...at guitar. But you're crap ass at lying. Listen, I'm not going to betray you. Pluto never needs to know. Just don't annoy me."

She walked away and Cameron dutifully followed. He paused to take one last look at the tree and a smile crossed his face.

■■

The next day, after morning classes, Cameron wandered into the hallway and overheard Senza and Pluto talking.

"You made him out to be the Seventh Coming," said Pluto.

"I merely said he's only 10 and amazing for his age," replied Senza. "I didn't say he was better than everyone else."

"You implied it," said Pluto, relentless.

Senza let out a sigh of exasperation. "What does it matter?!"

"He wasn't very good yesterday," said Pluto.

"He's still new," said Senza. "And these guitars are new, too. They take time to master. Let's not forget how well he did with the old guitar when he first visited. In fact, you gave him the nickname of C Sharp then."

"Beginner's luck," said Pluto.

"You and I know that using these guitars is nothing but skill."

Pluto smirked. "I think you recruited the wrong person."

Leaning on the railing, Senza replied "Well, we'll see, won't we?"

Cameron heard the whole conversation. He quietly raced upstairs, not wanting to be caught eavesdropping. There, he waited several minutes until he heard them approaching. Nonchalantly, he headed downstairs just as they were headed up.

"Hi C," said Senza. "Did you hear what we're doing today?"

He was unaware of anything planned for the day.

"You all have a mini mission this afternoon. Z3 wants to have you visit a school nearby right after lunch."

He nodded and descended the stairs, encountering Flipper.

"What's up?" Flipper asked.

Cameron didn't respond.

"I'm not going to bite you," he said

There was a slight echo given off by the marble floor.

"You get easily upset," said Cameron.

Flipper laughed. "I ought to flip you off for that remark. But I won't."

"You're the closest in age to me," said Cameron.

"I'm 14," Flipper replied. "How old are you? Six and a half? Seven?"

"Ten."

"I'm glad not to be the youngest anymore," said Flipper.

"I don't see the purpose of having us all here together except that we have guitar-playing in common," said Cameron.

"Things are going to be made clear soon," said Flipper. "At least that's my understanding."

Cameron whispered "Is this is a cult?"

"If it is, it's not so bad. Good food. No real school, just tutoring. A lot of guitar. I'd take it."

Cameron glanced up at the huge crystal chandelier overhead, figuring it was probably recording their whole conversation. He needed to be more careful about discussing his "cult" theory.

"Where are you from?" Cameron asked.

"The desert."

"Arabia?"

"Arabia?! Do I look like an Arab to you? No. I grew up in a different desert. Nevada. Las Vegas to be precise. You ever heard of it?"

Cameron nodded.

"Did you have a good life there?" he asked.

"My father was a professional poker player," he said. "We once lived in a mansion or at least it felt like one."

"You left that mansion to come here?"

"Well, my dad had these people who were after him down at Glitter Gulch. So, he got rid of the mansion. He said we needed to live quietly. He found a trailer park on the way to Red Rock Canyon that we lived in."

"And they discovered you there?"

"By 'they,' I assume you mean Z3 and Senza," said Flipper.

Cameron nodded.

"Yes."

"And your father was okay with them taking you away?"

"Not sure. One day, I came home from school and he was gone."

"Gone? No note or anything."

"Nothing. I think he had to go into hiding," said Flipper. "At least he left the guitar behind."

"Did Z3 find you and the others at School of Rock?" asked Cameron.

Flipped smiled. "The only one of us who did School of Rock was Fireball," he replied. "I never set foot in the one in Vegas. But yeah, a logical place to find great young guitarists is in their All Stars band. The thing is, School of Rock has programs all over the damn world. You know, Australia, South Africa, South America. On and on. Did they check out every one of those places? Damn if I know. But he did find some of us in other countries."

"So how then did Z3 find you? And the others?" Cameron persisted.

"I have no idea. Nada. It's not enough that you play the guitar well. Plenty kids do. There's this phenomenal girl in LA. Like phenomenal. She's 17 or so. Called Jasmine Star. She can shred as well as anyone. You can check out her videos on YouTube. But somehow, she wasn't chosen."

"What's with that?"

Flipper shrugged and said "I read she envisions the music in her head and can play it effortlessly. While that's something most of us can do, she also reads music. And if that weren't enough, she plays drums and a mean keyboard and on top of all that, she has a great voice. And she's sexy cute. But she wasn't picked by Z3?"

"Why?"

"They're looking for people whose brainwaves can be in sync with an electric guitar. How they find people like that I don't know. Maybe there's some brainwaves radar detection kit."

"Maybe Z3 didn't know about her".

"No, he did. We showed him some videos of Jasmine and he felt she was incredibly talented. But not what he was looking for. Beats me. I would have chosen her."

"I can't wait to check out her videos," said Cameron.

Flipper reached into his back pocket and took out a folded up photo made from a copier. It showed the image of a pretty long-haired brunette teenager holding an electric guitar. It was of Jasmine Star. He held it up to show Cameron but wouldn't let him touch it.

"But don't think she'd be interested in you," said Flipper.

"What do you mean?"

"If she's dating anyone, it's me not you," said Flipper.

Confused, Cameron replied "I'm only 10, you know. She'd be super old for someone like me."

"Lunch!" yelled Senza from another room.

Flipper looked at Cameron and said "Don't take things personally, okay? But I have a reputation to uphold." With that, Flipper raised his fist, peeling back one finger and giving him the bird. Cameron tried not to take it personally but being flipped off was bothersome.

Lunch today went in a normal manner, everyone staying above the table.

Afterward, they congregated by the front of the mansion where a rack of eight black Fender guitars awaited them. They each took a guitar.

"These have no special powers," said Senza. "What they do have is a built-in amp so you can play loud without plugging into anything."

They boarded a shuttle bus that could seat a dozen people. Senza drove them out through the gate and along some back roads. After a 15-minute drive, they arrived at their destination – a red brick high school called Eli Whitney High. In front of the school stood a statue of a man dressed in Revolutionary War attire. Flying above him on a towering pole was the American flag, flapping limply in an anemic breeze.

"Today is a lesson in effective protection through disciplined restraint," said Senza. "We have learned of a ninth grader who has been relentlessly picked on by upper classmen, i.e. football players. What we want to do is boost his self-confidence and let him achieve respect. Now, you have your guitars but not the ones with the special power as that could be too dangerous."

"How do we know if this kid is going to be bullied today?" asked Viper.

"Because this has been a daily thing, so I'm told," said Senza, holding up a photo. "This is who we want to help. His name is Leonard Scoggins. He's a music student here. His music teacher informs us that he's a good pianist and also plays some guitar. He's not as good as any of you by a long stretch. But then again, this isn't a mission of recruitment."

The photo showed a boy with brown hair, his bangs touching the rim of his thick lensed eyeglasses.

"Now, that looks like a perfect victim," observed Flipper.

"So, how do we do this?" asked Brick.

"You need to huddle amongst yourselves and figure out the best way," said Senza.

"I'd like to take this over," said Pluto, leading the others behind the shuttle bus and away from Senza. He shut his eyes and went into a state of deep thought.

Opening his eyes, he exclaimed "Okay! One of us will meet Leonard as he comes out of school. They will befriend him then tag along until he encounters the jocks. The rest of us will join in. As for the guitars, well, we'll let them speak for themselves. We'll play the rest by ear."

"How do you know when he'll be coming out?" asked Quake, sporting the lone bass guitar.

"Senza got some reports from a music teacher at the school," said Pluto. "Who will meet this kid?"

No one immediately volunteered so Cameron raised his hand. "C Sharp? You're going to do it? A ten-year-old protector. That's amusing," said Pluto. "But so be it. When he comes out, introduce yourself briefly and say a few words of support. Then stay by his side."

Cameron took one more glimpse of the photo as did the others.

Cameron walked over to the main entrance to the school, a black electric guitar slung over his shoulder. He looked particularly puny as the high school students emerged in clusters through the main entrance, each sporting overstuffed backpacks and eager to leave the school. Cameron tried scanning faces as they passed, hoping to recognize Leonard. He only focused on boys with glasses of which there weren't a lot. Students continued to stream from the building and as those exited thinned out, Cameron wondered if he had missed him. But if he had, one of the others would have spotted him.

Moving slowly, a bespectacled boy appeared, his eyes aimed shyly down at the ground. His posture was sloped no thanks to his heavy backpack. This was clearly Leonard.

"Excuse me," said Cameron, trying to get his attention. Leonard kept walking, pretending not to hear him.

"Excuse me, Leonard," said Cameron, finally getting his attention.

How did this young boy know his name, Leonard wondered?

"I'm a musician," said Cameron. "And me and some friends are here to accompany you."

"Accompany me? To where?" Leonard asked.

Uncertain how to answer, Cameron said "Accompany you to...a better life."

Leonard was completely perplexed. He swept back his bangs and got a closer look at Cameron. "How old are you?" he asked.

"Ten."

"And you're going to help me? I don't think so."

"I'm not alone."

"And what does that mean?"

"There are others who will be joining us. Our combined age is like 200."

Leonard stutter-stopped, his eyes locked in on two rather stocky jocks in white and blue patent leather letterman jackets. "Hey Lenny," said one of them named Paul. "You're late. And who's this with you? Your date?"

Leonard didn't know how to respond as he had no idea who Cameron was.

"We're going to ask you again, politely, to do our math homework for us," said Paul.

Fireball and Viper ambled over while Viper soon followed on her skateboard, circling around them twice before coming to a stop.

"And who do we have here? The Jackson Five?" said Paul in a voice laced with sarcasm. It was reminiscent of the bullying Cameron had endured with Scott and his friends.

"Nice counting. There's only four of us," snapped Viper.

"Okay, the Bangles, then," said Paul. "Isn't that a bunch of girls? So why have you all come out for Lennie today? And what's with the guitars?"

"We're guitarists," said Viper, fearless as ever. "And I happen to skateboard."

Paul lowered his backpack, settling it on the ground. His fellow jock, Howie, did the same. They possessed a lot of testosterone between the two of them and their confident manner bordered on obnoxious. Paul kicked at the ground like a bull getting ready to charge.

Paul and Howie faced Leonard, Cameron, Viper and Fireball. Unbeknownst to them, creeping up behind and sporting their guitars were Flipper and Quake.

"Why are you tormenting this guy?" bellowed Quake, startling them badly. Paul and Howie spun around to see Flipper and Quake; their guitars aimed like rifles directly at them.

"God damn. Where are you all coming from?" said Howie, speaking for the first time.

"He's a fellow musician," said Quake. "And we protect fellow musicians. So, what's your issue?"

Uncertain which way to face, Paul and Howie pressed their backs together so they each faced different guitarists.

"What is your problem?" persisted Quake.

"Our problem?" laughed Paul. "Well, we asked Lennie to help us with our tests and homework. And he did so for a while. But then he told us he wasn't comfortable doing it anymore. And when we insisted he continue, he did a very bad thing. He gave wrong answers on our homework so we looked like fools. We now want him to fix the situation and help us with our homework."

"And why do you focus on him?" asked Viper.

"Because," said Howie, floundering for an answer.

Paul and Howie felt cornered.

"Why do you care about Lennie?" asked Paul.

Pluto and Brick positioned themselves on opposite sides of Paul and Howie.

"Oh my God, how many more of you are there?" said Paul.

"Many more," said Pluto.

"Who are you?" asked Paul, annoyed.

"Lennie is my brother," said Pluto, surprising the other guitarists as well as Paul and Howie. Of course, that wasn't at all true. "And what he deserves is respect. We all deserve respect. A small thing to ask, wouldn't you say?"

"Listen," said Paul. "I know how we can settle this."

"Without fists," said Pluto.

"Of course."

"Go on."

"You're all musicians. I like music. Rock in particular. I listen to it 24/7. What if Howie and I name some songs. If one of you knows how to play each song we name, we'll leave Lennie alone. If we stump you, Lennie has to help us and I mean really help us with our homework and tests for the next month"

"How many songs?" Pluto asked.

Paul surveyed the guitarists and said "Seven."

Pluto's colleagues gave a comfortable nod.

"Leonard, tell me brother, are you okay with this?" Pluto asked.

Leonard's options seemed quite limited so he gave a reluctant nod.

"Now," said Pluto. "What guarantee do we have that you don't bother Leonard if we prevail?"

"Just our word is all," said Paul. "But we aren't going to lose."

Then for no apparent reason Paul focused on Cameron and said "And peewee here has to play one of the songs. And it's not going to be Twinkle Twinkle Little Star."

Cameron's face remained placid and calm though he seethed inside. It all reminded him of his encounters with bullies.

By now, a dozen students had gathered around to see just what was happening. All the colorful guitars got them curious.

"Deal," said Pluto. "Name your first song."

"How many do we get again?" asked Howie.

"Seven!" said Paul, annoyed by his dimwitted friend.

"Let me go first," said Howie. "Monkey Wrench by the Foo Fighters."

Without hesitation, Viper broke into the song with Quake plucking some bass chords.

When she finished, Viper said "And the Foos are the rock messiah Dave Grohl, Pat Smear, Chris Shiflett, Nate Mendel and the ever hot Taylor Hawkins."

Howie smiled. "Good," he said.

Paul nodded. "Okay, we got six picks left. I'd like to see you do 'American Idiot' by Green Day."

"Greatest album ever made," said Flipper, kicking off the lead guitar while Quake rocked the bass.

When they finished, Flipper said "Next time pick 'Jesus of Suburbia', greatest song ever."

Paul said "How do these damn guitars make such a good sound without any amps?"

"These guitars have built in amps," Pluto replied. "But we have even better ones just not with us."

"Can I pick another song?" asked Howie.

"Whisper it to me first," said Paul. "I don't want to waste our choices."

Howie whispered into Paul's ear and got an affirmative nod.

Smiling, Howie said "Snow by the Peppers."

Fireball knew the Red Hot Chili Peppers and volunteered to play it.

"What's with the hair?" asked Paul in a snide tone, staring at Fireball's violet dye job.

Fireball countered "And what's with your nose?" Paul's battered nose had clearly been broken several times.

Fireball played the opening of the song to everyone's satisfaction.

"Four..to..go," said Pluto.

Paul said "Spoonman by Soundgarden."

Brick absolutely loved Soundgarden. He knew most of their catalog, especially Spoonman.

To him, Chris Cornell was the ultimate rock God. A man so talented in his songwriting and singing, boasting a four octave range. And he looked the part with his long dark hair, haunting eyes and chiseled face.

"My friends," said Brick. "Thank you for allowing me the honor of playing a song by the greatest rock star ever, Mr. Chris Cornell."

Brick held up his guitar and shred one mean solo.

When he was done, Paul acknowledged him with a smile but then added "And no more of this commentary from any of you. It's getting annoying. Also, no more grunge. You clearly know it well. We're going to go further back. How's about the Allman Brothers 'One Way Out.'"

Pluto remembered this as one of the first rock songs he ever learned to play on the guitar. And he'd played it so much when he was younger, it was fresh in his mind. Several of the others hadn't heard it so they waited to see if Paul acknowledged it was done properly which he did with a glum nod.

Biting his lower lip and wanting to avoid defeat, Paul gave extra thought to the last two choices. Howie suggested a few titles but he nixed everyone. Finally, he suggested "Crossroads." "I believe I heard it done by a group called Cream," he said.

The guitarists looked at one another. Quake leaned over to Pluto and said "The Robert Johnson classic." Pluto concurred and the two of them played the song. It became immediately familiar to all who heard it.

"Enough," said Paul, cutting them off. "You got it. Okay, I've got one last pick."

"All or nothing on this," said Pluto.

Paul glanced at Cameron. "You're awfully quiet," he said. "Probably hoping I'd pick Mary Had A Little Lamb or something. But looking at you has given me the perfect idea, Chicken Little. The final song this kid has to play is The Sky is Crying by Stevie Ray Vaughn."

Pluto objected. "You didn't specify that you could pick who got to play the song."

"True," said Paul. "But I did specify that the little kid here had to play something. And he hasn't played a note yet."

Cameron looked uneasy. He started sweating and then wheezing. He knew exactly what was happening but he couldn't find his inhaler in any of his pockets.

"Come on, kid," said Paul. "We don't have all day. We want to leave enough time for Lennie to do our homework."

Cameron glanced over at Lennie who looked forlorn. He truly felt bad for him. But he couldn't perform. Not the way he was feeling.

"Looks like we win," said Paul. "The kid don't know it."

Cameron's chest tightened and his breathing became more rapid and forced. He felt like he was suffocating, unable to get enough air. Fumbling for his inhaler, he realized he'd forgotten to bring it. He fell to the ground, his skin pale and clammy.

"He needs an inhaler," shouted Viper, resourcefully patting down his clothes then beckoning passers-by. "Does anyone have an inhaler?" she asked, desperate.

The first few people that passed didn't. But then a girl came by and pulled one out of her purse. Viper rushed over to Cameron and let him take several puffs. In short time, his lungs opened up and the color returned to his face.

"It's been nice doing business with you all," said Paul. "But your little friend here just lost the contest for you."

Cameron knew he had let down Pluto as well as Leonard. Standing up, he steadied himself and took hold of his guitar. As he stepped forward, the neck of his guitar jutted right into Paul's groin, causing his knees to buckle as he bent over in pain. It was an accident but then again maybe it wasn't because Cameron sported a smirk on his face.

"Christ, watch what you're doing you little asshole," said Paul. "Man, that hurt."

Cameron quickly tuned his guitar. He knew the requested song as it was a blues classic first performed by Elmore James but made particularly memorable by Albert King and then Stevie Ray Vaughn. It was a 12-bar blues tune in the key of C with a slow tempo. In an effort to free Lennie, Cameron began to play. He made his guitar sound like it was crying as he bent notes, making the sound of each and every note carry a long time. And during parts of the song, he employed a slide which he kept in his pocket. "Okay, okay, enough, you can stop, you win," said Paul.

Cameron kept on playing.

"I said you win, you can stop," said Paul.

Cameron was so into the song, he paid no attention to Paul. He totally zoned out, feeling the music in his soul.

"Let him finish," said Viper.

When Cameron wound down and plucked the last note, he looked up at Paul, tempted to say something. Instead, he let a moment of silence pass.

"Impressive," said Paul. "Really."

The 20 students now watching, all applauded loudly and spontaneously.

"And you're going to keep your word?" asked Pluto.

Paul walked over to Leonard and put his arm around his shoulder. "Dude, you got yourself some peace thanks to your friends here."

"And what about an apology?" snapped Viper, feisty as ever.

Paul beckoned for Howie to come over. "We're sorry," he said. "Right, Howie?"

"Yep," said Howie.

"Well, we'll keep tabs on you," said Pluto, turning to leave. "Thanks for the audience."

The seven guitarists headed back to the van where Senza waited. Flipper couldn't help himself and as he was walking back, he held up two middle fingers aimed at the two jocks. He never turned around to see if they saw him. Leonard started to follow the group before stopping and wondering where he was going.

"Do you need a ride?" asked Pluto

"No. No, I don't. But thank you. Thank you very much whoever you all are."

"We don't even know who we truly are," said Pluto. They exchanged smiles and each walked in opposite directions.

Pluto was the last to board the shuttle bus. As he passed Senza, who had been waiting in the bus, he said quietly, "I don't think little C Sharp is going to make it."

Senza replied "I heard he did great."

"The kid has breathing problems," said Pluto. "We can't have him slowing us down. He's a major liability."

"Well, that's not your decision to make," she said.

"I called him C Sharp but he's really C Minor," said Pluto.

Senza knew this wasn't the time or place to argue with Pluto. He was in the minority as the others seemed very pleased with how Cameron performed.

Senza closed the door, pressed down on the gas and peeled out.

CHAPTER 10 FOOD FOR THOUGHT

A morning dew coated everything outside the mansion from glass top tables to the leaves of shrubs and trees. It misted the windows with an opaque fog, hindering any view. By noon, it all evaporated, disappearing as fast as it came.

Cameron sat on a stonewall by the back terrace watching Viper skateboarding, admiring her incredible balance and agility as she carved sharp turns, stopping on a dime whenever she liked.

"Yesterday was fun," she said.

Cameron agreed.

"Showed we can sometimes get things done without going to extreme measures," she said. "You had me scared there."

"I knew the song," said Cameron.

"Not that. It was your asthma attack," she said.

"I recovered."

Cameron always knew he had no chance whatsoever of ever being a superhero. Such a glorified role was just not in the cards for him. He often imagined stepping into a bank robbery to stop it when he'd suddenly be felled by an asthma attack. Someone would scrunch up his cape to prop up his head while the bank robbers would undoubtedly step right over him on their way out.

Senza emerged with the others. "We have a simple test to perform this afternoon," she said. "Non guitar stuff."

"I didn't know boredom was an activity," snipped Flipper.

Around the corner sat three large tubs, each about four feet tall, filled with ice and water. A small step ladder with three rungs rested against each tub for easy access. Next to each tub was a clock.

"Okay," said Senza. "We need you to strip down to your skivvies and hop into a tub."

"That sucks," said Flipper.

Pluto glanced over at Cameron. "Hey C Sharp, something you're good at. Stripping."

Viper glared at Pluto.

"Well, it's true," he said.

Senza looked around and said "Why don't we start with the younger members. C Sharp and–"

"I'll do it with him," said Flipper. "I want to get this over with."

Flipper and Cameron stripped down to their underwear. Cameron's body was so frail and scrawny, there wasn't an ounce of body fat. This was not an exercise for skinny people.

"Just get in when you're ready and we'll start the timer," said Senza.

Flipper got in first, his panicked expression displaying just how cold the water really was. By the time his timer hit a minute, he got out. Cameron had yet to try it.

"Come on C, you're up, "said Senza.

"I know a minute's not great but at least I survived," said Flipper, flipping off the tub. "I'm going to have to eat a ghost pepper to warm up. "

Cameron dipped in his toe. Ironically, the icy water felt like fire. As he climbed into the tub, Senza started the timer. Within seconds, his face turned a ghastly pale and his breathing accelerated. He gasped for air, unable to breathe.

"Get him out!" shouted Viper as Quake and Brick hauled him out and placed him on the ground. Senza stopped the timer. It read 15 seconds. But that was clearly irrelevant.

"Where's your inhaler?" Viper asked in a panic.

Cameron was unable to speak. He pointed to the mansion.

"Quake, go to his room and get it!" she ordered.

With long strides, Quake raced up to the house. While they waited for him, Cameron's skin turned a deathly blue tint. He grimaced as his chest felt like a thousand pounds of pressure weighed on top of it. Viper cradled his head and wrapped a towel over him.

Quake returned as fast as possible, clutching the inhaler like the baton in a relay race. He handed it to Viper who placed it up to Cameron's mouth and pressed it down. "Breathe!" she shouted.

Cameron obeyed and soon felt relief as his throat opened up and his color returned. His fear of suffocation subsided.

"Maybe we do this another day," said Senza.

Cameron shook his head. He didn't want this incident to spoil the whole activity. His mind was racing as he realized he didn't fit into this "cult." He had never fit in with any group before and this was no different. He clearly didn't belong to such cliques as jocks, nerds, stoners, popular, cool or good-looking kids. And though music was his friend, musicians at school rarely gave him the time of day. He even felt he'd be rejected by those labeled loners. They wouldn't want him. Why should they? He envisioned a rare gathering of loners at school who unanimously decided to reject Cameron Foster outright. It was just a matter of time before this group here would either kick him out or make him conveniently" disappear" altogether. No one would know.

"You heard him," said Pluto. "Let's do this now. I want to own another guitar."

Senza looked at Cameron. "Okay," she said. "Viper, why don't you, Fireball and Quake go."

"I'm bowing out," said Viper as she helped Cameron sit up. In a motherly way, she wrapped the towel tightly around him and then sat behind him with her arms wrapped snuggly around his waist. Senza, though a very good leader, lacked any maternal instincts.

"Fireball, Quake and Brick, you're on," she said. "A piece of advice. You need to get your mind from fixating on the cold and have it fixate on something else."

Flipped smiled. "Oh, now you tell me."

"You're welcome to try again," said Senza.

"I'll take a rain check," said Flipper, wrapped in a towel. "Make that an ice check".

Fireball, Quake and Brick got into the three tubs at the exact same time. At the two minute mark, each of them remained in the icy water but with teeth chattering.

At four minutes, Brick got out. The air warmed him instantly. "Note to self: Prefer hot showers," he said. "I once swam in the Yangtze and this beats it hands down. "

A minute later, Fireball climbed out. "Holy Jesus, Mary and Nanook," she said in an amplified Southern twang, looking at her timer. "I can't believe that six and a half minutes isn't enough to win."

All her fingers and toes felt numb and her teeth chattered uncontrollably.

"You're purple," observed Flipper.

"That's my color, baby," she replied.

Quake leaned back, grimacing towards the sky. "In, Sweden, ice baths are a big thing. Invigorating cold immersion therapy used to slow your metabolism, reduce muscle pain and close every single pore of your body. But I never quite got into it over there. What's my time?"

"You are now at eight minutes, my sweet Quake", said Fireball.

"Well, eight's my lucky number, at least today it is," he said, lifting himself out of the tub. He then ended with a quick rap "This chilling loss hurts me like a big screaming cavity. "Freezing my body in this game of depravity, Unlike when I win and my feet defy gravity."

Fireball said "You're still the man even though it's hard to tell."

"I will admit that running up to the house had warmed me enough to get to eight," confessed Quake.

"It's just Pluto left," said Brick. "Got to beat eight minutes".

"Aren't you doing it Senza? " asked Fireball. "Come on. Show that you're one of us. It will be a battle of the old people."

"Fine with me" said Pluto. "If I'm going to win, it might as well be against the person whose guitar I'll soon own."

Senza and Pluto got down to their undergarments and climbed into different tubs as Fireball hit the timers.

The timers soon hit five minutes, then six, then seven. Quake could see his victory slipping away. The color had drained out of their faces as Pluto and Senza passed the nine minute mark.

Senza detached her mind from feeling the cold and let it wander into other thoughts. To her, the water no longer felt as cold as when she first entered. Her body and mind had become acclimated. Her eyes no longer teared. She looked at peace in a completely calm and restful state. The timers passed 10 minutes then 11.

Pluto was going on sheer determination. He struggled with the cold as waves of shivers swept throughout his body.

At the fifteen minute mark, Pluto gave up. He climbed out of the tub.

"Some things in life just aren't worth winning," he said in his sour grapes style. " Like winning an oversized stuffed animal prize at a carnival or giving yourself frostbite for the sake of a musical instrument that you really don't need."

He grabbed a towel and sat on the ground, defeated. "You won," he said to Senza. "You can get out now."

Twenty minutes passed, then 25. At the 30 minute mark, Senza finally got out of the tub. She grabbed a towel, dried off and got dressed.

"Whose idea was this anyhow?!" she said with a perky smile.

"Welcome to the Rock 'n Roll Polar Bear Club," said Fireball. "Amen."

Viper helped Cameron get to his feet. He wobbled, his equilibrium off.

"Is he going to be okay?" asked Senza.

"I hope so," said Viper.

"Let's get some hot chocolate," said Brick.

"I'll carry him" offered Quake, cradling Cameron in his arms and heading up to the mansion. The others followed with Viper and Pluto trailing behind.

"What do you want?" asked Viper, standing still as Pluto grasped her arm.

"You know what your little friend is good at? Losing," he said.

"Well, I know someone who's not a good loser and it's you", she snapped.

"I'm just telling you as a friend, he doesn't fit in," said Pluto.

"You're no friend of mine," said Viper. "Just because you lost out on getting a new guitar, it doesn't mean you can lash out at everyone. It's not attractive."

"I'm just lashing out at him," said Pluto. "The loser."

Having heard enough, Viper shouted "Adios pendejo". Although Pluto didn't know Spanish well, he probably knew she was saying 'goodbye asshole.'

He watched as she ran back to join the others.

■■

Most people eat three often unmemorable meals a day.

In general, meals were forgettable occasions whose main purpose was providing fuel for the body. On this particular night dinner fell in the memorable category but not for the reasons one might surmise.

Inside the mansion, the dining room looked special with two candles on the table bestowing a calming and warm yellow illumination. The tablecloth, ironed white linen, coupled with quality china plates and polished silverware, gave it a formality it usual didn't have. On the sideboard were several large serving bowls – one containing spaghetti, another with meatballs, a third with fully cooked whole tomatoes and the last held mashed potatoes.

On the other side of the room were the desserts – six individual pies from blueberry and strawberry-rhubarb to lemon meringue and Boston cream. A special pie cutter and server lay before each one.

Cameron was the first to arrive. Then, Pluto entered and with his thumb and index finger pinched the flames on each candle, stifling them out, leaving a small tail of smoke. He moved the candles off the table.

"A bit too fancy, wouldn't you say?" he grumbled.

Cameron could only nod, having little interest in contradicting him.

As the others arrived, they noticed there weren't any place cards so they sat randomly at the table.

Conversation kicked off with a lively discussion of amps. "Is there anyone here who favors solid state over tube?" Pluto asked, almost defying anyone to answer solid state.

"I see where you're heading," said Quake "The only thing I'll add is that tube amps don't travel so good. Fragile buggers. And they can't handle distortion at low volumes the way solid state can."

"But what about the sound itself?" said Pluto.

"I like the warm sound of a tube amp. It's so much more natural," said Fireball, weighing in. "You get softer highs and mids."

"What amps do you all use?" Pluto asked.

"Fender Vibrolux Reverb," said Flipper.

"I have a Fender, a Vintage Deluxe," said Brick.

"Which artist do you feel is best at producing a really original sound thanks to the amp they use?" Pluto persevered with more questions.

"The Edge," said Brick without hesitation.

"What's he use?" Pluto asked.

"I know he has played with a Strat and used an Electro Harmonix Memory Man delay pedal with Vox AC30s," she said. "He gets that great echo sound that is so distinctive. If he played 'Mary Had A Little Lamb,' I'd know it was him."

Pluto nodded in agreement. "He sure does have a signature sound."

"What about you, C Sharp?" asked Pluto, putting Cameron in the spotlight. Cameron's cheeks flushed with embarrassment.

"Vox," said Cameron. "A very small Vox."

"Maybe you can upgrade to a Marshall stack someday," said Viper smiling.

"That's my choice," said Fireball. "Marshall all the way."

"Did you know that Marshall, the guy who invented that amp, was a drummer," said Brick. "And the whole idea of the Marshall stack was suggested by Pete Townshend and Richie Blakemore?!"

"I'm surprised it didn't come from Keith Moon. He loved to stack things up and knock 'em down. Big time," said Brick.

"I've got to tend to something," said Senza. "Back soon. Please keep things orderly while I'm gone."

She left the room, rather mysteriously.

"Let's get some grub," said Pluto, walking over to the side table and loading up his plate. The others dutifully followed until everyone had a full plate of food.

"Should I say grace?" Pluto asked.

"Sure," said Fireball.

"Grace," said Pluto, digging a fork into his spaghetti.

Pluto stopped after one bite, then exclaimed, "La Tomatina!" He grabbed two of the tomatoes on his plate and hurled them. One hit Cameron right on the neck, splattering red goo all over his shirt. Another sailed past Viper's head, smacking against the wall, leaving a bloody stain as though someone had been shot. Without missing a beat, everyone at the table started throwing food. They tossed handfuls of spaghetti, catapulted mashed potatoes with soup spoons, threw more tomatoes and every other piece of food they could find. And when they had cleared the food off their plates, they raced to the side table and started throwing the rest of the food. The pies made for a particularly sloppy mess as they were either thrown or delivered smack into someone's face or back of their head. Everyone engaged in the food fight, except for Cameron. He sat, stunned, watching the mayhem until the room was totally wrecked.

"Come on," said Viper, egging him to join in. "Throw something. Get Pluto. It's your big chance."

Cameron was coated, head to toe, in food. Pluto had dumped a blueberry pie on top of his head. Cameron wiped it off his forehead so it didn't creep into his eyes. Hesitating, he reached for a small tomato on his plate and threw it, narrowly missing Pluto but hitting Senza square in the face as she re-entered the room. Suddenly, everyone stopped what they were doing and all eyes centered on Cameron.

"What the hell?!" she exclaimed, pushing remnants of tomato off her cheek. She grabbed hold of a napkin and cleaned her face. "Who started this?"

No one said a word.

"Pluto?" she demanded. "Who started this?"

"You saw who started it," he said, implying it was Cameron. "I mean, Senza, how many people did you see throwing food? One, right?"

"C," she said. "Who started this?"

Cameron's eyes lowered.

"Look at me," she said. "Who started this? If you don't tell me, then I will assume it was you."

Cameron surveyed the dining room. The place was a catastrophe. "It was..." he said, deciding not to finish his sentence.

"You are going to face some heavy discipline," she said. "Everyone else, out of here now. Go clean yourselves off."

As Pluto passed by Cameron, he said softly "Be prepared for a dark chapter ahead."

A dark chapter? thought Cameron. What did that mean? Not good. That's what.

The Asian man entered, his head turning from side to side at the mess, uncertain where to begin.

"He's going to clean this up," said Senza, gesturing towards Cameron.

Senza left the room, re-emerging with a mop and bucket as well as two large sponges and some towels. She also had a large plastic garbage bag. "These are for you," she said, handing them to Cameron.

"Where do I begin?" Cameron asked.

"I don't know," she said. "You need to figure that out. I will come back here in an hour to see your progress."

Cameron scratched his head. Cleaning all this up was an overwhelming assignment. He started by tossing the emptied pie tins into the garbage bag. The Asian man went to help.

"I don't think you're supposed to help me," said Cameron.

"But it is a big mess," he said. "Break down the cleaning process. Toss all the debris into the garbage bag. We can pile all the linens over there by the door. We'll then work on cleaning the tables, windows and walls."

"I don't know how I'm going to reach all of the walls not to mention ceilings," said Cameron.

"You should have thought of that before you started this food fight," said the old man.

Cameron whispered "I didn't start it. Honest. I only threw one thing. A small tomato. That's all."

"Then who did?"

Cameron wouldn't answer.

The two worked on cleaning the room for close to two hours. Cameron had to refill the bucket with clean water several times and filled several trash bags with soiled paper towels. When they were done, Senza emerged for inspection.

Nodding her head in a sign of approval, she said, "Good job. But I told you to do it alone."

"I insisted on helping him," said the Asian man.

"Is that right?" she asked.

"Yes," he said.

"Well, I learned that..." said Senza, pausing mid-sentence. "Pluto started the food fight, didn't he?"

Cameron shrugged his shoulders, feigning ignorance.

"He did," she said. "He confessed."

"Well," said the old man. "This young boy here is very honorable. He took the fall. He never blamed anyone. Not even to save himself. I have the highest respect for him."

"And I heard that C only threw one item and it happened to be the tomato that hit me," she said. "Sorry, C for blaming you. I'm heading upstairs. I'll see you tomorrow."

Senza strode out of the room, a blur of black leather.

Cameron stared at the old man. "Thank you for always being so kind to me," he said. "Ever since I got here, you have been the one person to treat me with respect all the time."

The old man gave a solemn nod.

"I'm embarrassed to ask after all this time but what is your name?" asked Cameron.

The old man smiled, pausing, before saying "Z3. You can call me Z3."

"WHAT?!?" asked Cameron, surprised at what he'd just heard.

"I know," said the old man. "Sounds like a piece from a Bingo game. But that's what people call me here."

Cameron was utterly baffled. He had envisioned Z3 as being this all-mighty, all-powerful being. How could this frail Asian man be Z3, the person who owned this mansion and everything in it?

"How could you be Z3?" he asked.

"And how can you be C Sharp?" he replied.

"It's just a nickname."

"Precisely."

"Why didn't you say who you were when I first met you?"

"You never asked," he replied.

"True," admitted Cameron. "But why are you going around cleaning and stuff?"

"It's just a ruse. My way of getting to know you and understand you and see how you treated someone who appeared in an inferior position to your own."

"So, everyone else here knows who you are?"

Beaming, Z3 nodded.

Cameron let out a deep sigh.

"Have a good night," said Z3, quietly leaving the room.

Cameron sat cross-legged on the floor, his mind spinning, wondering if he was truly going insane. He spotted a small piece of pie crust under the table. He plucked it off the ground and slipped it into his mouth.

At breakfast the next morning, the room was serene and spotless. They all sat, wordless, eating their food. All except Pluto. He was nowhere to be seen. Yet, no one seemed to ask about him.

Back in his bedroom, Cameron wondered if the words Pluto uttered right before the food fight meant anything. La Tomatina. Sounded Spanish. Cameron went online and read a description. 'Many years ago, at a parade in Spain people threw tomatoes at some woodland animals eating their food; one person missed and hit another person which precipitated a major food fight. It became an annual event with more people joining in every year. People started to come prepared, wearing goggles, gloves and hats for protection. The whole fight lasted an hour with tens of thousands of tomatoes being thrown'. Why didn't Pluto just say 'food fight'?

Cameron felt a need to build a relationship with Pluto. Maybe he could impress him by talking about La Tomatina. He wandered over to Pluto's room, noticing the door slightly cracked open. He knocked. No answer. So, he pushed open the door. No one was there. The bed was made, the sheets pulled tight and nothing looked out of place. Either Pluto had somehow left or was perhaps being punished for starting the food fight last night. Maybe this 'cult' did him in. Time would tell.

■■

A week passed with no sign of Pluto. Stranger still was that no one had even asked about him.

Cameron met Senza outside by the guitar shed. Using a special tool, she was busy opening the back plate of a guitar then removing a large yellow crystal with a tongs. She dipped it in a beaker filled with a bluish liquid. There was an electrical flash, purple and yellow, as she removed the crystal and gently placed it back into the guitar.

"What are you doing?" said Cameron, startling her.

Caught by surprise, Senza said, "You shouldn't sneak up on people that way."

"What way should I sneak up?"

"You shouldn't. If I'd dropped this, Z3 would not be pleased," she said.

She tightened the plate back onto the guitar, held it upright and turned it on.

"You never told me that man was Z3," Cameron said.

"And I never told you that the sun sets in the west and the black rhino is an endangered species and the lowest part of the ocean is the Mariana trench," she replied. "There's a lot of stuff you've got to discover on your own. I don't think you want me being your mother. Or do you?"

He looked at her, quizzical.

She pulled over a chair and straddled it, stretching her legs out, the black leather taut and shiny. Sliding over a chair next to her, he took a seat.

"Can you tell me something about him? I mean, anything?" he asked.

"Oh God, what did I just tell you?"

"You said to discover things on my own," he said. "So that's what I'm doing."

"Why don't you ask him directly?" she said.

"I thought I'd start with you."

"Okay. I'll give you five," she said.

"Five minutes?" he asked.

"Five questions," she said. "And that's all. Make them count."

Cameron collected his thoughts.

"What does Z3 mean?"

"It's short for his real name Ziam Zen Ziam. Next question."

"He seems really rich. How did he make all his money?"

"Semi-conductors then cloud-based computing systems," she said. "Built his own company and made billions. And he's been a major supporter of musicians. Major. Done a lot for them and many of their causes. Next question which would be your third."

"Did he invent these guitars and what does he plan to do with them?"

"Well, that's kind of a sneaky two-part question but I'll allow it. Yes, he did invent them and he has a definite use for them which he plans to reveal. Next."

"Is he married and does he have any kids?"

"Again, sneaky. Two-part question. But I'll allow it. No and no. Last question."

"What are we all doing here," he said. "I mean, why is he housing us and why did he bring us all together? And what is my role?"

Senza reached her hands behind her head and yawned. "He's a very generous and caring man. He's brought together a unique group of people who all are skilled in ways that only he sees the true value of. He has a plan that involves everyone. And he hasn't revealed it yet because he doesn't do things prematurely."

"But it seems he told you, didn't he?" asked Cameron.

"And that, my little friend, would be question number six which, as we know, isn't permissible. Five questions only."

She stood up from her chair, locked the guitar shed and ambled back to the mansion.

Cameron felt like a small pawn in this game of life.

CHAPTER 11 A DISTANT PLUTO

With a day's worth of stubble and his clothes disheveled, Walter Matthews looked like he'd slept in the bar that night. He started straightening out bar stools and cocktail tables, giving some semblance of order to his dingy hole-in-the-wall bar.

The Florida paneled walls had a random mix of framed pictures, some of duck hunters and fishermen, others of baseball and football players. Called Walter's Watering Hole, the words dangling precariously over the entrance, it was located a few miles south of Caribou nestled in northern Maine where it carried the boast as the most northeastern city in the United States. In other words, damn cold most of the year.

Having lived there virtually his entire life, Walter spoke with a fairly thick Maine accent, barely opening his mouth when he talked as though his lips were frozen in place from one too many winters. He'd only left the state twice in his five decades and the most recent time was when he accidentally crossed the border into Vermont after a night of heavy drinking.

Caribou was heavily forested and lowly populated. It differed from the rocky coastline with its lobster boats, seagulls and native beauty attracting a stream of tourists all summer-long. There was a creepy beauty to it, a feeling that although you were in a seemingly tranquil environment, dark evil things lurked out there.

One of Walter's closest friends was Shep Landon, a willowy man in his late forties with long prematurely grey hair tied back in a ponytail. Shep tended bar there and was noted as the most talkative barkeep for miles around.

"Have you seen your new boarder yet?" Shep asked.

"Did Canada take more land back?" asked Walter facetiously. He knew that Shep meant "boarder" and not "border."

"No, I mean the person who's rooming upstairs."

"No. Can't say I have," said Walter. "He's just catching up on his sleep I guess."

"The noise carries upstairs something bad," said Shep, remembering the years when he lived above the bar.

"But it's cheap to live here," said Walter.

"Cheap until your renovation is done," said Shep. "I still can't figure how you have the money to do it and how you plan to get that money back."

Walter smiled. "May never get it back," he said. "But it's been a dream of mine to expand this place."

"But you're expanding a place in the middle of nowhere," observed Shep.

"And someday this little piece of nowhere may be somewhere," he said. "You been out back lately."

"Nope."

"Follow me," said Walter, heading towards a door in the back that opened up onto a vacant lot, where a large cement foundation had been laid down, occupying a lot of space. It was incongruent that a remote locale such as this would have a major construction project going on.

"This is much bigger than I imagined," said Shep.

"Well, I'm hoping if we get big enough, we can lure folks from Canada and other nearby towns. Would love to lure entertainers here just as they do in Vegas. That place was nothing more than a desert and now it's a prime destination."

"When's this supposed to be ready?" asked Shep.

"Supposedly before winter," said Walter. "Of course, it all depends on when winter wants to rear its head. Gets earlier every year."

Standing on the back porch, Walter pointed to two long crates. "You know what's in those?" he asked.

Shep smiled. "I was here when they came," he said.

"You remember that proposal I put together?"

"You mean the one for the rifle range?" asked Shep.

"Yep. I hadn't thought that through so well. And I shouldn't have been surprised when the town nixed my proposal. I can't blame them, though. Not the smartest idea to have a rifle range attached to a bar. But it would have been a helluva lot of fun."

"So those boxes have---"

"Rifles," said Walter. "I ordered them before I found out my proposal didn't go through."

"So, what do you do with two boxes of guns?" asked Shep.

"Find a buyer," he said. "And I got me one."

The two men went back into the bar. "Nice to have something to look forward to in life," said Shep.

"Aint that the truth," said Walter. "I was depressed in my twenties because nothing was going right for me. I had no direction. Nothing that gave me any joy. This bar, even in its current state, has been a godsend. You been depressed before, Shep?"

"Yep."

"And when might that have been?"

Shep hesitated, counting on his fingers. "My teens. Then also my twenties, my thirties and now my forties. I hope my fifties breaks the string."

"You need to have a dream, Shep."

Walter took a seat on a bar stool as Shep proceeded to pour corn nuts into small bowls.

"You know," said Shep, pointing at a sign on the wall. "In all the time I've been here, and it's been a while, I always wondered where you got that sign."

The sign he was talking about featured a palm tree with coconuts falling off and three people beneath trying to run from them. The sign read "Beware of Falling Coconuts."

"Death by coconut," said Walter. "No laughing matter."

"Seriously?"

"Oh yeah."

"It's just a funny sign to have here in Maine, you know," said Shep. "There's not a coconut within 1000 miles of here. I guess you have it to evoke a laugh now and then."

Walter shook his head. "Nope. Not the case. When I was about 7, I left the state of Maine with my mother and visited an uncle down in Miami. I was playing in the sand when a coconut fell and hit me square on the right shoulder fracturing it. Had it fallen two inches over, it would have hit me on the head and probably killed me. When I got back to Maine, I just never wanted to leave the state again."

"All on account of killer coconuts."

"Yep. All on account of killer coconuts. Those things weigh about 3 pounds each. And they fall from 30, 40, 50 feet high. A recipe for concussions."

"Wasn't Keith Richards hit on the head by a coconut when he was in Australia?"

"That was just a rumor," said Walter. "He actually fell out of a tree and hit his head."

"Speaking of musicians, "said Shep. "That new boarder plays guitar. He had three of them."

"Yep," said Walter. "And I'm working on a gig for him. Seems like a nice enough guy."

The two men heard a door close upstairs then some footsteps. The new boarder was coming downstairs.

"Here he comes," said Walter. "Just act natural."

The footsteps stopped midway on the stairs and then headed back up again.

CHAPTER 12 THE AUDITION

Cameron felt lost.

While he liked his new home, he didn't feel he deserved such a place because he really hadn't done anything to earn it. He went to talk to Senza.

She came to her bedroom door, sleepy-eyed, in a pink Dear Kitty bathrobe – a most uncharacteristic outfit for someone who usually wore black leather. Noticing Cameron's look of surprise, she commented "They don't make leather bathrobes. Come in."

He stepped over piles of leather clothes strewn across the floor and sat on the lone chair.

"One moment," she said, stepping into her bathroom and soon re-emerging in her trademark leather outfit.

"Safe to talk?" he whispered, his eyes moving from side to side. Her room was sparse except for a poster of Chris Cornell and one of, who else, Joan Jett.

"Follow me," she said, leading him out of the mansion.

They walked down the back slope towards a tall hedgerow. It felt like a secure place to talk, acting like a barricade. But maybe there were cameras there. Who knew.

"You look concerned" she observed.

"I want to know why I'm here."

"You don't like it here?" she asked.

He shook his head.

"Then what's the problem?" she asked.

"Pluto."

"He's not your problem anymore."

"He just disappeared like that," said Cameron.

"So? He hasn't been particularly nice to you."

Cameron let out a deep sigh. "Why isn't anyone concerned that he just disappeared?"

"What do you think happened to him?" she asked.

Cameron stared directly into her eyes. "Something bad."

"Z3 isn't concerned. So, I'm sure we'll learn where he is in good time," she said.

Cameron took a deep breath and exhaled. He turned to survey the impeccable surroundings--the well-manicured lawns, the forest of giant pines, the magnificent gardens, the beautiful lake and, of course, the mansion itself. This was a far cry from the "haunted house" he'd grown up in all of his life. And yet he felt he belonged there more than here.

"Can you tell me where Z3 lives in this big house and if he ever has visitors?"

"Those are more questions than the five you were allotted," she replied.

Cameron felt a degree of exasperation.

"Alright," she said. "He's upstairs. Third floor."

"And visitors?"

"He might. Or he might not," she said, providing no clarity at all.

He shook his head.

"You excited about tonight?" she asked.

He squinted, thinking. What was so special about tonight?

"Guitar contest," she said.

"Here?"

"Right after dinner."

"Who's in it?"

"Every musician in this house," she said.

"Except Pluto," he said, then under his breath, muttered "Because he's probably dead."

■■

At Walter's Watering Hole, two burly men stood up as the one with the goatee pulled out a black and blue handkerchief.

"A blindfold?! Really?!" said Pluto.

The goateed man gave one short and definitive nod.

"Isn't just being in Maine enough? No one's gonna see me and I don't know my way around up here," said Pluto.

"Can't take any chances," said the goateed man.

The blindfold was secured tightly over Pluto's eyes. For added measure, a burlap bag was placed over his head.

Unable to find his center of gravity, Pluto walked unsteadily as they escorted him to their car. Opening the door, they slid him into the back seat. He heard two car doors slam shut as the motor turned on and the car rolled out of the driveway.

Dozens of fleeting thoughts entered Pluto's mind but one made him chuckle more than the others. 'Never go on a job interview where they put a bag over your head,' he thought.

When your vision is hindered, time moves slowly as you are often disoriented and claustrophobic. Pluto could practically taste the burlap over his head. It tickled his nose almost provoking a sneeze. He resisted, feeling his own warm breath. What he wouldn't give for a cool dose of fresh air. To make matters worse, he felt every bump in the road, jostling his spine.

For all he knew, the trip could have been 45 minutes although it felt interminable. Finally, the car rolled to a stop and he heard voices exchanging a few words. There was a momentary pause before he heard a clanking sound, most likely a metal gate grinding open. The car crawled ahead slowly and he heard the clanking again as the gate closed. The car drove a short distance before coming to a stop.

The car door opened and the bag and blindfold were removed, causing him to blink uncomfortably as he had become unaccustomed to light. As his vision adjusted, moving in and out of focus, he saw he was in an underground garage.

"Where am I?" Pluto asked.

The driver chuckled. "Now, if I was going to tell you that, then we wouldn't have needed the blindfold."

Pluto felt his door open. He shuffled across his seat and got out of the car with some assistance.

The garage went right into a building, a concrete compound, sterile and unfriendly with a brightly lit hallway. They approached a security checkpoint where they held up i.d. cards.

"Not sure why we need to show i.d. cards each and every time we come in," said the driver.

"Rules are rules," said the guard at the security checkpoint.

They held the i.d. cards against a scanner, triggering a heavy door to open.

"He obviously doesn't have an i.d.," the driver said, referring to Pluto. "He is our special guest."

They headed down the hallway and stopped in a room with a table and chairs facing each other on both sides. It looked like a room for an interrogation. A man in a wife beater tee shirt entered.

The driver said, "This is that guy who could provide some entertainment. Really good guitarist. Has a band, too, if you're interested."

The driver left the room and the man in the tee shirt closed the door. "Well, well," he said. "What's your name?"

"Pluto."

"And I'm Mars. Seriously, though, what's your name?"

"That's really my name," he said. "It may be a little odd but it's not as strange as Moon Unit."

"Who's Moon Unit?

"One of Frank Zappa's kids."

"Frank Zappa?"

Did this guy really not know who Frank Zappa was? he wondered. "He was a very good rock and jazz guitarist. One of the very few who could actually read music."

"Have a seat."

Pluto did what he was told.

"You want something to drink?"

"What are you offering?" asked Pluto, realizing how foolish that sounded. After all, it's not like he was in a restaurant or a bar.

The man in the tee shirt seemed amused. He did the jock strut across the barren room and replied "What am I offering? Pina coladas, sea breeze, margaritas...."

"Um, well...."

"I'm kidding," he said. "I meant do you want something to drink such as water or coffee or tea or soda?

"I'd love a coke," he said.

"Lime?

"Excuse me?

"You want a wedge of lime?"

"No thanks.

The guy stood up and yelled out the door then sat down again.

"You probably want to know who I am," he said. "I am Domenick. Although I don't know you worth a rat's ass, you can call me Dom if you like. I think having to say three syllables is crap. Dom is more efficient. That work for you?"

"It does."

"Before we get down to the nitty gritty, I'd like to hear you play."

He gestured to a guitar leaning against a large Vox amp. "I'm sure you'd prefer to use your own guitar so I hope this will suffice."

Pluto knew instantly what an amazing guitar this was. For starters, it was a Gibson Les Paul with a high gloss finish and a classic double cutaway. And it had a sunburst color, dark on the outer edges and a light vibrant orangy red on the interior. Clearly, a special custom order guitar that cost at least $5000. He'd never played a guitar as nice as this one.

"This will do," said Pluto, matter-of-factly, concealing his true feelings of amazement.

He checked each string. It was perfectly tuned.

"What would you like to hear?" he asked.

"I'm not the best person to ask. I mean, you probably play rock music. It's not my thing. I like country or classical."

"You like Spanish guitar?" asked Pluto.

"Sure."

Pluto started plucking notes and playing a wonderful melodic and familiar Spanish song. Domenick couldn't help but get into the song, rocking his head and swaying back and forth. When Pluto finished, Domenick asked "Wow, man. Great stuff. What's the name of that piece?"

"Malaguena," said Pluto.

"Whatever that means, it's good."

Pluto gave an appreciative nod.

"So now, tell me about yourself. A quick sketch of your background."

"Well, I grew up in a broken home. Learned to play guitar really early in life. Bounced around a lot. Music is the one way I know I can make money with. But music is a tough business."

"Unless you're the Beatles or Frank Zappit."

"It's Zappa. Not sure he was that rich cause he wasn't mainstream."

"Which of his songs are the most famous?"

Pluto tried to recall some song titles. "Well, there's Willie the Pimp."

"Never heard of it."

"I am the Slime."

"Nope."

"Don't Eat The Yellow Snow?"

"Funny title but no. No need to go further. I don't know this guy's stuff. Tell me about your band."

"We're composed of a lot of runaway kids," said Pluto.

"Runaways?"

"Broken homes like me."

"And they're all good musicians?"

"Very."

"And where do they live?"

"Well, that's the thing," said Pluto. "They don't live anywhere specifically. They move from place to place. If I ever got a full time gig, I'd try to have them move up here with me."

"How old are they?"

"The youngest is, I think, ten," he said.

"And the oldest?"

"17. Although there is a girl who's 27."

"We wouldn't be interested in the 27-year-old," he replied. "That takes away from the whole novelty of a young band. What we also like is kids from foster homes or no homes. We want to give them a new place to live if they're interested. Now, can you get these kids here?"

"Oh yeah. I'm sure I can."

"And could they come for a while?"

"Sure. They don't have anything tying them down."

"I like that. You like young kids?" he asked.

Pluto paused. "You mean as musicians?"

"Whatever," he said.

Pluto stared at the white concrete walls. "Can I confide in you, Dom?" Pluto asked, conjuring up a lie. "I'm not necessarily proud of this but I like young kids. Let's leave it at that."

Dom nodded. "Understood."

Pluto looked solemn.

"Can I ask you one other question? Very important. Have you ever had trouble with the law?" Domenick asked.

"You mean, do I have a criminal record? No."

There was a knock on the door. Dom went over and unlocked it. In walked a very pretty young girl with startling blue eyes and brownish blonde hair tied back in a ponytail. She was carrying a tray of food with a teapot, two cups and a plate of crumpets. She was dressed in what could best be described as hospital attire – a peach-colored jumpsuit.

She set down the tray and poured a cup of tea for Domenick.

"Thanks Sasha," he said.

She handed the coke to Pluto who tried to make eye contact but she never looked up.

"Thank you," he said.

"Introduce yourself," said Domenick.

Neither knew who he was talking to so Pluto and Sasha each responded at the same time, stating their names. Pluto chuckled, waited for a moment and repeated his name. Sasha didn't feign even the slightest smile.

She placed a plate of pastries on the table.

"You like these?" Domenick asked.

"What are they?" asked Pluto.

"Crumpets. My favorite."

Pluto turned to Sasha and asked "Do you live here?"

She appeared very upset by his question.

"She's a bit shy and uncomfortable as you can see," said Domenick, stating the obvious.

Pluto couldn't remember seeing a woman as pretty as Sasha. He guessed her to be 17 or 18. Without even a tad of makeup, she was striking with sensual pursed lips, high cheekbones, sparkling teeth and a slim physique.

"Play that song for her," said Domenick. "The one you just played for me. Maladjustment or something or other."

"Malaguena," said Pluto.

He picked up his guitar and started playing, looking directly at Sasha. Her eyes never looked up and she never showed the slightest trace of a smile which was odd as it was a song so infectious that people often danced along to it on a tabletop.

When Pluto finished, he expected her to say something, a polite response for etiquette's sake but she didn't respond at all.

"I'm glad you liked it so much," said Pluto, sarcastically.

She remained silent and unemotional. Domenick broke the awkwardness, saying "That'll be all, Sasha."

Pluto hated to see her leave.

"Anything else, Dom?" Pluto asked.

"Yeah," said Domenick. "If we decide to have you come here, how long would it take to get your group together?"

"Well, I'm ready now," said Pluto. "But probably a few days for the others."

"A week," Dom repeated. "Okay. I just got to do a bit of due diligence."

"Background checks?"

"Yeah. That kind of thing. And then I'll get back to you."

"Okay," said Pluto. "Can I make a request?

Dom listened.

"Is there any way I could leave here without being blindfolded with a suffocating bag over my head?"

"Precautions," said Dom. "I'll tell you what. I like you. I'll have them just do the blindfold."

"Thanks."

Domenick walked over to the door and turned to Pluto. "We'll get back to you. And if you don't hear from us, well, that's because we're moving on."

Pluto walked down the hallway. Out of a window, he caught a glimpse of a river running close to the building. He paused.

"Hurry along," said a guard.

The driver approached with a blindfold and started to put it over his eyes. Right before he did, Pluto caught a glimpse of the goateed man holding the burlap bag.

"No bag," he said. "Right Dom?"

"Yeah. No bag," said Domenick.

When he was first blindfolded at Walter's Watering Hole, Pluto didn't realize how disorienting it would be. It made him feel nauseous. At least they honored his request to skip the burlap bag over his head on the return trip. But he felt they all had bad intentions and it disgusted him. Why would Z3 have Walter introduce him to these questionable people? There was a lot that wasn't clear.

Blindfolded, Pluto was led to the garage for the long drive back.

CHAPTER 13 NO CONTEST

The Big Room brought everyone together with their guitars in hand. Several Marshall amps were scattered around, one for each of them.

Senza arrived last, dressed in full leather. Her extra dark eye shadow showed she meant business.

"Are you ready?" she asked.

"Yep," said Flipper. "Just one thing. Since Pluto isn't here, can we still proclaim a winner for the night?"

"Yes, we can," she replied, putting on some black fingerless gloves and holding a hat. "So, here's what we're going to do. Everyone will draw a number out of this hat. That will determine the order of performances. Flipper, you can go first?"

Flipper reached in and announced his number "3."

Fireball was next and picked "2." Quake got 1, Viper 4, Brick 5 and Cameron 7. Senza got the remaining number which was 6.

"How many of you can play a leftie guitar?" she asked. "And this excludes Brick who I know is leftie. Come over here, Flipper."

She handed him a leftie guitar and he played but his fingering was way off. The others tried it with slightly better results but not by much. When they got to Cameron, he deliberately stumbled, unable to play well. He didn't want to stand out as he felt the others would resent him.

"That's sad," said Flipper.

As Cameron put down the guitar, Viper whispered to him "You're not fooling me. I've seen how well you can play leftie. You're doing yourself a disservice. There are some here who don't feel you belong. They haven't seen your skills. I'm telling you this as a friend."

"Brick, try a rightie," said Senza. Brick picked up one of the rightie guitars and played fairly well.

"I have a confession to make," said Brick, wearing a shirt with Chinese characters on it.' "I have played a rightie before."

"And now you, Senza," said Viper.

Senza took the leftie and played outstandingly.

"That was just for fun," she said. "Now, we want to get down to business."

Senza brought out an electronic device and plugged it into an iPad. On the screen were listed three categories: Song Title, Speed, Accuracy.

"What is that?" asked Brick.

"This is something that Z3 created," she explained. "You type in the name of a song. This little device measures just how quickly and accurately someone plays it. It's a very objective way to judge a guitar contest although I will admit that it doesn't give any value to someone taking a song and doing creative things with it. Let's keep the same order. To be fair, I thought we might want to all play 'Eruption' so we can judge based on the same song."

"Can't we do something different?" asked Fireball.

Senza put her hands on her hips. "Like what?"

"Like Dragonforce," said Fireball. "'Through the Fire and Flames' is awesome."

"How many know that one?" she asked.

Only Fireball and Flipper raised their hands.

"What about Cliffs of Dover by Eric Johnson?" said Flipper.

"How many know that?"

Only Flipper raised his hand.

"You guys suck," said Flipper. "How could you not know that one."

"What about Jordan by Buckethead," said Quake.

Flipper was the only one who knew that song.

"Welcome to the Jungle?" suggested Viper.

"I've seen you skateboarding to that," said Flipper.

"Show of hands?" asked Senza.

All hands rose.

"Well, we could do that," she said. "Or maybe we do the guitar solo for Free Bird."

"Yeah, I like that," said Flipper.

"That's like a 10-minute song," said Brick.

"14 minutes for the live version," noted Flipper. "But if we're just doing the guitar solo part, well, it's more like 5."

"I will find a backing track," said Senza, going over to an amp and receiver set up to the side of the room. "Okay now, I have a backing track set that will automatically speed up if you go fast and slow down if you go slow. Let's start it off. Quake. Start Free Bird about 4 minutes in."

He nodded.

She held up the iPad so everyone could see it. "Whenever you're ready," she said, shushing everyone.

Quake started playing the familiar solo. Not as dexterous a guitarist as the others, he still managed to do well. He ended by rapping his own lyrics.

"This bird that's free is rather feathery but it's song is lacking in brevity. My darn fingers once had dexterity but now they should be taken into custody. The bird's so high you need astronomy to find it flying in another galaxy. But a recipe for joie de vie is eluding me. Don't give me the third degree, I feel as useless as Tweedledum and Tweededee."

"89%," said Senza, announcing his score. "And you did the whole piece in 6 minutes."

Fireball and Flipper came on one after the next and performed identically, each receiving a 92%. It rattled Flipper as he recounted how he played, losing to Fireball by a note or two. As for speed, amazingly enough, they both came in at 5 minutes 40 seconds.

Viper sneered at the iPad, intimidated by its note-counting. She started playing, making an early error that threw her off. She got near the end when again she got lost in the song. The iPad showed her at 87% with a speed of 5 minutes and 30 seconds. She refrained from kicking the damn thing.

Having taken a cue from the previous performers, Brick took a Zen approach, closed his eyes and visualized the whole song. He started playing with incredible accuracy, scoring 99% through the first half of the song. But in trying to play faster to elevate his speed score, he started making errors, necessitating him to slow down. He finished at 5 minutes and 28 seconds with an accuracy of 89%.

Now it was Senza's turn. She looked ready to rock the house. She peered around the room, waiting for complete silence. Brick commanded the receiver and waited for her signal to start the backing track. She gave a quick nod and the music began. The iPad registered 100% for the first three minutes. Somehow, barely noticeable she missed a note and her accuracy went to 98%. But she kept a really fast speed, fastest so far, and finished with a 98% accuracy and a speed of 4 minutes 42 seconds.

"That was rad!" Viper exclaimed. Several others tossed out compliments.

Last up was Cameron, aware of what he needed to win the contest. Senza waited for his signal to begin. He closed his eyes, gave a subtle nod and began. He tore through the song with a 100% accuracy rate, playing so fast everyone wondered if he could finish with a perfect score. As he neared the last minute of the song, his face blanched as he had a sudden change of mind. He didn't want to beat Senza. He honestly didn't care about the contest at all. So, he suddenly stopped playing.

"Why'd you do that?!" shouted Viper. "You were going to beat everyone."

He meekly replied, "I forgot the ending."

"Oh man," said Flipper. "Dude, you were going to bring that in under four minutes, easy, with a 100% accuracy."

He just shrugged his shoulders.

"So, it looks like you're the winner Senza," said Flipper.

Senza knew she had played well but didn't feel she deserved to win. She clearly saw Cameron's performance as superior to hers.

Viper angled her way over to Cameron and quietly said, so only he could hear, "I know what you did. But in my book, you won. You proved you belong here."

"Turn off the amps and take your stuff with you," said Senza. "This is a wrap."

CHAPTER 14 YOU'VE BEEN HIRED

At Walter's Watering Hole, the low-talking owner Walter busied himself scheming new ways to expand his business.

Having dropped the idea of adding a shooting range, Walter contemplated an ice skating rink before realizing that it, too, would pose problems when combined with a bar. Drunken people gliding over a rock-hard skating surface was a recipe for disaster. He contemplated an archery range but, though not as lethal as guns, it, too, was dangerous.

Pluto overheard them discussing ideas when he offered one himself. "What about bowling or bocce?"

"Bowling's a good idea," said Shep. "I'm surprised we hadn't thought of that. And what's this other one, batchy, all about?"

"Bocce. It's Italian," said Pluto. "You roll a small hard ball and try to get it close to another small ball. You take turns. You can knock the other guy's ball away. I played it once and it was harder than it seems."

"You're an ideas person," said Shep. "Good to have one of those around here. I hope you stay a bit."

Pluto actually missed life at Z3's place as Maine felt remote. "Well, I'm waiting to hear about that musical job I applied for," he said. "If that doesn't work out, I'm not sure what I'll do. But I do appreciate your kindness."

Rubbing his hands together, Pluto took this opportunity to learn more about Walter. "How do you know the folks at the compound?" he asked.

Walter looked up from the notes he was taking on a pad and said "A bunch of their employees have frequented my place even though it's not that close. They knew I was a conduit for entertainment."

"I see," said Pluto.

"And regarding you, your boss, who I've known many years, asked if I'd make an intro for you at the compound," said Walter.

Pluto nodded.

"You ever been there?" he asked.

Walter shook his head.

Pluto felt more comfortable, believing that Walter didn't know what was going on at the compound.

Walter handed Pluto several sheets of sandpaper. "Here's that sandpaper you wanted," said Walter, lips still not moving much. "Hope it's not to wipe your ass."

Walter chuckled at his own humor.

"It's for my guitar," said Pluto, lifting up the blue Stratocaster.

"Looks in good shape to me," said Walter.

"I want to get a better sound," said Pluto. "Watch."

Pluto placed the guitar on a side table and started sanding away at the blue lacquered finish until he exposed a patch of wood the size of a fist.

"You may know how to play that thing real good but you sure aint good at polishing it," said Shep.

"It's not about the sight," said Pluto. "It's about the sound. I've been wanting to do this for a while. "

"Ruin your guitar?" said Walter.

"No. Giving it a heavy relic," said Pluto. "I sanded down the neck for a better tone and now by exposing the wood I not only get a better tone but more resonance."

"Let me ask you this," said Walter. "Why don't they just make 'em that way from the start if it's so much better?"

"Good point, Walter," noted Shep.

Pluto tried to come up with an analogy. "Sometimes things get better as they get older and broken into," said Pluto. "Like a car. It may be a bit tight when you first get it but after some time it gets real smooth and comfortable in its handling. Or a pair of jeans. New ones look uncool. Everyone loves older jeans even if they have tears in them. In fact, some companies have gone out of their way to make them look old from the start."

"I know about those," said Shep. "Stone-washed."

"Or washed stoned," added Walter. "I mean, we are talking rock n roll here."

Pluto looked down at the floor where a fine sawdust had piled up.

"I'm happy to get a broom and clean this up," he said.

"No need, son," said Walter. "It's just a bar. Not some kind of hoity toity place."

Pluto looped the guitar strap over his shoulder. "Gents, I 'm going to go upstairs, play a bit, then take a nap. If you need any help, let me know." He wanted to leave the bar area as the dim lighting there was starting to bother his eyes.

When Pluto got to his room, he started playing his Strat. He expected to hear a difference and he did, a finer and clearer sound than before. He played several songs and found it worked better on each and every one. He lay on his bed, strumming away, staring up at the ceiling which needed a paint job.

He thought he heard a knock at the door but kept playing. He heard it again and jumped off the bed.

"Yeah?" he asked.

"It's me. Shep."

"Am I too loud?" said Pluto talking through the door.

"Not at all," he said. "We just got a call from the folks you met the other day. The ones you went to visit. They liked you very much and want to hire you."

"Really?"

"Yep.'

Pluto opened the door and Shep took two steps in. He cleared the ceiling by a few inches. It was quite low like in those historic homes.

"That's good news, I guess," said Pluto."

"They're also real interested in having your young bandmates join you," said Shep. "They'd love it if you could get them up here real soon."

"You mean in a day or two or three?"

"Yep."

"I'll do my best."

"And one other thing," said Shep. "They'd really like you there starting tomorrow."

"Tomorrow?"

"Seems they want you pretty bad."

Shep reached up his arms to yawn but the ceiling prevented him from being successful.

"Nice to be wanted," said Pluto, then, muttering to himself he added "Except I don't really know who it is that wants me."

"Nice having you here," said Shep. "If this whole thing doesn't work out some, you're welcome back here."

Shep went downstairs.

Pluto felt a sudden urgency. He knew what needed to be done.

■■

Cameron and the others were getting ready to leave the Big Room and head off to their bedrooms for some sleep.

Senza appeared in the doorway, her arms stretching across, blocking anyone who tried to leave. "Z3 would like to talk to all of us in his room now," she said.

Baffled by the sudden request, Flipper, Brick, Fireball, Quake, Viper and Cameron glanced at one another, wondering what was going on. They dutifully followed Senza to the third floor.

Two security guards stood in an anteroom, preventing anyone from going further into Z3's main quarters. The room had huge red satin pillows situated along the walls, offering the only seating. They all found a pillow and sat.

Z3 emerged, looking calm and stoic. He, too, sat on a red pillow, crossing his legs in the lotus position.

"Thank you all for coming on such short notice," he said, scratching his head.

He paused, a long silence, effectively holding everyone's attention as they anticipated what he might say.

"Let me begin at the end. Then, I can end at the beginning."

Viper let slip a slight giggle prompting a glare from Senza who attempted to quiet any future giggles. This gathering was all business. They all were very respectful of Z3 and waited a beat after he spoke before asking any questions or making any comments.

"So," said Z3. "Tonight, I heard from one of you."

They wondered who he was referring to.

After another lengthy pause he said "Pluto."

"You heard from Pluto?" remarked Quake with surprise. "That's a relief."

Z3 gave a soft nod.

"I could feel the bad moon rising," said Brick.

"What does that mean?" asked Fireball.

"Trouble's on the way," said Brick. "Is Pluto alright?"

"He's perfectly fine and has been fine since he left here," said Z3. "I have remained in contact, sporadically."

"Why'd he just up and disappear so fast?" asked Fireball. "Not even a simple goodbye."

"He wanted to be discreet," he said. "In fact, he needed to be discreet. It was vital that no one knew where he went."

"Why?" asked Flipper.

"I asked him to leave quietly."

Z3 scanned the room, looking at each one of them.

"None of you know much about me," said Z3. "Senza knows the most. But not even she knows everything."

Senza wondered what she didn't know.

As though pre-planned, one of the guards stepped to the center of the room where some incense had been placed. He took out a lighter and lit it. Soon, the whole room had a calming lemongrass aroma. Cameron had never been to church before but this gathering felt very religious to him. Instead of a rabbi, priest or minister presiding, they had Z3 who commanded just as much authority.

Z3 continued "Life should have purpose. Meaning. A desire to make it better for you and for others. Do any of you know what your purpose is?"

No one responded.

"I have a strong purpose, one I hope you'll embrace," he said. "I saw something very special in each of you which is why you're here to help."

As he paused, Senza spoke. " Z3 took me in a long time ago for which I'm eternally grateful. He has asked very little in return until now. I completely stand behind him as he tries to make the world a better place."

"Sadly, there is evil in the world," said Z3. "And it can't always be eradicated through traditional outlets such as law enforcement and the legal system."

Intrigued, Flipper asked "Are you talking about one or many bad people?"

"One very bad person surrounded by other bad ones," he replied.

Z3 pressed his palms together in prayer then brought them up to his mouth. "This person has taken in runaway kids just as I have. The difference is he abuses them," he replied solemnly. "And his vast wealth has allowed him to get away with it."

"How do you know this?" asked Quake.

"I have known this man all my life," said Z3.

"You actually know him?" asked Viper with surprise.

"All too well," said Z3, and after a lengthy pause added "He's my brother. My half-brother."

There was complete silence.

"What my brother has done is to build a compound and somehow qualify it as a new religion so he pays no taxes. Many con men have done this over the years. He manages to get like-minded people to follow him and they create their own rules. Drugs flow freely. No one can leave on their own volition. It's all sick and demented."

"What is the religion called?" asked Fireball.

Z3 replied "Shock. My brother took the last name of Shock. Strong and memorable."

Shock?! What a downright eerie name, thought Cameron. He couldn't help but wonder what this evil man looked like. Did he look peaceful and normal like Z3? Or was he some green-skinned monster who lurked about, drooling and cackling? Cameron caught himself as he didn't mean to insult those with green skin like his former frog Robert.

"And law enforcement's done nothing? " asked Fireball who loved asking questions, seeing herself as a talk show host someday.

"Growing impatient, many years ago I went after him myself," said Z3.

"You?" asked Quake.

"I hired some former military folks," said Z3. "We went up there with a lot of weaponry and too small a plan. We failed. It was a big setback. Fortunately, I had a very good lawyer who protected me from a prison sentence. But my determination to pursue my brother has never been greater. Unfortunately, he has become more powerful than before which makes this very difficult."

"So how do you plan to go after him with us?" persisted Quake.

Z3 smiled. "My brother has a strange attraction to young people like you. That's your ticket to getting into his compound. Pluto got in because he pretended to be one of them. And you'll avoid the mistake we made ten years ago. Instead of coming in with guns, you'll be coming in with a different kind of weapon, your guitars. As you've seen, these guitars harness immense power and you all have learned to use them in such different and effective ways. And if the police appear at his compound, you can't be charged with carrying a weapon. You can't even be charged with trespassing as you were invited there."

"How many people are in this compound?" asked Flipper.

"I've heard reports there's anywhere between 30-40 people who work for him and another 30-40 children of varying ages."

"And how do we get invited there?" asked Viper.

"Pluto," he said.

Brick looked confused. "What do you mean, Pluto?"

"Over the past few days Pluto has managed to insinuate himself into the compound. He's supposed to go there today to stay and has been asked to bring a band —and that band is you."

"But we're not really a band," observed Fireball.

"Yeah," said Viper. "We can all play really well but we haven't played together. Not as a band."

"I have great faith you can learn fast," said Z3, squinting with a smile. "You're all very special."

"But we're all guitarists," said Viper.

"Yeah, we don't have a drummer or vocalist," added Fireball, slipping her fingers through her purple hair.

The incense started to bother Cameron. He glanced around and saw that no one else was bothered by it. And because Z3 had arranged for it, he didn't want to say a word. His breaths became shorter and shorter. His asthma was creeping back. He tried not to panic, sitting still and listening.

"Isn't that a bit weird," agreed Flipper. "A band with nothing but guitarists?"

"There are some groups with nothing but guitars," noted Senza. "Crosby Stills and Nash."

"They had Dallas Taylor as a drummer," noted Flipper.

"Peter, Paul and Mary," said Senza.

"Who the hell are they?" snapped Viper.

"Way before your time," said Senza. "And way before my time."

"Maybe one of you becomes the drummer," suggested Z3. "Several of you play drums, keyboards and sing. Or just bring along a drum machine. That might work best. We have some here."

"When is this all happening?" asked Flipper.

"Soon," said Z3. "I've constructed a model of the compound so you'll have a rough idea where everything is. You'll each have a different role. The main goal will be to capture or incapacitate as many of these people as possible and release those in captivity."

"Is everyone in?" asked Senza, glancing around the room.

Everyone raised their hands except Cameron who remained remarkably still and quiet.

"C Sharp?" asked Viper. "You in?"

Cameron felt an impending asthma attack. His hands fumbled in his pockets in desperate search for his inhaler. He took three deep breaths from it and felt instant relief.

"You okay?" asked Senza.

As his breathing stabilized, he raised his hand.

"We're all in," said Flipper. "Can you tell us where this place is located?"

"In Maine," said Z3. "That's where he's always lived."

"When the police arrested you, didn't they notice those held against their will"

Z3 nodded and said "The only ones around were too frightened to say anything. Understandably, the children there have been either brainwashed or so intimidated that they would never testify against him. And without their help, it's very difficult to build a case against my brother. My brother needs to be removed. Ideally, I'd love it if you captured him and brought him back here. At the end of the day, those kids need to be separated from him permanently."

"Aren't you coming with us?" asked Viper.

"In spirit," he said. "As much as I'd like to, if I showed up, he'd have me arrested on the spot."

Senza herded the group from Z3's chamber. As she started to leave, she turned and said "I'm looking forward to this."

Z3 hesitated and said "You need to stay behind."

She glared back at him. "What? Why?"

"You're older than what they want," he said.

"Then let them kick me out," she replied, defiantly. "But I'm going."

"To be discussed," he said.

"There's nothing to discuss. You must let me go," she insisted as she stomped angrily out of the room.

CHAPTER 15 MOVING DAY

Walter waited outside with Pluto for his departure to the compound.

Two men drove up in a van to get him. While Pluto's request not to be blindfolded was honored, the van that picked him up was designed so passengers in the back couldn't see out. All its windows were dark and opaque except, of course, the front windshield. But the back was partitioned off from the front by the same plexiglass barrier used in taxis to separate the driver from potentially dangerous passengers. This plexiglass, though, was not transparent but spray painted black.

When they arrived at the compound, Pluto went through a security check where one guard dressed in camouflaged fatigues frisked him, then checked his backpack and guitar. Finding nothing suspicious, he waved him by.

Escorted by another guard, Pluto came to a metal door. The guard there waved his i.d. by a scanner on the wall and the door slid open like the ones in a Star Wars movie.

Entering the main compound, Pluto heard the door close behind him and a feeling of claustrophobia set in. There was no easy escape.

A man named Joffrey, fortyish, with curly reddish brown hair led him down a long corridor which turned right and then right again. They scaled a stairway to a bedroom on the second floor, its décor stark white. It had a single bed, neatly made, with a lamp, a small desk and its own adjoining bathroom. Pluto pulled the shades up by the lone window only to reveal it was boarded up from outside, offering no view, just a feeling of imprisonment.

"Come with me," the guard said, leading him down two levels to a large restaurant-style kitchen, with multiple stoves, ovens and refrigerators. Three chefs were already cooking that day's meal. The aroma betrayed a rich spicy pasta sauce.

"How many do they cook for?" asked Pluto.

"A lot," said Joffrey.

"What's a lot?"

Joffrey counted in his head before replying "70, give or take."

"That's impressive."

"Follow me," said Joffrey.

He led Pluto down another long corridor which connected to a large gym. Inside were rows of fitness cycles, elliptical trainers, running machines, Stairmasters and weights of all shapes and sizes. There was a juice bar with a row of stools and stacks of towels.

"This is as good a gym as you'll find anywhere," said Joffrey. "All state of the art."

They walked past a room with two large locks on it. "What's in there?" asked Pluto.

"I wouldn't get too nosey if I were you," he replied. "Let's just say this room offers security."

Pluto quickly reasoned the room might be full of weapons. Why else would it need two locks?

"What's down that hallway?" he asked, pointing to a corridor they passed.

"That's where many of the ones you're going to entertain reside," said Joffrey. "You and your band are going to be performing, aren't you?"

"Yes," said Pluto, reminding himself why he was really there.

"There's a dormitory down there where the kids live," he said.

"Cool," said Pluto. "How many are there?"

Joffrey started to get suspicious of all the questions. "You ask a lot of questions," he replied.

"Would you rather I act completely bored and not ask anything?"

"Touché," said Joffrey.

Although Pluto wanted to ask more questions about the kids, he refrained from saying another word.

"Let me show you where you'll be performing," he said, approaching another heavy metal door. He swiped his i.d. card and it slid open effortlessly. They entered a room with a stage in the front and fixed seating for 100 people.

This was a state of the art theater. As you entered, you could feel in your ears how soundproof it was. And all along the walls were speakers, set up to provide surround sound.

"This is where you'll do the show," he said.

"Impressive. Do you use this theater often?"

He shakes his head.

"What a shame."

"Mr. Shock is not comfortable having outsiders here," he said. "This is a big honor for you to use it. And I've heard it may be a long-term thing. Let me show you the game room."

A long term thing? thought Pluto. Interesting. That's the first time he heard that. They probably had no intention of letting them go.

They entered the game room, which was lined with a series of video games, pinball machines, air hockey, hand shuffleboard and ping pong as well as a billiards table in the middle.

"I may never want to leave here," said Pluto, impressed.

"Let me take you back to your room," said Joffrey.

"Thanks. I'd never find it otherwise," replied Pluto.

"The fact is you can't go on your own."

Pluto nodded.

"You can catch some rest before dinner," he said.

Their footsteps reverberated down the long corridor.

■■

That morning none of Z3's recruits ate a full breakfast. They were too eager to discuss their upcoming mission.

They met in the communications room in the mansion's basement where Z3 awaited them. Cameron had only been down there once before when Z3 had shown it to him. Of course, at the time, Cameron thought Z3 was a cleaning man.

Several of Z3's guards watched the TV monitors which captured images both inside and outside the mansion.

On a long oak table sat a re-creation of the compound done to 1/50 scale. The model depicted the exterior but the roof was removable to see inside. Because there were so many different levels, Z3 had designed illustrations depicting the interior of each floor. These drawings were tacked to the side wall and labeled accordingly, showing all five levels -- three above ground and two below.

"How do you know what the inside looks like?" asked Viper.

"Architectural Digest?" said Flipper facetiously.

"I was there once," said Z3. "Ten years ago. I'm sure things have changed. But this is as close a replica as we were able to put together. When you get there, you will have to determine what is accurate and what isn't."

Viper walked around the table, soaking it all in.

"And what's that?" she asked, pointing to a wide blue line to the back of the compound.

"That's a river," said Z3. "It runs along one side."

"Take seats," said Senza as they pulled up chairs around the table.

Z3 waited for everyone to stop moving. Cameron felt like he was sitting in the war room of some major nation, awaiting instructions.

"My preference, to do what Sun Tzu would do -- win without fighting," he said. "But in this case, that is not possible. So, what we are doing is attacking without warning. You will integrate yourselves into the compound posed as a rock band. What we have working for us is the element of surprise. We have two primary goals. The first, to secure all the children living there and herd them into a safe area until they can be rescued. The second, to disarm or destroy those captors."

He pointed to the theater in the model. "This is where you'll be performing," he said. "The theater is accessible by four different doorways. Two at the top and two down below by the stage. We will go through several possible scenarios. But as you may know, with any plan, it generally all gets thrown out the window. You will need to ad lib."

Senza stood up from her chair. "Let's review how you can be most effective. Flipper. You can render a person defenseless by creating ear-piercing sounds. This disarms people. How many and for how long, well, that is uncertain."

Walking over to Brick, she said "Brick, you are the master of the force field. That will be invaluable in protecting hostages once we get them to a secure area."

She looked over at Quake and Viper. "Quake, you got that powerful rumble that can knock things over and break down a door or maybe even a wall. And Viper has that amazing serpentine shot that she can direct around objects."

Viper and Quake nodded.

"And let's not forget Pluto," said Senza. "He's got many skills, including great accuracy at a far distance. Who am I forgetting?

"C Sharp," said Viper.

Cameron felt left out. But perhaps that was for the best. Everyone here was older and more experienced. And the last thing he wanted to do was hold them back.

"I'm sorry," said Senza. "If his asthma holds off, he can help. And I'll be there as well."

"We need to discuss that," said Z3. "They don't want anyone older than Pluto who's 20. You're almost 27."

"But I --" she said, firmly.

"We'll talk later," said Z3. "I've given this mission the code name Chixalub."

"Chick-a who?" asked Viper.

"I happen to know this," said Quake. "Chixalub was some big ass crater caused by an asteroid several miles long. It crashed into the earth and caused a hole more than 100 miles wide."

"When was this?" asked Viper.

"If it was last week, I didn't hear about it," said Flipper.

"This happened like 65 million years ago," said Quake.

"Before my time," said Flipper.

"This dang asteroid wiped out all the dinosaurs that had been roaming the planet for millions of years," said Quake.

"How does one asteroid do all that?" asked Viper.

Quake smiled. "When it hit the earth, its power was the same as a billion atom bombs."

"Crap," said Brick.

"Yeah. Dinosaur crap. And lots of it," said Quake.

Senza piped in. "Our mission is aptly named. We want to wipe out these dinosaurs."

"Chixalub is the code word to let you know when to begin the attack," said Z3.

"Who's going to give it?" asked Brick.

"I hope they can pronounce it," added Flipper.

"Pluto for one," said Senza. "He'll be most familiar with the compound and its inhabitants. But you all could use it, too."

"I am going to suggest a few different strategies," said Z3. "You may end up using some of them or none of them. There is the pincer maneuver whereby you allow your opponents' forces to come straight at you while you surround their flanks and attack from the sides. Or one where you have minimal people up front while you prepare to attack strongly from the rear. we don't want to overextend ourselves which is why we'll be at full force when you're all in the theater together."

Scratching his head, Brick asked "The one thing I don't see is how we're going to get all of them in the theater. I can't imagine the guards are going to be leaving their posts."

Z3 nodded. "Pluto is figuring that out."

For the next two hours, they memorized the design of the compound, closing their eyes and reciting where each room was. They quizzed one another until each and every one answered the questions correctly.

"I have a question," said Brick.

"Of course, you do," said Flipper.

"What if they turn off all the lights and use night vision goggles?"

"I like the way you think," noted Z3. "Remember, the guitars you all have can produce immense amounts of light. You will never be in the dark for long."

They stood up to leave, finally understanding their role and why Z3 had brought them all together.

CHAPTER 16 THE MAINE THING

For Pluto, it was difficult to tell when morning had arrived. With no window allowing sun into his bedroom, he lay on his bed in his darkened room longer than normal. It was only because he wore a watch and saw how late it actually was--9:15am--that he leapt out of bed and got dressed.

There was a knock on the door. He opened it and there was Joffrey.

"I guess you're assigned to me," said Pluto.

"Lucky me. Breakfast is being served."

Pluto knew roughly where the dining area was but he still was required to have Joffrey as an escort. Inside the spacious eating area were a number of other late-risers. There was a clear separation of those who worked at the compound – dressed in regular attire be it jeans and plaid shirts – and those younger ones who wore clothes the same color -- pants and shirts in a pastel shade, either green or blue or yellow or peach.

"What's with the colored outfits?" he asked Joffrey.

"Easiest way to keep track of the occupants and the workers," he replied.

Confused, Pluto asked "But why? They look like they're dressed in prison garb for an Easter celebration."

"You know what's going on here, don't you?" asked Joffrey, puzzled that Pluto would ask such a question.

Bluffing somewhat, Pluto replied "Of course".

"It's how we do things here," he replied. "Go get your food and we can catch up afterwards."

Pluto took a tray and went through the cafeteria selecting a breakfast of orange juice, fried eggs and toast with jam. He went to find a table. He didn't know anyone there so he planned on sitting alone. But then he noticed her, the woman he saw when he first came to the compound. The one who served him tea and crumpets. Sasha was her name. She was seated alone and appeared to be done with her meal.

"Hi," said Pluto. "Remember me?"

She glanced up but didn't utter a word.

"Mind if I sit here?" he asked.

She didn't respond. He hesitated and then, imitating a girlish voice, said "I'd be mighty honored to have your company." He replied to himself "Well thank you much, ma'am. It's been a mighty hard day and I just need to get me some grub."

Pluto sat down and started eating. She started to rise from her seat when he loosely grabbed her arm and urged her to stay. At first, she acted uneasy, startled to be touched.

"You really don't want me to eat alone, do you?" he asked.

Hesitating for a long moment, she sat back down, her clenched lips displaying her discomfort.

"Listen, I'm not here to hurt you," he replied.

Her head tilted back and she stared into his eyes for the first time. He had a kindness in the way he looked at her, something she obviously wasn't used to and different than those she'd been around. She felt his spirit, loving and sincere.

"Your name's Sasha," he said.

She nodded.

"You're hard to forget," he replied, looking into her amazing blue eyes. "I'm Pluto."

He could see by her response that she didn't believe him.

"Seriously, that's the name I've gone by for the past ten years," he said. "Named after the distant planet not the dog. Some say Pluto's not a planet at all. Just a ball of flying ice hurtling through outer space. That would be me. You don't talk much. Not a bad habit. I guess you avoid saying foolish things that way."

She remained silent.

"Anything you want to ask me?" he said, then imitating a girlish voice, added "Nothing really, sweet sir."

He continued a mock conversation, switching from the girly voice to his own.

"You are so annoying," said Pluto in his own voice.

"Aren't I now," came Pluto's girly reply.

"Well, I guess I'll just eat alone," said Pluto. He started to work on his egg, expecting her to get up and leave. But she remained seated, oddly intrigued.

"Who are you?" she asked, catching him by surprise.

"Oh, my!" he exclaimed. "You can speak. Well, I'm, um, a musician."

"What brings you here?"

"To perform for everyone," he said. "I have a band that will join me soon."

"Do you know anyone here?" she asked.

"No one, really," he said.

"Then how did you come to this place?"

"I was approached about a job opportunity," he said. "Playing music. How long have you been here?"

She took a moment to think then replied softly in a pained voice, "Four years."

"Do you like it here?" he asked.

Her lack of a response said it all.

"And where did you come from?"

Sasha glanced around the room to see if anyone was watching their conversation. Feeling comfortable, she replied "I came here after being in a series of foster homes and orphanages. Are you in their club?"

"Club?" asked Pluto.

She stared at him sternly, not believing he didn't know of the club.

"I honestly don't know what you're talking about," he replied.

"Really?"

"Yes really. Something tells me you don't care for me."

Sasha peered down at the floor, somewhat ashamed of her behavior. It was rare that she encountered someone nice like this. Looking back up, she said, "Not true."

"Maybe we can start this relationship anew," he replied, stretching out his hand. "Hi, I'm Pluto."

She gave his hand a shake and said "And I'm Sasha."

"Pleased to make your acquaintance," he said.

At that moment two dozen kids entered the cafeteria, all wearing pastel-colored clothes that resembled prison attire. Their ages were as young as 8 to upwards of 16 or so. Pluto had never seen such a sad group in all of his life. They came in robot-like, taking trays of food and then sitting quietly at tables.

"We should go now," she said.

Pluto bussed his tray and left the cafeteria. Waiting outside was Joffrey ready to escort him.

"Where do I go?" asked Pluto.

"I'm going to have you meet him," said Joffrey.

"Him?"

"Yes. Him."

■■

"Chixalub. Tomorrow," said Viper, standing by the lake on Z3's property and holding a guitar skyward like a warrior.

A breeze blew across the lake, sending a wave of ripples and creating a small whirlpool of water at one end. Several ducks landed on the other side, smoothly floating along in a mini armada. And the staccato ribbit of frogs got Cameron's attention and made him want to go down there and search for one of Robert's relatives.

Brick added "At least I now understand why we were all brought to this place."

Viper and Brick were soon joined by Cameron, Flipper, Quake and Fireball who all came with guitars.

Only Pluto and Senza were missing. They all now knew where Pluto was. But Senza's absence felt strange.

"Where is Senza?" asked Viper.

Flipper shrugged his shoulders.

"Should we wait?" asked Viper.

Cameron cleared his throat and said "She's in her room with the door locked. I knocked but she told me to go away."

"Is she really not part of this mission now?" asked Brick.

Nobody quite knew.

The afternoon sun reflected off the lake, causing several of them to shield their eyes from the brightness.

"So, how are we getting there?" asked Quake.

"And where exactly is there?" added Viper

Fireball said "A van."

"And who's driving?" asked Quake. "Senza?"

Fireball shook her head. "I think Z3 has that guy Harvey taking us."

"Whoa!" said Quake.

"Last chance for some practice with these guitars, " said Brick.

"And act like the ducks are hostages that need to be protected," said Viper. "Do not injure them."

They took their wireless guitars, put on their headsets and started practicing. Cameron got to go first. He had problems getting the suction cups to stick to his head. Fireball helped by wetting them first. He saw her tongue licking at them and hoped his head didn't short circuit. He aimed at the dummies and started to play. But he couldn't produce a powerful surge.

"Let me try," said Viper, lifting her guitar and aiming. She spun two of the dummies around and then aimed for a pine branch and snapped it in two.

Fireball, Quake, Brick and Flipper all took turns, exhibiting much improved skills and dexterity. They left just two dummies standing.

"C Sharp, try again," said Viper. "Use a different headset."

Cameron borrowed Viper's headset, turned on his orange guitar and started to play. He focused hard and soon the surge came. He nailed both dummies, redeeming himself for the time being.

"Must have been the headset," he said.

The ducks remained in the pond, not bothered at all.

■■■

Pluto sat in his stark room, waiting for his meeting with the man named Shock.

Two guards led him to a room one level below. Why did they need two guards, he wondered? One would suffice as they were very strong and armed.

"Take a seat," said a guard, pointing to a lone metal chair. Pluto obeyed, nervously rubbing his hands together and noticing two cameras mounted in corners of the windowless room. The second guard left the room. The heavy metal door slammed shut. The remaining guard, cold and unfriendly, remained in the room.

Pluto caught his first glimpse of Shock as he emerged from a secondary room. Clad in a black kimono with red dragons on it, he was average height with black hair tied in a ponytail. Wrapped around his face Bono-style was a pair of green-tinted eyeglasses.

"Welcome," said Shock.

Pluto gave a polite nod.

"We know all about you and your plans," he said.

What?! Pluto stopped breathing as panic set in. How could he know everything? The plans were secret. He tried his best to remain calm.

"Eisenhower said 'When you make a plan, be prepared to throw it out the window," said Pluto.

Shock smiled. "A student of history," he said. "I like that."

"If you know all about me," said Pluto "Then tell me how I got the name Pluto?"

Like a caged tiger, Shock walked across the room, stopped, turned, then walked back, all the while studying Pluto.

"I don't know," said Shock. "What I know is that you're a stellar musician. And you have some special musicians who will be joining you here to perform for everyone."

Pluto nodded.

"Can you tell me anything about these other musicians?" he asked.

"I thought you knew everything," said Pluto, feeling more confident that his cover wasn't blown.

"I know what I've been told," he said. "But I wanted to hear from you."

Pluto noticed the walls of the room had a lot of dings in them.

"Fair enough," said Pluto. "I happened to have gotten to know some kids, mostly foster kids, who play really well."

"How old are they?"

"Well, as young as 10 and upwards of 17."

"And where do they live?"

"Some were living on the street and some were runaways from bad foster homes," said Pluto. "They'll like it here."

Shock's voice modulated from low to high in a very disconcerting manner. It was the voice of a mad man.

"How are they getting here?"

"I got a friend to rent a small bus and drive them up," he said. "Because of your secrecy, I may need to have them dropped in a nearby town and picked up there."

Shock replied, "Hmmmmm. Okay. And is the friend hanging around?"

"Only if I ask him to," said Pluto.

"No need."

Shock shuffled across the room to a mini kitchen and poured himself a glass of a thick green liquid.

"Wheatgrass," he pointed out. "Helps with longevity. When might your friends come here?"

"As early as today," said Pluto.

"So, they could perform tomorrow then?"

"I don't see why not."

Shock swigged down the juice, let out a satisfied sound and threw the glass against the wall. It shattered into pieces, shards flying everywhere.

"Do you have any questions for me?"

Scratching his head, Pluto remained calm. He felt Shock was trying to rattle him. He asked, "Do you own this whole house?"

Shock nodded. "I call it a retreat. A religious retreat."

"And what do you do for a living to have such an impressive place?"

"I had a series of very successful startup companies in biotechnology."

"And you've been living here for a while?"

"Yes. Oh. How rude of me. Would you like some wheatgrass?"

Pluto vigorously shook his head. "It's not my kind of thing."

"Well, I'm glad you're here. We can always use entertainment. And I hope you stay as long as you like."

Shock gestured to the guard that the meeting was over. Pluto stood up and reached to shake hands.

"I never shake hands. Vile custom. A simple nod will do," he said, bowing his head, respectfully.

Pluto returned the gesture.

■■

A small purple bus with a capacity of 12 sat in the driveway, its motor purring. Everyone except Senza had gathered near it, loading their guitars and backpacks. Z3 came down to see them off.

"I have arranged for one of my people to drive you," he said. "This is Harvey. He has worked for me for 10 years. He knows the way and will be dropping you off."

Harvey was a nondescript man in his fifties with a tinge of gray hair and a French beret angled on his head.

"And Harvey's bringing us back?" asked Flipper.

"Let's hope so," said Z3. "Good luck to you all."

All their luggage fit in the rear storage area as well as the overhead bins.

They boarded and gave a final wave as the bus headed out. There was a center aisle between the plush bucket seats so one could move around during the ride.

On the long drive, Cameron found it greatly puzzling that Senza wasn't along for the trip. More than anyone else, she was their leader. He couldn't think of a single good reason for her absence but assumed it was a decision she made with Z3.

The bus stopped for gas midway and they were all able to take a bathroom break and get some snacks. Harvey picked up the tab.

For Cameron the seven-hour trip didn't feel long as his mind wandered and wandered. He started off thinking about cell phones and all the invisible radio waves traveling through the air. That couldn't be healthy. But it also wasn't healthy to not have a cell phone like every kid at middle school. Of course, at the mansion, being the oldest, only Senza and Pluto had them. But this is the 21st Century. Give a kid a break, he thought.

The gently jiggling of the ride pushed him into a dream-like state. How did he get here, he wondered. Going to the mansion was such a radical change in his life. He felt like he was growing up too fast. Was this just the beginning? Or was his whole life winding down very soon? A short life and a forgotten one at that. But he did hold some fond memories? His frog Robert. The variety show. Meeting Bono, The Edge and Jack White. Playing these amazing state-of-the-art guitars. Senza and all the others, except maybe Pluto. On the downside he still recalled his many confrontations with bullies. Why did he have to be a constant target of their wrath? Why couldn't everyone be nice and just get along? Maybe if he scowled more, they would leave him alone? Or maybe he needed to build more muscles and get a skull tattoo. That would keep them back. The problem was he tried desperately to build muscles but all his exercising produced--nothing. He was just as scrawny as ever. And as for a skull tattoo or even one of a snake, well, for some reason 10 year olds can't get them. Not even if they wanted Sponge Bob. Apparently, it's the law.

He wondered how tall he might be. Height could help his cause. Get him some level of respect. Certainly, he wasn't done growing. Or was he? With his luck, maybe this was it.

And being burdened with asthma was annoying. What else was he allergic to, he wondered. There must be plenty of things. And one of them might just kill him. The ultimate bully could be something like asparagus.

Is there another planet out there where he would fit in better, he thought? There had to be. And maybe it had a lot of other different unusual musical instruments beyond woodwinds, strings, brass and percussion. The thought of new weird Dr Seuss like instruments made him giggle as did his ticklishness. He let out a loud "eeeeeeeh" and then opened his eyes. Seated next to him on the bus was Viper who was tickling his ribs.

"Welcome back to earth," she said.

"Are we almost there?" he asked.

"Almost."

Prior to leaving, Quake had a briefing with Senza which he shared on the ride. "Three of you will not perform."

Flipped asked "What's that mean?"

"Just what I said. Those three will have another duty to perform. Freeing other hostages."

"And how do we know who the hostages are?" asked Viper.

"Based on info from Pluto, the hostages are easy to spot. They are wearing pastel colored clothing. Like pajamas. And they're all basically kids. Now part of the task will also involve neutralizing the guards."

"Are there a lot of them?" asked Fireball.

"Couple of dozen," said Quake. "There's a command center they use that will be critical to take over. It's near the rear entrance and has a lot of video monitors. "

Throughout the ride, some stretched, others napped and a few peered mindlessly out the window. There was a stretch of complete quiet before Flipper broke the silence.

"Who's performing?" asked Flipper, quite curious.

"The performers are Pluto, Viper and Brick," said Quake. "Flipper, you and Fireball will stay with me in getting to the hostages."

"What about C?" asked Viper

"Oh yeah. Sorry, Sharp. Forgot about you," said Quake. "You'll, um, well, you'll perform."

Feigning a smile, Cameron once again felt like an afterthought.

When they arrived at their destination, two vans were waiting near the entrance of this sleepy town. It was ten at night. Everyone got off, feeling stiff and tired, stretching and yawning. Harvey waved and soon left.

Several guards from the compound escorted them into the vans which drove to the compound located 15 minutes away. No one was blindfolded. As they arrived, the vans drove into the garage and released the passengers who were greeted by six guards. When they got inside, they were officially registered as guests with photos taken and photo i.d. cards issued. They were instructed to carry the i.d. cards at all times.

A guard tried to take Viper's guitar case but she clung tightly to it. "These stay here," the guard said.

"You can't ask a musician to leave their instrument behind, "snapped Viper.

The guard looked at his supervisor who shrugged his shoulders and said "Fine. They can take the guitars after we check each case."

They proceeded to open every case and found nothing suspicious.

Because it was so late, they were escorted directly to their rooms, down a phalanx of hallways.

"We are going to lock you in tonight for security purposes," one guard announced in a Slavic accent. "Each room has its own bathroom facility."

"A lock down," muttered Flipper. "Welcome to Supermaxx."

"Is our friend here?" asked Viper.

"Who would that be?" the guard remarked.

"He goes by Pluto," she said.

"Mr. Pluto is here," he said. "You'll see him in the morning."

Cameron settled into his barren room, feeling completely isolated. He could feel his heart beating as he felt a sense of dread. If he knew how to pray, he would have done it then and there. Tired from the long ride, he fell asleep quickly, fully aware that tomorrow was going to be the scariest day of his life. And he hoped it wouldn't be his last.

■■■

The next morning, Senza awoke in her room at the mansion, furious to have been left behind. All her blame went to Z3.

Z3 had stringent rules and usually very sound reasons for them.

She really didn't want to abide by his recent decree that she stay behind and away from the action. Well aware of the danger the others faced, she wanted to be with them. It should be her choice. What was worst was that Z3 never gave her a specific reason why she couldn't go beyond age. Did it really matter that she was older than what they wanted? The easy fix there would be to lie about her age. And if that didn't work, so what if she gets turned away?

Her relationship with Z3 stretched back a decade. During that time, she had little to complain about as he gave her tremendous freedom to come and go as she pleased. No one had as much liberty as she did. She was one of the few with a smartphone. And he had provided her with room and board for a long time. But she wanted to confront him one more time to see if he would change his mind.

They met in the dining room where a map of Maine was spread out on the table.

"Where in Maine are they exactly?" she asked.

He pointed at the map then opened a Mac book to home in on the compound.

"So, the compound has all of this property?" she asked.

"My brother has a lot of money," said Z3.

"As much as you?"

"He can buy whatever he wants," said Z3. "Do you remember being at his compound?"

Senza stood perfectly still, almost frozen.

"Come on, Senza," he said. "Please tell me. Do you remember the compound?"

She clearly did and not fondly. She gave a solemn nod.

"We've not discussed this as it's very sensitive," he said. "What do you remember?"

"I'm not really sure. I didn't know it was in Maine. I don't have any positive feelings about it."

"It was a while ago."

"Yeah," she said.

"You were young and some awful things happened to you."

The bad memories, which she'd repressed, started to come back.

"I don't think you're ready to return to that place."

"I appreciate that," she said. "But maybe I should be allowed to return and deal with those demons. That might be the best therapy."

Z3 wasn't conceding a thing. "If this mission is a success and the compound gets shut down, then I might entertain the notion of your returning. But not until then."

"You are a stubborn man," she replied.

"We're both stubborn," he said.

Senza returned to her room.

She kicked over a chair, letting out her frustration. She felt guilty knowing the others were endangered and she was safely ensconced here.

She took out her phone and looked at a map of Maine. She had a vague idea where the compound was. It was too long and tiring a trip by motorcycle but she didn't have another option. She was now more determined than ever to go there and face the consequences later. Throughout her relationship with Z3, she had never disobeyed him but there's always a first time.

She packed a light knapsack, slung it on her back and headed down to her motorcycle. Both tires were flat. Shaking her head in disbelief, she checked the sparkplug and saw it was gone. Anticipating correctly that she was a flight risk, Z3 took the precaution of hindering her preferred mode of transportation. She didn't have any spare tires nor sparkplugs and the time it would take to repair the bike seemed too long as time was of the essence.

On her iPhone, she opened up an app for Uber and waited for a ride to appear. An Uber driver came to the gate of the property within 15 minutes. The driver was in his twenties, but prematurely bald with a baby face. His skin was pale as chalk and he wore wire-rim granny glasses.

"Are you the Uber driver?" she asked.

He pointed to a sign on the passenger window that read 'Uber.'

Senza climbed into the car, a grey Nissan Maxima, its enamel badly scraped. Hubert was impressed by her appearance. She looked like a genuine rock star. He wanted to say something but refrained. She'd probably heard that a lot before. He pulled out of the driveway.

"And you are?" she asked

"It's on your phone."

She checked her phone. "Hubert?"

"Yes."

"That's a crappy name."

"This is a test, isn't it?" he replied. "I'm relatively new and you're here on behalf of the company to deliberately provoke me. To see if I get rattled and scream. Well, I'm not going to. Even if the video footage ends out on a reality show."

"It's not a test. And I apologize for using the word crappy. I've been on edge lately," said Senza.

"Really?"

"Really."

"Okie dokie."

"Hubert, do away with that expression. Not cool."

"Okie dokie. I mean, okay."

Hubert always kept a stash of food in the car. It was mainly for himself. But because this was a long ride, he offered some to Senza. She gladly accepted the salted almonds, raisins and Evian water but passed on the twizzlers and jelly beans.

"I need a little quiet," she said. "I've got to rest my mind."

"Okie---" Hubert refrained from finishing that sentence. For the next three hours, he didn't say a word. Then, Senza broke the silence, saying softly "Hubert of Uber. Sounds very 14th century. And catchy. A bit Game of Thrones."

"I thought you didn't like my name," he responded.

"It's very old sounding. Like a name no one uses anymore," she said.

"It's a family name," he said. "I am Hubert the Eighth."

"The Eighth? Impressive," she said.

"Nothing I've ever done has been impressive," he said, sadly. "Unlike my parents, I'm a flop. I can never achieve what they did."

"Really?"

"The plain and simple truth is that no one cares much about me," he said, forlorn.

Senza tilted her head back, resigned to her fate with a needy driver. "Why do you say that?"

"Because no one has ever asked about me," he said.

"Well, I'd love to learn more about you."

"You're just saying that," he said.

"No, Hubert. Really. Tell me about yourself. We have the time."

"Okay. Before I begin, are you going to need a lift home from Maine?"

"Can I let you know when we get there?"

"Sure. I accepted the job of driving you there because I have an uncle who lives in the area. I thought I might visit him."

"Cool with me. So, tell me about yourself."

"Sure. Okay. My name is Hubert Everett Inge the 8th. My father has a very moving story."

"Good start," she said, noticing the smell of pine in the car. Hubert had bought a pine pillow in Vermont which he kept on the passenger seat.

"I was born in Dover, Delaware. When I was two, we moved to Philadelphia. At age four, we moved again to West Hartford in Connecticut. At six, we moved---"

"Why all the moving? Was your dad in the military?"

"No. He was in the moving business. I told you he had a very moving story. He kept moving other people's stuff and falling in love with the cities he moved them to."

"And your mother?"

"She worked as a cleaning lady," he said. "And she was the best there ever was. She could get a place so clean and free of dust that kids with the worst allergies seemed better after she had been to their homes."

"I don't quite see why you feel you can't achieve as much as or more than your parents did. No offense to them. But a cleaning lady and a moving man?"

"They were great at what they did," he said.

"You have any brothers or sisters?" she asked.

"Not a one."

"Well, no competition, that's a good thing," she said, putting a positive spin on things.

Hubert started to cry.

"Are you crying?" she asked.

"I cry often," he said. "I don't quite know why."

"As long as you can see the road, it's fine with me if you cry," she said. "Pull over if you have to."

"You're so kind. It makes me want to cry even more."

"Please don't or I'll be mean," she said with a smile. "So, go on."

As he drove and darkness set in, his Uber light sign started to glow an electric blue. Senza found it comforting.

■■■

When morning arrived at the compound, each room had to be unlocked and the occupants escorted to breakfast. Although there were no prison bars on the few visible windows, the whole place felt like a prison.

At breakfast, they sat together. Pluto joined them, inspiring a lot of hugs and smiles. All except Flipper who just wasn't a hugger and Cameron who still felt uneasy around him.

"Nice of you to join me here," said Pluto, his eyes gesturing that they needed to be careful what they said as they were being monitored.

"When do we perform?" asked Viper.

"I think we're going to do it late afternoon," he replied. "They've given us some time to practice after breakfast."

"This place is very—" began Viper.

Pluto cut her off from saying anything negative by saying "Unique!"

She got the point.

The very presence of guards made it feel like a military state. Eight were visible guarding various areas around the eating area.

Quake found an empty table and he and the others took seats there. A bit crammed but better than spreading out with people they didn't know. They all spoke cautiously, knowing that everything they said could quite likely be overheard. Being watched on the monitors and by the guards themselves, they avoided saying anything negative about the place.

After bussing their trays, they were escorted back to their rooms by individual guards.

■■

Senza slumped in the car seat, half-listening to Hubert as he rambled on about his life. He started to get redundant and her interest faded.

"So, enough about me," he said. "Tell me about you."

"What do you mean?" she replied, caught off guard.

"Well, where are you from, are you close to your parents, do you have siblings..." he said.

Senza stared out the window at the passing scenery. Gazing at the split-rail fencing that probably corralled some mottled cows left little doubt this was a rural farming area.

"I don't know," she replied.

"You don't know what?" he asked.

"I don't know where I'm from nor who my parents are," she said without an ounce of emotion.

"Seriously?" asked Hubert. "You're not just trying to protect your privacy?"

"I grew up in a foster home and an orphanage," she replied. "There weren't any records I know of that disclose my past."

"Did you try to trace back where you might have been born?" he asked.

"You mean with those DNA kits?"

"Yeah."

"No, I didn't," she said. "But I don't know if I really want to know."

He fiddled with his radio but got nothing but static so he turned it off.

"That house you live in is amazing," he noted.

"I don't own it," she said. "I'm merely a guest. But yes, it is nice."

"We're all just guests on this planet," said Hubert, very philosophical.

"That's a good title for a song, Hubert of Uber," she said."

"Thanks, Hillary," he replied, catching her off guard.

"How'd you know my real name?"

He smiled. "It's on your Uber account."

She started to laugh. "Of course, it is. Nothing's private nowadays."

CHAPTER 17 CHIXALUB

"This is the longest Uber ride I've ever given anyone," said Hubert as his car came to a stop on the shoulder of the deserted road. "Are you sure this is the place?"

They truly felt like they were in the middle of nowhere. Senza looked at her texts and said "Yep. One of our bandmates got in with their iPhone. They probably took it by now. But it allowed me to see where exactly they were."

"It looks like there's a gate and fencing all around the property," said Hubert.

Senza nodded.

Hubert scanned the area "Do you want me to drive up to the main gate?" he asked.

Senza drummed her fingers against the car window, thinking and thinking. She hadn't had time to come up with any sort of a plan.

"They'll never let us in," she said. "This place is like a fortress."

"Never say never," said Hubert. "What if I'm just dropping you off."

"Dropping me off for what?" she asked.

"Well, whatever your friends are there for."

"To put on a concert."

"Yeah," said Hubert. "And the guard there can vet you by calling your friends inside. Worst case, they don't let you in."

Senza smiled broadly. "Thanks Hubert. Let's give it a go."

"Great," he replied. "And after I drop you off, I'm meeting my uncle not far from here. My uncle was actually fascinated that I was coming up here. I mean, he likes me and all, but was very curious about my visit up here. Anyway, I can be back to get you anytime."

As they approached the gate, a guard stepped from a booth and walked up to the driver's side door. He did not seem at all friendly.

"You lost?" he asked.

"No," said Hubert.

"What are you doing here then?"

"I'm dropping off someone," said Hubert. "We're not expecting anyone that I'm aware of. Who's your passenger and what's her business?"

The guard peered into the car at Senza.

"I'm Senza," she said. "I'm a surprise guest. My friends are here to perform and I often join them."

"I'm aware of the performance but no one mentioned you," the guard said.

"I told you I'm a surprise," she repeated.

"Your friends came up the other day. Tell you what. I'm not letting your driver in but I'll let you through. Just walk up to the guard at the compound. I'll let him know you're on the way."

"Okay," said Senza. "That would be fine."

Senza stepped out of the car. The guard couldn't help but notice her black leather rock star attire which made him feel all the more comfortable. Of course she was in the band.

"Good luck," said Hubert as he waved and then drove off.

Senza had to do some fast thinking. There was a guard waiting for her but clearly she would need to be vetted. That made her uncomfortable. As she walked along, she thought of running off into the brush. But then what?

She decided it best to walk to the compound. As expected, a guard met her and brought her into the security area.

"Who here can vet you?" a security officer asked.

"A guy named Pluto," she said.

"I remember him," the guard replied. "Let me see what I can find out."

The guard got on the phone. Senza waited and waited. Soon, she heard the guard saying "Okay. Okay. Yeah. As long as he remembers her."

He hung up the phone. "You're cleared," he said.

"Thanks," she replied. "Before I go in, you mind if I step outside for a smoke?"

"Not at all," said the guard, "I'm glad some of us are keeping smoking alive."

She stepped back outside the compound and started walking around the corner towards the river that flowed nearby. She knew there were probably cameras watching her every move so she tried to act nonchalant.

A few minutes later, two guards emerged outside. They walked a few steps, looked from side to side and then shrugged. They didn't seem at all concerned.

"Where is she?" asked the first.

"No idea," said the other guard. "I can't even smell her cigarette smoke."

"She was heading towards the river," said the guard.

"She can't get very far then. "

"Yeah, we'll find her. That water's too cold for anyone to endure."

"Welcome to Maine," laughed the other guard.

They started walking around the corner towards the rushing river with guns drawn.

■■

"This is the day," thought Cameron as he sat up in his bed at the compound. "Could be my last. Or not." He understood why Z3 had to wait so long to confide in them all. This was extremely sensitive and high risk. Everyone embraced the idea with a mix of fear and anticipation.

He waited in his room for a guard to escort him to breakfast.

The other band members sat together for breakfast, careful not to openly discuss anything that might prompt suspicion from the guards. They spoke elliptically, feeling they were under surveillance the whole meal which they were.

Brick appeared serious. "I checked all of your horoscopes last night," he said.

"And?" asked Viper.

"And for many of us, the planets don't align so good," he replied.

Playing with the spikes in her maroon hair, Fireball responded "Say no more. I want to be surprised."

"I just don't buy into this horoscope crap," said Flipper. ""Where I come from, we go to the oddsmakers and let them tell us our odds.

All I want to know is what are my odds of being alive tomorrow? 50 to 1? 3 to 4? You know."

Viper looked over at Quake. "Quake, you have anything to add?"

Quake nodded and went into a quick rap. "As we get ready to play, I feel my hair turning gray. We got to crank it to eleven, Could all end out in heaven. But just play, play, play, Hoping for another day, day, day."

Viper noticed Cameron looking forlorn. "C Sharp? You okay? You're awfully quiet."

"He's always that way," said Flipper.

Cameron gave an unconvincing nod.

A guard came over and signaled for Pluto to come over.

"What is it?" Pluto asked.

"You vetted this woman earlier," the guard said.

"Yeah. So?"

"Well, your friend seems to have disappeared. But she can't go far."

Pluto scratched his head. "Disappeared? How is that possible? There are cameras everywhere."

"We'll find her," the guard said. "But not very smart on her part."

Pluto stepped back to his table. His bandmates stood up.

"Everything okay?" Viper asked.

"It will be if Senza doesn't mess it up," he replied.

They all bussed their breakfast trays and were promptly escorted by several guards to a large conference room.

One guard took charge, addressing the band members. "In a few hours, you'll all be escorted to the main auditorium for the concert you'll put on. I want to forewarn you that we have strict rules in place that you'll all need to abide by. You must remain on stage after the show until a guard escorts you back to your room. You can have no interaction with anyone in the audience before, during or after the show. And we ask that you have minimal dialogue from the stage beyond the lyrics of the songs you've chosen to perform. "

Soon they were returned to their rooms, totally isolated from one another, until the guards returned two hours later. The inability to come and go as they pleased made this place feel like one big strange prison.

■■

Hubert sat in his car, driving down a back road not far from the compound. In the passenger seat was his uncle, Jon Haggerty, slightly balding with a dark suit and tie.

"Ritz," offered Hubert.

His uncle seemed confused.

Hubert reached down and pulled out a box of Ritz crackers. They each indulged.

"The place I dropped my friend off was this big--"

"Compound," said Haggerty, finishing the sentence.

"Yeah. It felt like it was in the middle of nowhere."

"I'm very familiar with it," said Haggerty."

He opened up his iPad and tapped away, soon bringing up aerial images of the compound.

"Pull over," he said.

Hubert drove onto the side of the road, the car brushing against some shrubs. He stopped the engine and looked over at his uncle's iPad.

"That's even bigger than it looks from the road," said Hubert.

The aerial photos showed the electric fence that ran around the length of the property and how closely the compound was to the river. In one image, Hubert spotted the guard station that he had driven up to with Senza

His uncle stared out the passenger side window, in deep thought. He chewed on a Ritz cracker, turned to his nephew and asked "What about the person you dropped off?"

Hubert nodded and replied "Hillary. She's this cool woman in black. Rock star-ish. I never found out what she really did."

"Did she tell you why she was going to the compound?"

Hubert thought a moment. "Well, she didn't give me an exact reason. She just said she had some friends in there. Young musicians. And she was going to surprise them., I guess."

"Did she mention how many friends?"

"No. Can't say she did."

Haggerty pressed his hand against his forehead. "Wish we had more time," he said.

"How so? " asked Hubert.

Haggerty looked glum. He shook his head and said "This is not good. Not good at all. Your friend is in major danger."

Uneasy, Hubert felt a shortness of breath. He really liked Senza, enjoyed her company, and now felt great concern for her safety.

Haggerty pulled out his iPhone and started dialing a phone number.

"We don't have a lot of time, " he said.

■■

Two guards stood by the river near the compound, glancing up and down. The current was so powerful, it exuded a mist all round it. The wet air smelled fresh and cool. No mold or algae could ever survive here.

They attempted to walk down the slope leading to the river but it was slippery and steep. They craned their necks, making sure Senza wasn't clinging to the side. Their view was obscured but they felt little concern that she was still alive.

"There's nowhere for her to have gone except in the water. And she'd freeze to death by now. I think we're cool."

"Yeah, her body's probably a mile or two down river by now. Foolish woman."

The guards tucked their handguns back into their holsters and adjusted the automatic rifles slung on their shoulders. They inhaled the fresh air. One yawned and then the other did the same. Yawning was contagious. They walked back towards the compound.

One guard stopped and the other soon did as well. He looked up at the video cameras then turned his back and whispered "We're best not letting Mr. Shock know about her."

The other guard nodded.

"I wish she'd have dropped her cigarettes as I could use one now."

The other guard reached into his pocket and took out a pack. They each lit up and took a moment to smoke.

"We better get back inside," one of them said.

They stomped out the remaining cigarettes and went back inside the compound.

Senza's head popped out of the icy water as she clung to a root on the side. She had remained submerged for much of the time, not taking any chances. She grabbed onto the root and managed to pull herself out of the water. It was a struggle to get back up the slope but she did.

Sitting on the ground, catching her breath, she grumbled "This is no way to make a living." Her leather outfit now felt tight and uncomfortable. She tried to warm up as she plotted her next move.

■■■

Several guards gathered up the younger occupants in the compound, ranging in age from 9 to 17, and brought them to the theater.

About forty children took seats while a dozen burly guards watched from the perimeter. It looked very odd that so many guards were needed to watch these kids. Now, these weren't all the children in the compound. Five were kept behind due to illness or disciplinary reasons.

Four band members-- Pluto, Viper, Brick, Cameron -- took to the stage. They adjusted their guitars and headsets and waited.

Soon, from the back of the theater, Mr. Shock appeared in his tinted glasses and red kimono along with two bodyguards. He took his seat in a large lounge chair situated dead center three rows back. He had a bodyguard on one side and the young woman Sasha on the other. Pluto couldn't help but notice her. She looked scared.

"Thank you all for coming," he said, speaking into a wireless microphone. "I have long wanted to have live entertainment here on a regular basis and am glad that is now a reality. I was hoping to have the full band. I believe there's seven or so of them, but I'm told that three are under the weather. However, they may be better tomorrow and we could schedule another concert then. I will now turn it over to the leader of the band, Pluto, who will take it from there."

Pluto walked up to the lip of the stage where a standing microphone awaited, his yellow guitar slung across his shoulder.

"Thank you, Mr. Shock," he said. "We are pleased to be here."

"What is the name of your group?" Shock asked, catching Pluto completely off guard as they had never come up with a name for the band.

There was a long awkward pause. Viper interjected "We've had several different names. It's hard to get the group to agree on one. I think we are now called, um, Garden of Sound."

"Sounds like Soundgarden?" said Shock.

"Actually, Garden of Sound confused people for the reason you cited," said Pluto. "So, we now call ourselves, um, Gods of Sound."

Shock smiled. "I like that much better. Gods of Sound. Very memorable. Very memorable indeed."

"We really hope so," said Pluto, nervously clearing his throat. "We haven't performed together recently so bear with us."

Pluto adjusted his special headset with the suction cups pressed on his forehead. The other three band members did the same.

"Standing with me for this set on the green bass is Brick. Then on red guitar we have Viper, on orange guitar is C Sharp and me on my yellow baby. We're also using a drum machine. I hope you'll forgive us for that."

He walked across the stage, holding his wireless guitar while surveying the room. Then he went over to Brick and whispered, "You need to separate the guards from the kids."

Brick, intensely serious, nodded.

Pluto then said to the crowd "We want to start with an instrumental."

Pluto struck the first chord and the others joined along.

The song was a version of Crosby Stills and Nash's Suite Judy Blue Eyes but with no vocals. Substituting for the vocals were the guitars, imitating the higher chords perfectly. The audience appreciated their virtuosity even if the younger ones were unfamiliar with the song. When the song was finished, audience sat motionless and speechless. Not a single child moved.

It wasn't until Shock stood up and clapped, nodding his approval, that they did as well.

Pluto waited for the applause to subside.

"For our next song," he said. "We'd like to involve all the kids here. If they could join us on stage, we need a chorus."

The main guard rushed over to Mr. Shock. "I told them beforehand that there was to be no interaction between the band and the kids."

Shock took a long time to think about it. He glanced out at the children in the audience and could see they were waiting his approval before doing anything. Finally, with a slow and steady nod, he gave his permission. The children obediently left their seats and headed towards the stage.

The main guard shook his head and returned to the side of the theater. Shock always had the final word.

Pluto stalled for time as the children made their way to the stage. "I appreciate this. Sometimes for our finale we like to get people on stage with us," said Pluto. "Audience involvement is always a big plus."

Once all the children were on stage, Pluto leaned into the microphone and said "Next up is... Chixalub."

And then all hell broke loose.

■ ■

Quake, Fireball and Flipper planned in advance to leave their rooms, using the excuse that they suffered from food poisoning and needed to visit the infirmary.

Food poisoning always earned instant sympathy and the guards who came to escort them were no exception. And the guards didn't think it strange when each band member insisted on bringing their guitars, not wanting to leave such a valuable belonging in their rooms. And when they also insisted on wearing their headsets with the suction cups on their forehead that too didn't beg any questions. The headset looked relatively harmless. There was no reason for the guards to think it could play a role in harnessing immense power from the guitars.

Nearing the infirmary, Quake turned and said "Chixalub."

Flipper and Fireball knew the signal well, raised their guitars and started strumming along with Quake. The guards watched, unaware of the power of these guitars. Within seconds, an enormous rumble of sound emanated from Quake's guitar, knocking down the guards.

Flipper's guitar then sent out a piercing screechy sound that caused the fallen guards to writhe on the ground, desperately trying to cover their ears. Flipper added some power chords that rendered them either unconscious or dead. It wasn't clear which.

They took off down the long corridor, encountering two more guards.

"Why aren't you with your escorts?" one guard said.

"They collapsed," said Quake. "Like this."

Flipper leveled both guards with guitar sound. They remained on the ground, motionless. He flipped them off for good measure.

"The odds of me flipping them off? 100%," said Flipper. "My prized trademark."

Quake then sent a rumble of bass for added insurance.

Quake, Fireball and Flipper next found their way to the security area.

Quake got his guitar rumbling low and loud as it shook open a heavy metal door revealing four guards watching security monitors. Quake and Flipper neutralized them with immense guitar power.

Then Fireball went to work, sending jolts of sound that exploded on impact, shattering every security monitor in the room and destroying the other surveillance equipment. The whole room caught fire, burning fiercely out of control until Quake stifled the flames by playing some heavy bass. He then took a fire extinguisher off the wall, surveyed the damaged equipment, and extinguished the remaining flames and perilous embers.

"We've got to find the theater," said Quake as they hurried down a hallway, taking wrong turn after wrong turn and seemingly going in circles. Suddenly, three guards emerged from behind, knocking them to the ground.

The guards overpowered them, ripping off their headsets. Quake, Flipper and Fireball tried playing their guitars but they didn't work anymore.

"Somehow, they can't operate their guitars without these headsets," observed one guard, stuffing all three headsets into his pocket. "If I hadn't witnessed it myself, I would never have believed guitars could do this."

"Get on your feet!" shouted the other guard as the three bandmates slowly got up. Quake looked despondent, knowing they'd failed their mission.

The guards marched all three to the theater.

∎∎

In the theater, with his green guitar, Brick had created an effective force field that prevented the guards from getting to the kids clustered on stage behind the guitarists.

Pluto and Viper divided the room in half, focusing their guitars on the guards within each area. Cameron had been assigned to watch their backs. But somehow Cameron couldn't get his guitar to work properly. He kept readjusting his headset hoping to generate power in his guitar but to no avail. Frustrated, he threw off his headset and felt an asthma attack coming.

Taking aim and strumming fast and furious, Viper knocked down three guards with her guitar's sound, incapacitating them. One tried to exit the theater and she sent a chord that bent round the door and nailed him.

Another guard raised his gun, taking aim at her. Pluto astutely hit a chord on his guitar, zapping the guard's gun out of his hand.

"Don't shoot anyone!" Shock shouted to his guards. "They don't have weapons."

"But they do!" said one guard. "Those guitars are weapons."

"I don't want any shooting yet," replied Shock.

Brick stepped to the side of the stage, rotating his guitar back and forth to keep his force field in place.

Three guards entered the theater with their captives -- Quake, Fireball and Flipper.

"Their guitars are useless without their headsets," said one of those guards.

Viper took a shot, sending her sound curving in a Bend it Like Beckham manner and knocking out that guard. Pluto leveled the other two. Although now free from the guards, Quake, Fireball and Flipper couldn't help. Without their headsets, their guitars had been rendered powerless.

Shock had a wicked smile on his face, now knowing their Achilles heel. He watched as three of his guards appeared from the back of the stage, surprising Pluto, Brick and Viper and pinning them to the ground.

"All you need to do is take their headsets," said Shock.

The guards did just that, aware that the guitars were rendered powerless without the headsets.

"Don't put them in your pockets," Said Shock. "Crush them."

The guards tossed the headsets to the ground and stomped all over them. They also crushed Cameron's headset which was already discarded on the ground.

Cameron stood there holding his guitar and feeling a rage from within like he'd never experienced before. Asthma be damned.

■■■

Senza noticed smoke coming from the security area. She walked over to the heavy door, the kind that locks ultra tight and secure through electromagnets. But the door lay slightly ajar from a lack of power caused by the now smoldering security center.

She stepped inside, unaccosted. Several guards lay motionless on the floor.

She wished she had a special guitar with her. She felt helpless without one.

Cautiously, she hurried down the corridor, stopping every few steps to listen and determine if it was safe to continue.

She heard a loud rumble and headed in that direction, soon approaching some double doors. She pushed them open, finding herself at the top of the theater. Walking in, she almost fell into the lap of Shock.

"And who are you?" Shock asked, unaware who she was although she recognized his voice and face instantly.

"Is it too cliché to say 'your worst nightmare?'" she responded.

"My dear I beg to differ," said Shock. "I think it's the other way around."

He signaled to a guard to grab her. For a moment, she struggled to get free but the guard was too strong.

Shock walked closer to Senza.

"You're wet," he said.

"How observant," came her sarcastic reply.

The carpeting underneath her had become damp.

"How old are you?" he asked.

She didn't respond.

"What's your name?"

Again, she remained silent.

"I'll get all this information from you eventually," he said, with an eerie cackle. "I just thought we could save a little time doing it now. So be it."

There was a momentary silence.

Suddenly. the theater doors burst open as police chief Captain
Eugene Dunphy arrived with one of his deputies Grover Smuggs.
Dunphy was overweight which contrasted in a comical way with his
deputy who was thin as a rail.

Senza felt relieved to see them.

"Everyone stop what you're doing," said Dunphy, holding up a badge
which wasn't entirely necessary as he was wearing a police uniform.
"I'm Captain Eugene Dunphy and this is my Deputy Grover
Smuggs."

"You heard the man," said his skinny deputy who sported a dated
handlebar mustache.

"Officers, I'm glad you could get out here so fast," said Shock.
"These people invaded my little home and should all be arrested."

"So, what seems to be going on here," asked Dunphy.

"I'll tell you, captain," said Shock. "You know how I stay clear of
trouble. Well, today we had some trespassers. They all broke the
law."

"Do you wish to press charges, Mr. Shock?" Dunphy asked.

"The maximum allowed," said Shock.

Dunphy surveyed the theater, seeing the children in their pastel garb,
some guards and Z3's guitarists. It was a strange amalgam of
people, he thought.

"Okay," said Dunphy taking out his notepad and pen. "These people
attacked you and your guards."

"They did," said Shock. "I want them all locked up for a long time."

"Did they come armed?" Dunphy asked.

"Well, yes. They came armed with guitars," Shock replied. "I know it sounds ridiculous but these guitars pack a lot of power when you wear a headset."

Shock picked up a guitar. One of his guards had an extra headset and handed it to him. Shock put on the headset and attempted to strum the guitar to show its power. But nothing happened.

Perplexed, Shock said "There's some secret to it."

Frustrated, he shook the guitar. Still nothing. Then he hit it with his fist. Again, nothing.

"Well, we'll look into that," said Dunphy. "Right now, we'll bring them all down to the stationhouse and book them for trespassing and destruction of private property. I think it best you hold off on the assault charge with guitars."

"How's your wife?" asked Shock, clearly familiar with Dunphy.

"Gladys is getting better," he said. "She appreciated your well wishes."

"Glad to hear that," said Shock. "I assume you got my contribution to your police fund."

"Very generous of you, as usual," said Dunphy.

Captain Dunphy turned to his deputy. "Deputy Smuggs, how many handcuffs do we have?"

"Not nearly enough," said Smuggs. "Oh wait, I do have those disposal zip tie ones. I'm just not sure how we're going to get them all to the station house," added Smuggs.

At that moment, Hubert unexpectedly entered the theater. With his wire-rim glasses, pasty complexion and balding pate, he looked like a disoriented accountant.

"Excuse me," he said.

"And who are you?" asked Dunphy, annoyed.

"My name is Hubert," said Hubert. "I'm an Uber driver. But right now, that's irrelevant."

"And why is that?" asked Dunphy.

"Because the person you need to know about isn't me," he replied. "The person you need to know about is my uncle."

Walking in behind Hubert is his uncle.

"Good afternoon folks," said Haggerty. "I'm special agent Haggerty and I'm here to place a number of you under arrest, starting with Mr. Shock."

"Can I see your identification?" Dunphy asked.

"You surely can," said Haggerty. As he pulled out his i.d., his shoulder holster came into view.

Dunphy walked over to Haggerty, looked at his billfold and saw an FBI i.d.

"He's legit," Dunphy said. "He trumps our jurisdiction."

"But there's just one of him," said Shock, annoyed.

"But it's the FBI, Mr. Shock," explained Captain Dunphy. "There are boundaries here."

Exasperated, Shock whispered to one of his guards who obediently seized Sasha, bringing her to him. Witnessing what was going on, Pluto started to make a move but Captain Dunphy warned him to stay put.

"Dunphy," said Haggerty. "I know you're a corrupt cop. You and your deputy Smuggs. You've been under surveillance for a while. And now, you've graduated. You're under arrest."

Haggerty applied handcuffs on the police chief and deputy. "I clearly didn't bring enough handcuffs tonight," he said. "I may have to borrow some of yours for the time being."

Appearing desperate, Shock said "You're just one guy. You're way out of your league here. Guards, neutralize him."

Two of his guards fired their guns at Haggerty, wounding him. He fell to the ground. Hubert rushed to his side. Taking advantage of all of the commotion, Shock disappeared through a side door along with two of his guards and an unwilling and frightened Sasha. Pluto's heart sunk as he saw her disappear.

With the FBI agent down, 15 of Shock's guards appeared on the scene with guns raised and ordered the guitarists to kneel on the stage with their hands behind their heads. One by one, they all obeyed. As Flipped kneeled, he flipped them off.

The only one still standing was Cameron.

"That goes for you, too, junior," the guard snapped.

"He has asthma, you asshole!" shouted Viper, defending Cameron as she always did.

Cameron stood perfectly still, grasping his guitar. He felt a surge of anger as he saw all that was dear to him in great jeopardy.

"I told you to put your guitar down and kneel," the guard shouted. "This is your final warning."

Cameron's mind raced. He closed his eyes then slowly reopened them, shifting his rage right into his guitar without a headset. With sparks spewing out, the guitar responded like the serious weapon it could be and sent an overwhelming force of sound waves at many of the guards.

But three guards rushed him from his blind side. They knocked the guitar from his grasp and began to subdue him, each taking an arm or leg to pin him down. His eyes widened and his face reddened as he telepathically lifted the red, yellow and green guitars into the air, sending a devastating surge of sound at the remaining guards.

The orange guitar went zooming out through the doorway, racing down corridors and reducing any threat whatsoever. Like a force of nature, it sent out bolts of electricity and powerful sound to fell every guard in sight. As it hurtled along, seemingly possessed, it ducked into every side room, clearing them of any threat. It soon returned to the theater, obediently hovering over Cameron.

Within seconds, each and every guard in the theater had been rendered unconscious. And for good measure, Cameron gave a surge of sound at Dunphy and Smuggs, knocking them out.

Cameron's mind eased and the guitars lowered to the stage.

He got to his feet, grabbed his orange guitar and checked it out. Then he placed it back on the stage, looking at what he'd wrought. He stood perfectly still, almost in shock.

For a moment, no one uttered a word. They were all stunned.

Then Viper shouted "Awesome, C!"

"Man, that was cool," said Flipper.

"Ultra rad!" added Fireball.

"Killer performance," said Quake.

Pointing to the door, Pluto said "We must get Shock before he escapes."

Pluto grabbed one of the guitars and found a discarded headset that wasn't crushed. Along with Quake and Fireball, he hurried around the interior of the compound, down corridors, peering into rooms. The place was one giant maze, difficult to navigate. And what made it more difficult was the number of bodies strewn around.

At one point, they emerged outside the compound. He spotted three guards running away. He put on the headset, turned on the guitar and aimed.

"They're too far," said Quake.

Pluto concentrated his anger into the guitar. He strummed rapidly. It sent a burst of sound. It didn't come close. The guards kept running, getting further and further away.

"It's okay," said Fireball. "You tried."

Again, Pluto focused his anger. This time the sound burst twice as far. He knocked down one guard and with a sweeping motion nailed the other two.

"Well, I'll be," said Quake. "Damn, that was sweet."

Quake and Fireball high-fived him as they went back inside the compound. Reality began to set in that Shock had escaped and had taken Sasha and at least two guards with him.

Returning to the theater, they learned from one child that five children remained unaccounted for. Shock had likely taken them.

By now, Agent Haggerty had been bandaged enough to stop the bleeding. Two FBI agents had arrived as well as two EMS workers. They wheeled him out on a stretcher.

"We'll take it from here," said one of the agents, herding Smuggs and Dunphy out of the theater, down the long corridor and eventually into an unmarked car. The other agent remained behind, surveying the theater, noting so many guards lying motionless on the ground.

Never one for great emotion, Senza spotted Hubert and gave him a big hug. "You're the best Uber driver I've ever met," she said.

"How many have you met?" he asked.

"Let me re-phrase that," she said. "You're the best ever."

"Really?" said Hubert.

"Without you, all would be lost," she replied.

"But I didn't do that much," he said.

"Getting the FBI here was key as these corrupt cops were going to lock us all up," she noted.

Viper stepped forward, clearing her throat to get their attention. Pointing to Cameron, she said "And this guy here needs special recognition. C Sharp gets an A plus."

Swallowing his pride, Pluto looked Cameron straight in the eyes and said "Listen, man. I apologize for any ill feelings I had about you. I was wrong. I know I started thinking of you as C Minus. You're C Sharp and you're Wireless. Thank you pal."

Cameron couldn't believe his ears. Up until now, nothing in his whole life had been as meaningful as those kind words from Pluto.

"I will never rest until we get that guy," Pluto said. "He must be caught and Sasha must be rescued."

"Did you know her well?" asked Viper.

"In the short time I knew her, I felt a special connection," said Pluto.

"I'd like to help you," said Cameron, evoking an appreciative smile from Pluto.

Pluto placed his arm around Cameron's shoulder. "And I would love your help." he said.

CHAPTER 18 NO ONE LIKES SURPRISES

The mission was a partial success. On the positive side, Shock and his operation had been exposed and shut down. Of the three dozen children rescued, Z3 had set in motion plans to adopt them which would take time. But on the negative side, everyone felt disappointed that Shock and some of his guards had escaped along with Sasha and five kids. Pluto was especially glum. He had wanted so badly to rescue Sasha but failed to do so. He blamed himself. People tried talking to him but he was too distracted to engage on any level. He wanted to find her but had no idea where she might be.

Cameron stood in the driveway with Senza, assessing the state of her motorcycle. Both tires were flat.

"I can fix the flats," she said. "I just don't know what else he did to disable my bike."

"Z3?"

"Who else?!" she said.

"Well, he didn't stop you from going to the compound," said Cameron.

"That was thanks to Uber," she smiled.

Through the front gate, Cameron noticed a Hispanic man, trying to get their attention. Senza and Cameron wandered over. The man stared at them through the wrought iron bars, looking like he was imprisoned. He kept his hands raised, holding the bars, to show he was unarmed. But just to be safe, Senza scanned him from head to toe.

"Hi," said Cameron.

"Hola senior," the man said.

"Can we help you?" asked Cameron, feeling a sense of déjà vu as he smelled the strong cologne the man was wearing. He recalled that very distinct smell from the night he collapsed while running around the rim of the property. Sometimes smell was its own fingerprint, he thought.

"I need talk to someone," the man replied, his eyes darting about.

"About what?" Senza asked with suspicion.

A squirrel grabbed an acorn and dashed along the wall by the gate. The man was so skittish, he stepped back as though the squirrel were a dangerous leopard. He tried to collect himself. He could feel that his frantic nature was a turn-off. "I came here before," he said. "And have tried many other times to tell you things but no one listens."

Annoyed that she had to step away from the maintenance on her bike, Senza impatiently asked "We don't have all day. What is it?"

"The man who own this house has brother," said the man. "The brother very bad man. I worked on his home in Maine."

"You mean, you helped build it?" she asked. "That large compound?"

He nodded. "Si. Mi amigos worked on it. And after, they disappeared. Never to be seen again. The man who owned the compound didn't want anyone to talk about the secret passageways built throughout it. I am sure he murdered them all so they wouldn't talk. I'm lucky he didn't get me."

"So, you're saying the house had a lot of escape routes?" asked Senza

"Si."

"And where did he escape to?"

The man shook his head. "I don't know," he said. "But he built another compound."

"In the US?"

"No. Argentina," he said. "And it's much bigger. Much much bigger than the one in Maine."

"So, you think that's where he went?"

The man shrugged his shoulders. "I have map of compound in Argentina."

"You mean, architectural drawings?" she asked.

Nodding, he reached into his windbreaker and pulled out several folded-up architectural plans. He waved them in the air like evidence.

Senza sensed he was telling the truth. She wished they had spoken to him earlier. But he had gotten scared off and they didn't know what he wanted. While it might have made a difference had they met before the mission, at least now they had a lead on where Shock may be headed.

Senza pushed a button by the wall and the heavy wrought iron gate opened. She gestured for him to come through.

"Gracias," he said.

■■

Later that day, Cameron was with Viper and Pluto in the dining room of the mansion.

Viper held up a newspaper clipping with the headline 'FBI Agent Haggerty Busts Up Child Abuse Ring.'

"Hubert sent this to Senza," she said.

Pluto turned to Cameron. "Does it bother you he got all the credit?"

Cameron shook his head.

"Good."

Viper tossed the article onto a chair. "You know, C," she said. "However you did what you did, it worked so well that every single person you disabled has no recollection of what happened. You created one big amnesia fest."

"Of course, there were witnesses--all of us, the kids there and Hubert--who remember everything," added Pluto.

"And Senza trusts Hubert," added Viper. "And the two kids who mentioned flying guitars lost any credibility," laughed Viper.

"That's funny," said Cameron.

"What amazed me," noted Pluto. "Was how you were able to wield those guitars so well without harming anyone that mattered. I mean, if you were going after people you were angry at, I'm surprised I didn't make the list. "

Viper smiled and said "Right now before you, I am going to use my mind to send an object across the table." She placed a glass on the edge of the dining room table. She crouched down so she was at eye level with it. She rubbed her forehead, took several loud breaths, then reached under the table for her skateboard which she rolled across the table. It fell off the other end, rolling into the wall.

"There," she said. "Quite simple. But seriously, C, let's test your telepathic mind. Make that glass move."

Cameron crouched down and stared at the glass but nothing happened.

"I think he needs to be angry to do it," said Pluto.

Pluto stepped on Cameron's foot.

"Ow!" he cried out.

Viper glared at Pluto.

"We're trying to get him angry, right?" said Pluto in defense.

"Try now," said Viper.

Cameron stared again at the glass. But nothing happened. He breathed through his nose and tried again. This time, he tried to block out everything around him so his complete focus remained on the glass. He envisioned moving it across the table so it stopped just shy of the edge.

"Well, you have an amazing skill somewhere," said Pluto. "Unless it was a one shot. "

Senza entered. She looked particularly serious today. "Hey, C. Z3 wants to see the two of us."

Cameron felt determined to make the glass move. He wanted to try again with Senza as part of his audience. But he sensed her impatience and he knew that keeping Z3 waiting was not a wise move.

Viper smiled. "Maybe you can try another day. I mean, maybe your telepathy only works with guitars."

Senza and Cameron headed to Z3, not saying a word to one another.

He met with them right away.

"Thank you for meeting me," said Z3 as if there was any other choice.

Wearing his black kimono, Z3 walked over to a table in the room. He pulled out a lighter and lit some incense. Cameron's eyes rose as panic took over. He recalled how badly he'd reacted before. Here we go again, he thought. He assumed the incense was important to

Z3. He tried to be reverential about it but this time he couldn't help himself.

"I'm allergic", he cried out.

Without any clarification, Z3 quickly snuffed out the incense. A waft of smoke rose up. Z3 scattered it with his hands, fanning the air until there was no more sign of it.

"I've always known you were allergic," he said, surprising Cameron with that revelation. "I was just waiting for the day when you would stand up for yourself and say something."

Cameron nodded.

"I really don't care for incense myself, " added Z3.

Cameron felt great relief. The air felt clear again.

"Today, as you're aware, we met a man named Juan Fidel Ameche," said Senza. "His English is passable. We understood most of what he told us."

"Yes. The way he discussed my brother rung true," said Z3. "Do we have the man's contact info so we can stay in touch?"

"We do," said Senza. "Pluto's holding onto it. He's determined to go to Argentina."

"He shouldn't do anything until we have time to figure things out," said Z3.

"I'll tell him," said Senza.

Z3 looked uneasy. "There's something big I need to talk to you about."

"Bigger than this?" asked Senza.

He nodded.

"I've waited to have this conversation a very long time," said Z3, looking solemn. "But I need you to try to be very understanding. This isn't easy for anyone."

He turned to Senza.

"Senza," continued Z3. "You know how much I care about you.'

She nodded and said "You've been kinder to me than anybody I've ever encountered."

"I took you in ten years ago," he smiled.

"I remember," she replied.

"You were in very bad shape," he said.

Somber, she appeared quite uncomfortable. Z3 reached for a pitcher of water and poured two glasses for Senza and Cameron. Feeling dehydrated, they gladly accepted it and drank it down. They had both been under a lot of stress the past few days.

"Do you remember what condition you were in?" he asked.

Senza sat quietly thinking back. "I think," she said, hesitating. "I think I do."

"Go on," he prodded.

"I was pregnant," she replied.

Cameron tried to contain his surprise, sipping the few last drops of water in his glass.

"Yes. And how old were you?"

"16."

"Sadly, that is right."

"And the man who did this—" she hesitated.

"Do you remember?" he asked, watching her pained expression.

"I do," she said, resigned.

"The man who did this to you was my half-brother," said Z3. "That is one of the reasons I didn't want you to return there. He had raped you as he had many others."

She exhaled deeply, feeling ill.

Cameron felt incredibly awkward listening in on their conversation. He half-expected at any moment for Z3 to ask him to leave. That would be the appropriate thing to do, he thought. He wouldn't be offended at all. But Z3 kept talking, paying little notice to him.

"I was fortunate to get you out of that place," he said. "It was only through my legal team that I was able to keep you."

"Thank you."

"I'm not looking for thanks," he said. "Just truth and justice. Do you remember coming here? Shortly after you arrived, you had the baby."

She closed her eyes, the memory too painful to dwell on.

"And because of all you had been through, we felt it wasn't wise for you to keep it. So, the baby went into foster care and you went into my care."

She nodded solemnly.

"But I kept an eye on that baby," he said. "I felt a certain responsibility. And I knew someday you might ask about it."

"I don't need to know," she said. "I'm way past that. In fact, I hadn't thought about it until now."

"You should know," he said.

"Whatever," she replied. "Tell me if you want. It won't mean anything. So, what happened to the damn baby?"

"I can do this another time if you prefer," he offered.

"Now is as good a time as any, I guess," she said.

Z3 paused for the longest time, then took a deep breath and said "Your baby is in this room right now."

Senza and Cameron looked at one another. Aside from Z3, they were the only ones in the room. They each knew exactly what he meant but they had a hard time digesting it. Senza was Cameron's mother. There was not enough therapy in the world to unravel the effects of this news.

Cameron was completely slack-jawed. It hit him like a punch in the face. Senza being his mother was one thing to cope with. But the fact that Shock was his father made him feel sick to his stomach. It was incomprehensible to think that that awful evil man was his father.

"Please take your time reflecting on all of this," said Z3. "And I might suggest you keep it to yourselves. I don't plan to tell anyone else."

Cameron and Senza sat in stone-cold silence. There was nothing to say.

CHAPTER 19 REUNITED

For a solid week, Cameron stayed in his room as much as possible overwhelmed by what Z3 had told him. This dark secret would haunt him forever, he thought. How could he ever go on?

Being Shock's son was the absolute worst nightmare he ever could have conceived. And equally startling was the revelation that Senza, a woman he looked to as an older friend, was actually his mother. She must have been devastated at that news. Who wouldn't be?! How could she even look at him going forward, he wondered.

Because he had to eat, Cameron made a rare appearance downstairs but barely said a word, retreating to his room immediately afterwards. He played his guitar most of the day as it was the one distraction that took his mind off of everything.

There was a knock on his door.

Reluctantly, he asked "Who is it?"

"Me," said the voice.

He slowly opened the door. There before him was Z3. Up until now, he had never visited Cameron's room.

"Can I come in?" he asked.

Cameron nodded, stepping to the side and then closing the door behind him.

"They call you C Sharp," he said. "When I think of you, I have always thought of you as C Sharp Minor. That's the key Beethoven used for his Moonlight Sonata. But I now realize that you are Major. Very Major. Without you, this whole mission would have been a complete failure. I am sure of that."

He looked into Cameron's sorrowful eyes.

"I debated telling you everything," he said. "But I know the truth, painful as it may be, is freeing. And I didn't think it was right to go on any longer without you or Senza knowing the truth. I can see how upsetting it's been...on both of you. And I know it's going to take a long time to digest. My brother has become a very bad person but that doesn't mean you will be, too. This may not be that comforting but being my brother's son makes you my nephew. I am your uncle. We are related. And I promise to look after you, always."

Cameron smiled for the first time in a long time.

"What might cheer you up now?" asked Z3 sincerely. "What would take your mind off of things? Anything you can think of?"

Cameron chewed on his knuckles, uneasily, then shrugged his shoulders.

"Is there a friend you might want to see?"

Cameron didn't have a lot of friends. At least, not many beyond the ones here. He felt awkward not being able to cite a single friend. After a moment's silence, he thought of someone who was a true friend.

"There is one person," said Cameron, uneasy. "His name is Tommy. But he lives a ways away."

Z3 gave a wry smile as though he knew exactly who Tommy was and where he lived. "Well, we'll arrange to have you two meet," he offered.

"I don't know his phone number or anything," Cameron replied.

Z3 slipped a cell phone from his pocket, tapped a few numbers and handed the phone to Cameron.

"How do you know his phone number?" Cameron asked.

Z3 simply smiled.

Someone answered. "Hello, Tommy? It's me, C Sharp. I mean, Cameron."

Tommy was blown away by the sound of Cameron's voice. "Oh man, this is a killer surprise. I didn't know what happened to you, man. I honestly didn't think I'd ever see you again the rest of my life."

"Yeah and I didn't think I'd see you again. Anytime soon. Or anytime ever. Or never," said Cameron excited to hear his voice. "Do you want to get together?"

"That'd be cool," said Tommy.

"When can you do it?"

Tommy shouted to his mother then got back on the phone. "How's tomorrow? 12 noon at the mall. We can meet at the Starbucks there. That okay with you?"

Cameron looked over at Z3. "Can I have someone bring me to the mall near my old hometown tomorrow at noon?" he asked.

Z3 nodded. "Of course."

"Tommy, that is perfect," said Cameron.

"And Cam," said Tommy. "Remember the time we went to the mall and I told you to bring your wallet and you did."

"Yep."

"And it had nothing in it," laughed Tommy.

"Yep."

"I mean, nothing. Not a card or a single bill."

"Yep."

"So, don't forget to bring your wallet...with some money in it," said Tommy.

"I will. Promise."

"I'm so glad you called. I really missed you, my friend."

A smile slid across Cameron's face. "You, too. See you tomorrow, Tommy."

■■

Cameron really looked forward to seeing Tommy.

That morning he had time to waste before departing for his visit. He went outside and wandered around the vast property, balancing along an old stonewall like a tightrope walker.

Off to the side, he saw Fireball and Brick tossing a Frisbee around. While he liked them both, he didn't feel like socializing. But he was relieved that neither of them knew about his dark secret. And he hoped that Z3 and Senza would keep it that way.

Z3 promised to get Cameron a ride to see Tommy. Probably Harvey, their bus driver, or maybe he'd get that nice Uber driver Hubert. He didn't specify.

Cameron appeared at the front of the mansion at the agreed upon time and sat on the stoop.

Around the corner came a motorcycle driven by Senza. He cringed, uneasy just seeing her. She must absolutely hate him, he thought. And who could blame her? He stood up but was reluctant to walk towards her.

Straddling her motorcycle, she signaled for him to join her. He took a deep breath and walked towards her. She was clad in her usual black leather but wearing two red leather gloves.

"In case you were wondering, I'm your ride," she said matter-of-factly. "And I know where to go."

Speechless, he reached for the extra helmet and put it on. Uncertain what if anything he could say, he remained silent. Cameron climbed onto the bike, sitting behind her. But instead of wrapping his arms around her waist, he pried his fingers under a crevice in the seat.

"You're being kind of foolish," she said. "Wrapping arms around me is something you do for safety not cause you give a damn about me."

"I'll take my chances," he said, stubbornly.

She had no interest in arguing. She was half-tempted to floor it and let him take a tumble but she knew that could cause him severe injury so she refrained.

They began the ride, weaving in and out of traffic. Realizing his safety was at stake, Cameron wrapped his arms around her waist, giving him some security. At least he didn't have to talk to her as he might have in a car.

He remembered the ride to his former hometown as feeling long but this time it felt surprisingly short. It's not that Senza went any faster. It's just that his mind had wandered, wondering what lay ahead in his life.

Senza arrived at the mall fifteen minutes before his scheduled meeting with Tommy.

"How much time do you want?" she asked.

Cameron pondered for a moment. "How much can I have?" he asked.

"As much as you need," she said. "This is your special visit."

"Maybe a couple of hours," Cameron replied, his eyebrows rising to see if she reacted negatively.

"You got any money?" she asked.

Cameron pulled his brown wallet from his back pocket. He opened it and found it empty as usual. Senza unzipped her jacket, reached in and pulled out a thick wallet. From it, she tugged out three twenty dollar bills and handed them to him.

"That's too much," he replied, handing it back to her.

"Give me back what you don't spend."

"Okay." He took the money and slipped it in his wallet.

"No point in carrying a wallet if you have no money," she said. "Since you don't have a cell phone, I can't text you. So, I'll tell you what. I'll drive by here every hour on the hour. When you're ready to leave, just come out here on the hour and look for me. We'll connect somehow."

"Okay."

"And give me your helmet," she said, sounding motherly. "You don't need to lug that around."

He handed her the helmet and strode into the mall, never looking back.

When he arrived at Starbucks, Cameron looked around anxiously for Tommy. He was five minutes early. He took a seat at a table, hoping Tommy could spend a bunch of time with him.

Everyone there was gazing at their cellphones. He felt naked without one as all he could do was stare at the entrance. Tommy's father walked in with Tommy who pointed to Cameron. The father nodded, pointed to his watch and left. Tommy walked over, excited, as Cameron stood up.

"So cool to see you," said Tommy.

"You too."

"Let's get something to drink," added Tommy. "I usually get a grande double crunch caramel frappuccino double-blended with whipped cream. What about you?"

Cameron hadn't ordered anything from Starbucks before so he replied "That's what I usually order."

Tommy did a double take as he thought his order was quite unique. "This is a nutty store," he added. "First time I came here I ordered a Tall and it came in this tiny cup. I don't think the guy who started this operation knows much about size. And you go to the movie theater where it's just the opposite. Crazy."

They each got their drinks and slurped them down, sucking every last drop, as they circled the mall. Tommy took the lead, choosing which stores to drop into. They went to the Gap then Tommy insisted on a snack at Wetzel's Pretzels. Then they hit Van's and afterward Tommy wanted a frozen yogurt. They spent a long time at Barnes & Noble before coming to Game Stop.

"I've always believed in alternative universes," said Tommy. "Imagine every game in here is an alternate world. As real as the one we're in but a lot more exciting. Anyway, you've been kind of quiet. Maybe because I can't stop talking."

They both laughed.

"So, Cam, tell me about your life."

Shyly, Cameron responded "Well, what is it you want to know?"

"Like what you've been up to?"

"Well..."

"Do you still play guitar?"

Cameron nodded.

"That's good. Don't give that up. It gives you a purpose. Are you getting better?"

"I think so."

"That's good," said Tommy. "And don't feel bad if you don't do a sport. I'm not an athlete either. For me, sports are better to watch on TV than play. So, what else is new with you?"

Cameron shrugged his shoulders. "Nothing much."

"Cameron, I love you, man, but you have a kind of boring life, if I might say so. We'll have to liven it up."

Tommy checked the time on his cell phone. "I've got time for one last stop then I got to meet my dad. So, get ready as I'm going to liven up your life."

"Okay."

Tommy led Cameron over to the Victoria's Secret store.

"This is my favorite alternative universe," said Tommy.

"It feels kind of funny being in here," said Cameron.

"Why's that?

"Well, they know we're just kids and we aren't going to be buying anything."

"Not so true. They know we're future customers. And the more we visit, the more we'll probably buy some day."

"But for who?"

Tommy looked at him cross-eyed. "Your lady," he said, picking up a red lace bra. "You buy her one of these and she'll worship you."

"Because they're expensive," noted Cameron.

"She'll know you have class," he said.

A saleswoman passed by and spotted Tommy with the bra. "Young man, I don't know if it's appropriate for you to be holding lingerie like that."

Thinking quickly on his feet, Tommy responded "I'm getting married soon. I have to start somewhere."

He put the bra back and the two walked out of the store.

"Are you sure you have a ride?" Tommy asked.

"Yep. In fact, she should be coming around very soon."

"She?"

"Yep."

"My dad's running late. As usual. So, I'll go with you," said Tommy.

"No. That's really not necessary."

"Come on. I got the time."

"But you really don't need to do that."

"Well, I want to," said Tommy.

"But—"

"You're not trying to hide something from me, are you? We're best friends, right?"

Cameron let out a sigh. "Okay."

Tommy followed him to the agreed upon meeting place. And right on schedule, Senza pulled up on her motorcycle. Senza lifted the dark visor on her helmet.

Tommy's eyes popped out as he realized that this was Cameron's ride.

"I remember her," said Tommy.

"Yeah," said Cameron.

"Hi," said Tommy, staring at Senza.

Senza gave a subtle wave. She turned to Cameron and asked, "Aren't you going to introduce me to your friend?"

Cameron swallowed nervously. "Sure. This is Tommy," he said.

"Hi," said Tommy. "And who are you?"

Senza hesitated and replied "I'm his mother."

Cameron looked stunned by her unexpected response. Tommy was equally stunned. His eyebrows couldn't rise much higher.

"You're really his real mother?" asked Tommy.

"Yes, I am," she said.

"That's cool."

"You ready to roll?" she asked Cameron. "If you need more time, that's fine with me. I don't want to be accused of being a bad parent."

"I'm good," said Cameron, waving good-bye to Tommy.

Tommy muttered under his breath "I still can't believe that's your mother?! Holy whatever."

Senza handed Cameron his helmet. "Thanks...mom," he said, putting it on his head.

And with that, the two sped away

# # #

Many thanks for reading GODS OF SOUND THE PERILOUS PATH OF CAMERON FOSTER. If you enjoyed it, please leave a review online with your book distributor. You can also connect with me as follows:

Facebook: https://www.facebook.com/QMSchafferAuthor

Twitter: https://www.twitter.com/Qschaffer

Made in the USA
Las Vegas, NV
05 February 2021

17243228R00184